Murder Across the Ocean

Charlene Wexler

Books by Charlene Wexler

LAUGHTER AND TEARS SERIES
Book 1: Lori
Book 2: Murder Across the Ocean

COMING SOON!

LAUGHTER AND TEARS SERIES
Book 3: Milk and Oranges
Book 4: Elephants in the Room

FAREWELL TO SOUTH SHORE SERIES
Book 1: Farewell to South Shore
Book 2: We Will Not Go Back

NOVELS
Murder on Skid Row

**For more information
visit:** www.SpeakingVolumes.us

Murder Across the Ocean

Charlene Wexler

SPEAKING VOLUMES, LLC
NAPLES, FLORIDA
2023

Murder Across the Ocean

ISBN 979-8-89022-001-1

In honor of my three granddaughters,
Lily, Bella, and Sage.

Acknowledgments

A special thank you to my agent Nancy Rosenfeld/AAA Books Unlimited; my publisher, Kurt Mueller, Speaking Volumes; and my editors William S. Bike and Erica Mueller. They have helped me bring my work into the world. I also want to thank my family and friends who have read my drafts and encouraged me to keep writing.

Chapter One

Lori stood in the shower feeling sensuous and alive as she enjoyed the spray of hot water cascading over her body. She ran the bar of floral scented soap over every part of her skin, appreciating the fullness of her breasts and the mature expanse of her hips. She lingered longer than usual; it had been a long flight to London yesterday, and a rather physically challenging but wonderful evening. Remembering how she'd spent the night, she blushed at the thought of the wild sex she'd enjoyed—too wild for her years—and of how his hands and mouth had tenderly caressed her whole body.

She shrugged off her momentary embarrassment and, humming happily to herself, turned off the water and stepped out of the shower into the bright morning sun shining through the small bathroom window. As she reached for her towel, she heard a sudden pounding noise coming from the adjacent bedroom. She dismissed it as nothing more than the sound of room service bringing breakfast.

Lori ran her tongue over her lips and smiled while saying aloud, "Josh." Gazing at her reflection in the mirror, she realized she glowed. *Yes*, she thought, *last night with Josh was almost as wonderful as the senior prom.* At that moment, she felt like a teenager again instead of a seventy-year-old grandmother.

She toweled and then dabbed herself with Chanel No. 5, put on her expensive flowered silk dressing gown, slipped on her complimentary hotel slippers, and stepped out of the bathroom into their luxurious suite in the world-famous Palace Hotel.

Her eyes immediately stung from a smoky cloud hovering in the air; her nostrils twitched from the thick metallic scent of blood. Fear grasped her entire being. She slowly edged farther into the room while cautiously calling his name.

"Josh? *Josh!*

He didn't answer.

Slowly, she approached the bed, then stopped cold, gasping in disbelief. Bright red blood spattered the rich tan-colored wall and the mahogany headboard, continuing down to the unmade bed where Josh's body hung over the side of the mattress. White bone and gray-red brain matter dripped from the side of his head, staining the white silk sheets and the lush beige carpet. A burst feather pillow, also besmirched with blood and gore, lay on the floor.

Lori fixated on Josh's face; a shower of white feathers clung to his forehead and cheek. Where once was a beautiful blue eye, there now appeared a mangled, bloody hole. It took a few moments for her mind to gather this information, process it, and allow a scream to escape.

Once she began screaming, she was unable to stop.

Chapter Two

Lori ran out of the hotel room and through the hall, crying hysterically until she tripped on her flimsy slippers and ended up sprawled on the thick-carpeted floor in her dressing gown. Her horrific screams brought out everyone on the twenty-first floor.

"What happened? Why are you screaming? Are you hurt?" they shouted as they ran towards her.

All she could do was point in the direction of her room in between gasps for breath. Two women came to her aid. They helped her up, took her to a suite next door, and sat her on a soft, silk lounge chair while the other occupants of the suites took off in the direction she had pointed.

Lori sat there, not sure for how long, numb and shocked, while chaos surrounded her. A dizzying sensation swept through her. She took a deep breath. The two women—one dressed in a plum-colored, ankle-length dress and the other clad in black all the way down to her black orthopedic shoes—hovered over her.

"I'm Mrs. Putnam," the woman in plum said as an introduction, "and this is Mrs. Sweeney."

The older woman smiled sadly at Lori while the woman in the plum-colored dress left the suite for a time to see what all the excitement was about. Lori was unsure of time actually passing.

"Are you hurt?" Mrs. Putnam asked upon her return. "Should we call an ambulance for you? My dear, we've been told that the two men who checked out your suite have declared the bloke next door quite beyond the help of an ambulance, I'm afraid."

Lori stared at the women. They were either very calm or very English, considering the situation, though neither one had seen Josh's body.

At the thought of Josh, Lori gasped for breath, "No, no doctor . . . Oh, no, no . . ." Lori sobbed into her hands, letting the tears flow freely.

"Poor dear," the grandmotherly Mrs. Sweeney said as she patted Lori on the back in an attempt to comfort her. "To lose your husband in this manner is really . . ." At a loss for words, Mrs. Sweeney made a few sympathetic *tsk*ing noises.

Lori accepted the tissues handed to her by Mrs. Putnam and dried her eyes and cheeks before answering, "He wasn't my husband!"

Chapter Three

"Well . . ." Mrs. Sweeney pursed her lips, stepped away from Lori, and in an icier tone, said, "You've had a ghastly shock, whoever you are."

Lori's tear-stained eyes followed Mrs. Putnam as she walked over to a table near the window and picked up a cup and saucer. She turned back to Lori and handed it to her.

"I've made you a nice cup of tea. This should help calm your nerves."

Lori suddenly came to life. She looked in disbelief at these two English women with their polite and proper English accents. *A cup of tea! A bottle of whiskey and a handful of tranquilizers would be more appropriate.*

Mrs. Putnam and Mrs. Sweeney both busied themselves with the preparation of refreshments while a burly security guard and two Italian men from the suite across the hall entered the room. Color flooded the men's faces, and they quickly turned their eyes away from Lori.

Mrs. Sweeney and Mrs. Putnam looked at the poor, disheveled woman sitting on the sofa half undressed. They quickly set off to look for a throw blanket and, locating one, covered her with it. Neither woman could loan her any clothes. Lori was a petite little thing, barely five feet tall and no more than one hundred pounds. The two British women were both hardy and large-boned, of stout Manchester stock from the north of England.

They asked the security guard to take them next door, so they could get the poor woman some clothes.

"Absolutely not," he responded. "No one can go into a crime scene room."

Finally, the elder Mrs. Sweeney overpowered the guard with her five-foot-eight, one-hundred-eighty-pound frame, taking him by the arm and leading him out of the suite and into the hall.

"Listen, you young bloke. You need to help me get the lady some clothes. She's obviously absolutely gutted. Go in there and get her suitcase or some clothes from the closet, anything. I'll keep an eye out for the constables. That's a good lad. Ta, darling."

The guard quickly grabbed the suitcase from the bedroom closet, avoiding looking at Josh's dead body still sprawled on the bed. Mrs. Sweeney took the suitcase and pulled out panties, a bra, and a pair of trousers, a sleeveless blouse, and some shoes for Lori. The guard managed to return the suitcase right as other guards from the hotel, along with a crew of Scotland Yard police and forensic workers, descended upon the room, sealing it off from everyone.

Lori took the clothes to Mrs. Sweeney's loo. She tried to dress there, but at the thought of Josh's bloody body, she felt dizzy and nauseous. She quickly turned towards the toilet and heaved up the contents of her stomach.

Over the toilet flush, she heard Mrs. Sweeney knocking on the door. "Are you all right, love?"

"Yes," Lori answered weakly, though she was far from being all right. She leaned into the sink and washed her face with cold water, wiped it, rinsed out her mouth, and took a deep breath. She looked around the restroom. Mrs. Putnam had left her nylon stockings over the shower bar to dry. She smiled a little. What an old-fashioned thing to have, individual stockings instead of pantyhose. Lori frowned and wiped away a fresh batch of tears. She wanted so badly to be home, in bed. Maybe this was just a nightmare, and she would soon wake up. She threw on some clothes and returned to the women in the suite.

A constable stood there waiting for her. "Mrs. Brill, the MIT would like to speak with you at the station."

"The what?"

The constable answered, "The murder investigation team."

Like a zombie, Lori obediently followed the constable down the hall until Mrs. Sweeney stopped her.

"Love, your blouse is all wonky."

Lori, shoulders slumped down, just stared straight ahead and stood very still as Mrs. Sweeney turned her away from the men and re-buttoned her blouse.

Before continuing, Lori paused, her eyebrows knit in an attempt to focus. She turned to the constable. "Where is my purse, my passport, my makeup case with my pills?"

"Sorry, missus, I have them, plus your suitcase, but I can't be handing them to you now, as they may be evidence."

Turning away from the suite where Josh's body lay and where a host of police officers and other people had gathered, Lori seemed to move by rote. She found it hard to keep the tears from streaming down her face or to concentrate on anything. Still in shock, she was not about to argue with anyone.

"Could you at least give me a hanky?"

The policeman smiled kindly as he handed her some tissues. Lori saw sympathy in his eyes before he turned to lead the way down the hall. In order to avoid the crowd already gathering around the hotel, the two of them took the service lifts down to the waiting police car.

* * *

Mrs. Sweeney made her way into the Putnam suite and plopped down in an overstuffed, gold brocade chair.

"Margaret, I just can't believe the events of this morning. What was a woman that age doing in that man's suite? She surely wasn't a tart. Shameful! Do you think she knocked him off?"

Margaret Putnam raised her cup of tea to her lips and gazed away from her friend. "A bloke like Wheeler has a way of charming the best of women. Help yourself to some tea, dear."

"How do you know anything about him? What is his name again?"

"I overheard the men talking. He's someone famous. Well known, at the very least. I read all about him in the paper earlier. Some bank scandal or other. They said his name is—was—Josh Wheeler."

A knock at the door interrupted their conversation. Upon opening the door, they were met by a police officer.

"Ladies, we will need a statement from everyone on this floor, so please stay put. The hotel manager has been kind enough to arrange for a complimentary breakfast for each room while we detain you. You will be knocked up shortly."

He was halfway out the door when he popped back in. "Beg your pardon, ladies; we will also need statements from your husbands and anyone else who has been in your suite or on the floor this morning."

Mrs. Sweeney picked herself up from the chair and straightened out her black ankle-length skirt by pressing her palms along the front of it, smoothing out some wrinkles. "We better go find the men. Can't pass up a free breakfast from the Palace Hotel."

"Peter is in the bedroom, resting, and I believe your Stanley is in the hall, chatting up the other men," Mrs. Putnam said.

"How fortunate, Peter slept through the entire thing."

"Yes, he didn't sleep well at all last night, so he slept all through the morning. Since we haven't anything planned until the afternoon, I figured, why not let the dear man be?"

Mrs. Sweeney smiled and nodded. "Good heavens, they're all out there, playing at Sherlock Holmes, I imagine. I must have walked right past him. I didn't notice. My nerves are a jumble, Margaret. I believe this holiday has gone wrong."

* * *

Lori sat in the back of the police car, wrapping her thin arms tightly around herself in an attempt to warm up. The sleeveless blouse was a bad idea, but what choice did she really have? She wasn't prepared for the chilling, damp, below-normal temperatures, and she hadn't exactly picked out this ensemble herself. Somehow, she had believed it would be warmer in London in late April. The hot temperatures in Arizona had thinned out her blood and changed her thinking.

Oh, God. Oh my God, she mumbled to herself. *How did this happen?*

The whole trip had started so innocently. Two days prior, when she had left Arizona on a pleasure trip to visit her granddaughter in London, she had been so full of hope. Life had begun getting quiet and boring, and she felt excited about going abroad.

The flight from Phoenix, Arizona, to her connecting flight in Chicago to London had gone without a hitch. Then she spotted him. And chaos set in.

She had been standing in line at Chicago O'Hare International Airport, waiting to board her plane, when she saw tanned skin peeking through an open polo shirt, radiating up a dimpled face to those sparkling blue eyes she remembered so well. Excited, Lori pushed her way through the line until she finally reached him.

"Josh!" she said breathlessly.

He turned around, smiled, and briskly walked towards her. His strong arms engulfed her. She could feel her heart speed up, her face blushing. Releasing her, he held her at bay while slowly moving his gaze over her entire body.

"Lori, you look marvelous, so thin and young looking. Don't ever dye those shining silver locks," he said, nodding his approval. "My God, it's been years." He gave her a seductive smile.

"Yes, at least twenty." Lori knew the exact date she had last seen him. In fact, she knew every date going back to that first day when, as a fourteen-year-old high school freshman, she fell in love with a sixteen-year-old junior.

"Are you on the British Airways flight to London?" he asked.

"Yes. I'm visiting my granddaughter."

"Give me your ticket," Josh said, holding his hand. "I'll see if we can get seated together."

By the time the plane left the airport, Lori was sitting in first class beside Josh, sipping wine and reminiscing about old times. By the time the plane landed at Heathrow Airport, she was following him, like a puppy, through immigration and security, into a big black London taxicab, and then through the lobby of the luxurious, world-famous Palace Hotel to a grand suite with a large canopy bed.

Josh Wheeler, at seventy-two, still looked the model of the heartbreak male living off his charm, and Lori, at seventy, had fallen for it again, hook, line, and sinker.

And again, it had led to disaster.

* * *

As the police car moved along the Strand towards New Scotland Yard, Lori's mind wandered to the first day Josh came into her life.

Nervous about going to a new high school, she had been walking down the sidewalk on her way to the bus stop when someone bounded out of a house and literally knocked her down.

The arm that extended to help her belonged to a tall, slender, blond boy with gorgeous peacock-blue eyes.

"Oh, my gosh, I'm so sorry. Here, let me help you up. Are you hurt?"

Surprisingly, she was not angry, just startled and a little embarrassed.

After getting back on her feet, smoothing out her dress, and wiping the dirt off her hands, she looked up into those blue, blue eyes, and responded nervously, "No, just a little scrape. I'll be fine." She felt her face blush. "Hi, I'm Lori. I just moved here."

"Ah, so we're neighbors. Great way for me to welcome you to the neighborhood. I'm Josh." He extended his hand, this time for a greeting, and smiled a million-watt smile. "I'm so sorry. Did I ruin your pretty dress?"

Josh, a mere two years older, was already a man of the world. For the next three years, he took Lori to places and activities she would never have gone to on her own—some not so kosher, like the day he picked her up in a stolen white Cadillac and they drove seventy-five miles north to a beach on Lake Geneva in Wisconsin and then abandoned the car and took a train home, where, ignited by their adventure, they kissed passionately throughout the entire ride.

When her mother ignored her, which was most of the time, and her father was gone on business, Josh was there for her. He was her Peter Pan, and she was his Wendy. Those were their pet names for one another, a name he would often call her when pleading with her to take him back time and time again. Now Peter Pan was dead, and seventy-year-old Wendy was going to jail. Unable to help herself, she started laughing.

Chapter Four

Lori stared out the window of the police car at the crowded streets of London with their red double-decker coaches, beautiful parks, and shops. She smiled at all the mobile phone users. It was a craze worldwide, something she hadn't seen during her last visit thirty years ago. She thought of the historic theater district just east of the Palace Hotel, where she should have been enjoying a play and, later, lunch instead of heading to Scotland Yard. She shook her head as a horrid realization seized her: This was not another innocent high school prank Josh had conjured up. He was dead, murdered by someone, while she was just a few feet away from the bedroom. She could have been shot, too. She covered her face with her hands and cried anew.

The police car turned left onto Dacre Street and stopped before one of the station's entrances. It was a large, imposing, ultra-modern building made of glass and steel. Looking at it from the tidy, small side street, it seemed an unlikely place for such a building, with a quaint barbershop directly across from it. But Westminster was a bustling part of town, and the building was imposing enough to intimidate Lori.

A stout and serious-looking constable stood by the entrance. He waited for Lori to pull herself together before opening the door and leading her into the station.

Upon entering, Lori surveyed the interior of London's famous Scotland Yard. The Westminster District police station didn't look much different than stations in the States. The uniforms of the constables were slightly different—longer, with more buttons, but still black. Most of the constables wore high helmet-type hats and navy blue vests. The well-kept building housed the same inhabitants as most police stations: drunks, prostitutes, and parking ticket offenders. Unlike in past days,

Lori was now in one alone instead of with Jerry Brill. Yes, Lori had visited many police headquarters with her late husband, Jerry. She had a great track record regarding the men she picked; first, there was seductive, powerful Josh, who turned out to be a womanizer and a swindler, and then there was playful and loving Jerry, an alcoholic.

"What are you doing?" Lori jumped back as a constable grabbed her hand in an effort to fingerprint her. "Stop that! I'm not a criminal." She pulled away, her entire body beginning to shake nervously.

The constable conferred with someone on the phone and then walked her to the back of the station. He led Lori into a small room sparsely furnished with a couple of wooden chairs and an enormous old desk with scrollwork carved in its sturdy mahogany legs. She sat down in one of the uncomfortable straight-back chairs and waited. Presently, the door opened, and a tall, narrow-faced man with a prominent nose entered the room. He wore a long black trench coat over his thin frame, and his gray hair peeked out in small waves from beneath a black knit hat. He leaned an umbrella against the wall, removed his coat and hat, and opened his black leather briefcase after placing it on the desk.

He offered Lori his hand while saying, "Madam, Detective Chief Inspector Geoffrey Holmes from MIT, at your service."

Instead of accepting his hand, Lori broke out in nervous laughter. The Chief Inspector gently put his hand on her shoulder. "I pray I haven't offended you."

Sudden tears now replaced Lori's laughter. "I just came to London to visit my granddaughter. Since I walked off the plane yesterday, a friend has been murdered, and now I've been dragged into the police station to be interrogated by Sherlock Holmes." She pulled a tissue out of the box on his desk and blew her nose.

Geoffrey Holmes stood there stroking his chin pensively before speaking. "Yes, you've been through a terrible ordeal. And my name does evoke strange responses, but I assure you I am no relation to Sir Arthur Conan Doyle's fictional character. Now then," Inspector Holmes continued in a more serious tone, "since you are the only witness to the murder of Mister Wheeler, we need to ask you some questions, not interrogate you."

He sat down on a chair behind the desk facing her. "Could we get you some tea?" he asked as he handed her the tissue container. He tried to sound less intimidating, to put her at ease. A distraught witness might omit important information while being questioned.

"Coffee would be great," Lori replied, looking into his face.

"I am certain we could round up some." He pushed a button on his phone and asked someone named Tuttle to procure some coffee.

"Cream and sugar?" he offered courteously.

"No, black."

How bland, he thought. He liked loading his teacup with cream and two lumps of sugar. Turning towards his briefcase, he pulled out a passport and began reading it.

"Your name is Laura Brill, not Wheeler, correct?"

Lori answered with a simple yes.

He continued, looking up at her. "Missus Brill, could you tell me how long you've known Mister Wheeler, your relationship with him, and how you ended up in his suite at the Palace Hotel?"

"I'm no longer married. I'm a widow."

"Yes, of course, and you've known Mister Wheeler . . . ."

"I've known Josh Wheeler since I was fourteen. He took me to my senior prom in 1961."

She pursed her lips and looked away from the inspector as she recalled the night at the Drake Hotel when she lost her virginity to Josh, Northfield High School's football hero. *Silly,* she thought, *this man doesn't want to hear about that kind of teenage stuff.* But that Josh

Wheeler was still alive in her memory; her mind would not let her identify with the body lying on the hotel bed.

"Really?" he said, straightening up in his chair. He began again to stroke his chin. "We were under the impression you two had just met on the plane."

"Why would you think *that*?" Lori asked, surprised that in her emotional state, she could summon up a feeling of offended. What did they think she was, some kind of floozy, picking up strangers on a plane? At her age? These British must really be swingers.

"Pardon our assumption, madam, but this is 2013, after all." Holmes smiled shyly. "And you say you have known him for over fifty years? This throws new light on the situation."

Lori mumbled under her breath while looking down around the legs of her chair, searching for her purse. Her aggrieved mind was beginning to clear, and she analyzed the situation, remembering the authorities had confiscated her purse and its contents.

"Am I under arrest?"

"No, ma'am. But as the only witness to the murder, we need to hold you for questioning."

Lori straightened up in her seat. "I believe in England I have the same right as I do in America. I want to call my lawyer before answering any more questions."

"Yes, of course, you may make a call." Inspector Holmes handed her the station phone.

"I will need my cell from my purse. There is no way I can remember phone numbers now."

Holmes pushed back his chair and left the room, returning a few minutes later with Lori's mobile phone. "We need your things a little while longer, but you can use it to make a call to your solicitor."

15

* * *

After handing Lori the phone, Holmes walked out of the room to give her some privacy. He welcomed the time to think. This was going to be an international case, not just another run-of-the-mill murder, so, as Chief Inspector, he had been called back to work from his holiday. Too bad they hadn't reached him in time to arrive first at the hotel. It seems the hotel manager was tardy in calling his department; too many people had already tramped through the murder scene.

According to Inspector Sanders, the press had invaded the hotel. Holmes didn't know what to tell them. For sure, the *Guardian* and the *Daily Express* would post stories in their papers by this evening. He had better call them and make a statement. Geoffrey had been on holiday only two days when this chaos broke out. Too bad he hadn't gone abroad somewhere.

He wondered, could this petite seventy-year-old actually shoot her lover in the face? She was the only other person in the room. There was no blood on any of her things or on her. *When they find the weapon, the fingerprints will tell.* He understood the woman's agitation over being fingerprinted and pictured, but it had to be done. Her rights were read, though she'd appeared somewhat overwhelmed at the time. She did need a solicitor.

* * *

Alone in the tiny interrogation room, Lori almost punched the button on her phone for her trusted friend and lawyer, Bill Cohn, before it dawned on her that he would be no help thousands of miles away. She needed a lawyer in London. She knew one, but she wasn't sure if she wanted to call her.

Lori's granddaughter was living with a London solicitor while studying for her master's degree at the prestigious London School of Law. Lori had missed this delightful young woman for too long. Her Cate, half Jewish, half Irish, could make her smile, make her laugh, make life worth living. *Oh my God,* thought Lori. What would she say to Cate when she called her?

Help! I've been arrested for the murder of my ex-lover!

Chapter Five

Joseph lounged in his brown cashmere robe, drinking tea and nibbling on a scone while watching the news on the television. He stretched his full six-foot-plus frame along the length of the couch and ran his hand through his curly brown hair while yawning lazily. It was his morning to relax. No court today, and his first appointment with a client wasn't until noon.

Suddenly, his girlfriend, Cate, ran out of the bedroom and down the stairs, screaming hysterically.

"Now what?" Joseph asked in a calm manner. He was used to this. Cate went into hysterics over everything. She had probably lost her mobile again. He wondered how someone as intelligent as Cate could be so excitable and careless. He passed it off as being an American trait.

"It's my grandmother. She called from Scotland Yard!" As she explained, Cate hurriedly pulled on a pair of black, high-heeled leather pumps and straightened out her black knee-length skirt.

"Oh, yes. Wasn't she due in to visit us sometime this week?" Joseph placed his teacup on a nearby coffee table.

"She's in London *now*. She's in trouble." Cate buttoned her white silk blouse and tucked it into her skirt. Hoping it would impress upon her boyfriend the seriousness of the matter at hand, she repeated, "She called from Scotland Yard!"

Unaffected, Joseph continued to ask questions. "Isn't she the one you've called your Auntie Mama? The one who picks up strangers, loses things, goes on Indian retreats to the desert, climbs mountains, taught you to drive when you were only twelve, and buys—"

Joseph sarcastically rattled off all the idiosyncrasies Cate loved about her Gram until she cut him off.

"Joseph, listen to me." She stood over him with her hands on her hips. "My Gram—Lori— is being held at Scotland Yard for questioning about a murder, and she needs us to come down and help her!"

"Really? There's nothing on the news about it."

"Joseph!" Cate raked her hands through her blonde bobbed hair, thoroughly exasperated. Cate really hadn't understood her grandmother's story, but she knew Lori needed help.

"All right, Cate, calm yourself. There must be some sort of mix-up. Why, the woman is almost seventy. Look, you're a solicitor. Go down there and straighten it out." Joseph picked up a scone and resumed sipping his tea before stretching out once more and turning his attention to the television.

Frustrated, Cate leaned closer to him as he remained reclined and grabbed the scone from his hand before it touched his lips.

"Get dressed and come with me. Now!" Cate shouted. "She needs a lawyer who practices in London."

In a calm, steady voice, Joseph answered, "Please stop shouting. This is England, not America. We are *civil*." Joseph loved pointing out his Englishness to Cate whenever he felt she needed a bit of reprimanding. "I will come with you, but I must dress and then ring my office to cancel some appointments." He looked down at his robe, which was now covered with cream from the scone, shook his head with annoyance, rose from the couch, and slowly made his way upstairs to their bedroom.

Cate paced back and forth, knowing that nothing she did or said would hurry him. They had first met at court when her class participated in a practice trial, and they had been living together for almost a year. At first, she was charmed by his aristocratic mannerisms, but lately, they drove her crazy. Her proper English boyfriend would go through his morning routine no matter what was happening. Even now, with her grandmother in trouble, she could picture him neatly folding his pajamas, neatly placing them in a drawer, and then picking up her clothes, which were thrown all over the room.

At least his suits, shirts, and ties were all matched together in the closet, so he wouldn't spend time perfecting his outfit.

Up in his bedroom, Joseph behaved exactly as Cate predicted. He knew she wanted him to rush out of the house, leaving everything in disarray. It simply was not in his nature to do that; anyway, he was certain there was no reason to hurry. *In for questioning for a murder, indeed.* Most likely, Cate's grandmother was detained as an uninvolved spectator of a traffic accident. Cate had a way of dramatizing everything.

* * *

Lori waited patiently for Cate's arrival. She savored her strong black coffee, sipping it slowly. No one at the station tried to question her now that they were aware a junior barrister would represent her, especially one who was the son of a lord. She had calmed down some and now tried hard to remove the picture of Josh's dead body from her mind. She was in a state of denial, a survival mechanism she often used as an only child with an unavailable mother.

Lori walked into the restroom and rinsed her face with cold water at the sink. When she looked up at her image in the mirror, she became frightened. Her eyes were red from crying, and she had never retrieved her makeup case, so all her wrinkles and blotches were visible on her pale skin. She was frozen to the spot until a lady constable entered the restroom and asked if she was all right. She stared at the constable, thinking, *How could I possibly be all right after what I just went through?*

"Yes, of course," Lori replied. She walked back to her seat in Inspector Holmes' office and waited. She was determined to be calm for Cate, even though her pulse still raced.

When Cate walked in with Joseph, Lori's face lit up, and so did the faces of the police officers in the station. Her Cate had a way of turning heads wherever she went. She was a very attractive girl, but that wasn't the main reason; it was the energy she brought with her.

Cate ran over to Lori and wrapped her arms around her, almost lifting her off the floor.

"Oh, Gram, it's so good to see you. I was so worried you may have been hurt. What on earth happened? Whatever it is, Joseph will take care of this nonsense," she announced loudly enough for all to hear as she waved her hands in an effort to push aside the problem.

Lori reflected on Cate's statement; *I was worried you may be hurt.* Suddenly taut with fear, she realized she could have been murdered also had she been in bed with Josh instead of in the shower. She trembled at the thought and sat back down on the chair to compose herself. She need not alarm her granddaughter.

They hadn't seen each other in two years. Cate had tried to Skype and FaceTime her grandmother, but Lori wasn't current enough with electronics to try it. Now she was surprised to see how much older than her twenty-six years Cate looked. Maybe it was the professional suit and high pumps. Lori was accustomed to seeing her granddaughter in jeans. Cate's hair, normally long, thick, and honey blonde, now looked a darker shade of blonde and was cut in a short bob style. But the sparkle in her blue eyes and the broad smile on her face hadn't changed; they definitely belonged to the same lovely girl Lori knew.

Cate brought Joseph forward and introduced him to her grandmother. Lori relaxed slightly, thankful that the two of them were with her. She couldn't help thinking, *What if I were here alone?*

21

Joseph bowed slightly as he took Lori's hand. "Mrs. Brill, I am so sorry that you have been brought here. There must be a mistake." He then disappeared into the office of the superintendent of the MIT.

Cate sat down near her grandmother and squeezed her hand affectionately. They barely had time to discuss matters before Joseph emerged from the office and approached them. "Well, I guess the situation is a little more involved than I first realized, but I do have your release and most of the contents of your purse. They are keeping your suitcase and, I'm afraid, holding your passport for a while. You will need to give Inspector Holmes an initial signed statement and answer a few additional questions. You must understand, at this time, you are the only witness they have."

He didn't mention that she was also the only suspect they had, or that he was really worried about his father's reaction when this situation spread across the news.

Lori and Joseph went back into Inspector Holmes's office, where Lori described the murder scene and answered some more questions about her relationship with Josh Wheeler. When she shook violently and burst into tears, Joseph asked for her release until another time when she'd recovered from the shock. Taking Lori by the arm, Joseph said, "Come, let's get out of here."

Inspector Holmes stood up and smiled down at her with compassionate eyes. "Get some rest. You've had quite an experience."

Hearing sincerity in his voice, Lori felt a rush of warmth envelop her. She left Scotland Yard with a sense of relief and, following Cate's lead, settled into Joseph's black Bentley.

Joseph turned towards her. "Mrs. Brill—"

Lori stopped him in mid-sentence. "I'm Lori to you, not Mrs. Brill. What can I call you for short? You must have a nickname like Joe. Joseph sounds so formal."

Cate winced slightly at this, for she knew Joseph despised cutesy names. He believed one was born with a title and should respect it. It took him a few months to finally stop calling Cate Catherine.

Joseph hesitated. "Actually. . .everyone calls me Joseph. We never use nicknames in my family."

"That's only for the servants in the high and mighty Lunt household," Cate said with a smirk.

Joseph ignored her. "Mrs. Brill—I mean, Lori—you must be famished. Permit me to take you to Wiltons for lunch. It is one of our upscale establishments, having been around since 1792."

Lori, exhausted and still somewhat in shock, really didn't want to go to a public place, but she wasn't going to disappoint her granddaughter and her charming boyfriend.

They took a rather scenic route through London, passing St. James Park and making their way around Buckingham Palace and onto Piccadilly until they reached Wiltons. Once settled inside, Lori tried just to order coffee, but it didn't work.

"Mrs. Brill, you must try one of their fish specialties. This is one of my family's favorite lunch places," Joseph said.

The waitress stood politely waiting for her order, so Lori pointed to a shrimp special and nodded yes. She was sorry she had agreed to go out to eat. When the orders came, she found the food stuck in her throat; although she felt slightly nauseous, she didn't complain. Even in crisis, her inclination to please others took over.

Halfway through lunch, Cate looked at Lori's plate with the barely touched shrimp and then up to her grandmother's pale face and pursed lips. She reached over, patted her grandmother's hand, and then turned to Joseph.

"Let's get the check. This was a bad idea."

Cate and Lori exited and made their way to a waiting cab while Joseph got into his car and went to his office to take care of some things.

Lori sat with Cate in the back of the taxi on the plush leather seats, nervously tapping a hand on her purse while trying to block out the reoccurring image of Josh's bloody dead body. She tried to concentrate on the scenery out her window, but nothing helped. Her body started to shake nervously. Cate wrapped her coat around Lori, believing her grandmother was cold. The thought comforted Lori, and she calmed down some.

It was somewhere around four in the afternoon when they pulled up to Cate and Joseph's flat, located in a quaint section of Mayfair just west of Buckingham Palace.

After Cate's perfunctory tour of the apartment—showing Lori the kitchen, the living room, and the upstairs guest room with the adjoining bath she would be occupying for the duration of her stay—Lori excused herself, went straight to her bedroom, and plopped under the covers, never getting up to wash her face or brush her teeth. She immediately fell asleep, thanks to some sleeping pills Cate had in her medicine chest, and she didn't wake until around eleven the next morning when she heard Cate's cat meowing and scratching at her closed door. She ate little and spent most of the day in bed, refusing to talk to anyone, existing on a little coffee and toast.

* * *

When Geoffrey Holmes was called in on the Wheeler case, he had pictured dealing with the murder of a scoundrel who had cheated hundreds of people out of their life savings. He hadn't planned on someone like Lori Brill being involved. He expected to be interviewing a prostitute or, at the very least, the type of trophy girlfriend regularly seen hanging from the arms of high rollers like Wheeler, not a well-to-do American senior citizen. These thoughts scrambled through his mind as he drove home from the police station.

He lived in a red brick row house not far from the station in a neighborhood of police officers. He walked up three stairs, carefully avoiding the pot of geraniums on the top step. Upon entering his flat, two senior cats—one a brown tabby, the other an orange mixed-breed with a triangular cut on his right ear—met him in the hallway. Calling them by name—Patty and Casey—he bent down and petted his two companions before he filled their food bowls. He opened the fridge and closed it again, thinking, *I really should go shopping.* He reached into a cabinet and removed a can of lentil soup and a bag of crackers. He sat at his round wooden kitchen table as his soup heated in a pan on the stove, his computer and briefcase full of papers before him.

Geoffrey's gaze moved across the kitchen to the adjacent living room area and rested upon the photograph of his deceased wife, which sat framed in gold atop the gray stone mantelpiece.

My love, life has been lonely since you've gone.

Chapter Six

Early on the third day, Cate burst into Lori's bedroom holding a little black and white tabby cat who quickly jumped out of Cate's arms and spread out on the bed in an effort to reclaim possession of it.

"Scotland Yard called. They want you in for some more questions. Joseph will go with you." Cate sat down near the cat and lovingly stroked her back. "Do you need help dressing, Gram?"

"No, honey."

On her way down the stairs, Cate called, "Hurry up, Gram. I'm making blueberry pancakes, just like you used to make for me!"

Lori sat on the bed and looked around the room where she had spent the last two days. It was a comfortable, cozy bedroom decorated with Laura Ashley pink and green floral-patterned curtains and matching bedspread. She breathed in the scent of lilies, asters, and marigolds that rested in the cut-glass vase sitting atop a table by a nearby window. A picture of the room at the Palace with Josh's dead body shot through her mind, and her pulse began racing immediately.

Tigger, who had rubbed her face against Lori's arm in a friendly gesture, was adept at detecting change and tension and suddenly jumped down and ran under the bed.

Lori tried hard to erase the image of Josh as she entered the bathroom. The sight of the shower didn't help. She decided to take a bath instead. Cate had laid out new toiletries, as hers were missing. Her granddaughter had also purchased panties and a top for her to wear. They fit a little big, but she was grateful to have them.

After her bath, Lori dressed and even tried to look human again. She dabbed at her face with some make-up base and a red-orange lipstick and tried to blow-dry her hair. Her arms felt heavy, though, so she left her short silver hair to dry on its own. All her efforts to stay thin, healthy, vital and active these last few years seemed for naught. Had Cate not been here, she would have never left the bed. She thought back thirty years to when her seventeen-year-old daughter died, and she quickly became despondent. Avoiding the full-length mirror by the door, she moved out of the bedroom, almost tripping on the cat that quickly scampered back under the bed.

She joined Cate in the kitchen, sitting on one of the modern chairs that, to Lori, did not denote warmth and hominess but rather sterility and coldness. Lori was traditional, and the stainless steel kitchen and its modern furniture and digital appliances felt unfamiliar and unwelcoming to her. The high-backed chair with its curved seat was clever but uncomfortable. She was surprised to see so many electronics in the kitchen. There was a computer, a new thin-screen television, and several digital gadgets. Cate pushed buttons, and doors opened and shut. Recipes and lists of groceries to be purchased appeared on a computer screen attached to the refrigerator door while Cate gave verbal orders to the devices. The only clock present was the clock on the computer. Lori had been in the flat for two days, but since she'd spent most of her time in bed, she had not noticed any of this before. She felt it was something straight out of a science fiction novel.

While Lori cut into her three large blueberry pancakes, she noticed Cate's breakfast consisted of a bowl of oats, nuts, raisins, and a large glass of blended juice. No wonder Cate was thin and energetic.

Cate poured a cup of coffee for Lori and set it down next to *The London Times*. "I still like the feel of paper, though Joseph reads everything on his iPad or computer or mobile."

Holding her cup in hand, Lori stared at the paper. The headlines read: *Wealthy U.S. Real Estate Mogul on the Lam Found Murdered in London's Palace Hotel.*

"Did you know he was rich and famous?" Cate asked as she carefully watched her grandmother's reaction to the news. She was glad to see Gram finally out of bed, and she wasn't sure how far to go into Josh's murder.

"Not really. I knew he was successful. Charm and glory had always been his, but I guess as he aged, he felt the need for extreme wealth and the power it brought. His father died when he was in law school, leaving the family penniless, which may have contributed to his actions. Actually, he was always good at coming out on top at whatever he did, getting away with murder while the rest of us got caught for every little infraction."

"Not this time!" Cate answered before Lori realized what she had just said about Josh.

They stared at each other for a few seconds. Then Lori reached for the newspaper and began reading the article. Cate picked up a bottle of syrup with one hand and a cell phone with the other and gave them to Lori.

"Eat first. Your cell phone's been constantly ringing. I didn't answer any of the calls, but I did talk to Mom and Dad. Dad said he would rearrange his schedule and come out, but I told him I was taking care of you."

Lori swallowed hard as she looked Cate's way. Cate and her deceased daughter Julie were getting mixed up in her mind. She turned away, picked up the mobile phone, and checked for numbers and messages. She had received calls from three friends in Arizona, several unknown calls, a call from her son Barry (Cate's dad), and another, more frantic phone call from her good friend Rain.

Rain had left messages. The first one read: "Boy, do I have news for you about an old friend."

28

Lori realized Rain must have sent that message before the news of Josh's death. Her second one made it clear that she'd learned of his death and was shocked to hear he had been killed in London.

Out of the many calls Lori received, she only returned three: one to Scotland Yard to affirm that she and her solicitor would be back for another questioning; one to her son to assure him she was alright, and one to her good friend Rain.

"Yes, Rain, I know Josh was murdered. I was the woman he was with at the Palace."

There was a gasp on the other end of the phone before Rain asked, "What? When? Where? Oh, my God. Now I understand why some investigator was in our Arizona retirement community asking about you."

"Was he from the newspapers?"

"I don't know. He asked a lot of questions about you and Josh. I played dumb. He was Chinese."

"Chinese?" Lori asked, bewildered.

Chapter Seven

Torrents of raindrops pelted against the foggy windowpane of the car, making travel difficult as Lori, Cate, and Joseph drove to the station. Joseph turned the windshield wipers up to full force. The constant tapping noise produced the only sound in the car; each of the three passengers was silently assessing the situation.

After staring out the window for a few moments, Lori realized how much she longed for her home in Arizona, where there were three hundred and sixty days of sunshine and quiet. She vowed to never again complain about being bored.

Joseph let Lori and Cate out in front of the station while he parked the car. They entered thru the heavy double doors and walked up to the desk, Lori was asked to sign several papers, but she waited for Joseph's arrival and approval before doing so. They were then led into a large windowless conference room.

This time when Lori sat at a wooden table across from Inspector Holmes, they were not alone. Joseph represented Lori, Holmes represented the London Police Department, and a Mr. Jordan Gould from the FBI represented the United States' interest in Josh Wheeler.

Jordan, who stood about five feet nine inches, was much younger than Holmes, very American in speech and dress, and wore black pants and an open-neck blue polo shirt. Jordan's brown hair was cut short, and he was clean-shaven, per the FBI rules on appearance. He was a thin man with an abundance of nervous energy, which did not allow him to stay seated. He paced back and forth with his hands behind his back. He had a habit of stopping and staring intensely into Lori's eyes while waiting for an answer to a question.

This maneuver made Lori very uncomfortable, leaving her with the sensation of an executioner measuring her for the gallows. Her body seems to shrink down into the chair.

Cate sat in the back of the room, away from the conference table; biting her nails and squirming on the hard wooden chair as she listened to the men harass her grandmother.

Inspector Holmes, dressed in the English throwback uniform of a dress shirt, tweed jacket, and brown trousers, arose from his chair and walked in front of Jordan and over to Lori, where he leaned down and smiled gently at her. Instinctively, he used his calm, soft-spoken voice.

"Mrs. Brill, I know this is not easy for you, but we really need your assistance in sorting out what happened. Will you explain to us how you ended up in Mister Wheeler's room the night he was murdered?"

Jordan turned away in anger, roughly shoving his hands deep into his trouser pockets. He realized he'd just been told to lay off. His training in interrogation made this type of coddling of a suspect hard for him to deal with.

Lori smiled at Geoffrey Holmes and unfolded her story of how she had met Josh at the airport in Chicago and how they had renewed an old friendship.

Holmes rubbed his chin while slowly making his way around the room before sitting back down.

"I'm going to ask you to think back over a long stretch now. Are you certain you have had no contact, no phone calls, no letter, text, or perhaps an e-mail with Mister Wheeler in nearly twenty years?"

"I've had no contact with him until three days ago at the airport."

"Can you remember what type of contact you had with him last? Was it business? Pleasure, perhaps?"

Joseph spoke up before Lori could answer. "My client has already told you there was no contact in all that time. I don't think what happened that long ago is relative today."

Lori smiled. "That's okay, Joseph. I will be happy to answer that question. It was neither business nor pleasure. Josh Wheeler attended my seventeen-year-old daughter's funeral on September 11, 1991, and that was the last time I saw him until three days ago."

Lori looked down, her mouth twisted awkwardly in a half-smile while tears welled up in her eyes.

Both Holmes and Gould were at a loss for words.

Finally, Holmes said, "You were right, Mr. Lunt. Let's concentrate on the present. We don't want to intrude on hurtful memories."

Lori was in-between a sob and a laugh as she reached for the tissue box atop the wooden desk. *There go the British again, with their clipped responses to emotion*, she thought.

Inspector Holmes continued. "Did Mister Wheeler speak with anyone personally or on his mobile while you were with him?"

Before answering, Lori stopped and gazed around the room. "What's making that clicking noise?"

Geoffrey answered, "A device is recording your voice and typing it into the computer."

Lori shook her head and looked behind her at the computer and recorder. "Machines can do everything now. No need for us humans anymore."

Gould stopped pacing and stared down at Lori. "Mrs. Brill, could you just answer the questions?"

Lori ignored Gould and turned to Geoffrey. "Could you please repeat the question?"

After Geoffrey repeated the question, Lori answered, "He was very outgoing and friendly. He talked to the porters, the servers, and the cab driver. He used the hotel phone to order breakfast, and he did receive one call on his mobile in the morning."

Jordan asked, "Do you remember the conversation on that one call?" Jordan had traced Wheeler's calls and had also found only one call. It was from the San Francisco Airport and only lasted about two minutes.

Lori answered, "All I heard him say was, 'I'll be delayed by a day.' I went into the loo and missed the rest of the conversation."

Geoffrey continued with the questions. "Did you ever feel like someone was watching or following the two of you?"

Lori stopped to think about it. "When we had dinner at the Savoy Grill, I went to the restroom and had a strange conversation with a woman who was drying her hands under a hand dryer. She said the gentleman I was with looked like a famous actor. Then she asked his name."

"What did she look like?"

"I can't remember, maybe around forty with dark hair, probably American," Lori remembered how romantic the evening had been, how elegant the Savoy Grill was with its wood paneling and gold gilded ceiling, the delicious roast beef and Yorkshire pudding. She had basked in the glow of Josh's undivided attention, and it was a lovely surprise to receive the bottle of Chanel No. 5 he bought her.

She recalled the look in his eyes when he held her hand across the table and told her, "Lori, you were my first love and my true love." She felt like all her dreams had finally come true, like Cinderella being swept off her feet by Prince Charming. He had, to say the least, a very strong influence on her emotions.

"Mrs. Brill, are you absolutely sure you never saw or heard anyone in your room before the murder or after you came out of the bathroom?

Possibly you heard a voice or noticed a shadow of someone running, a cracking or popping noise?"

Lori looked up, startled, as she was jarred back to reality. "No, as I told you before, I was taking a shower. I thought the noise I heard came from the bellman bringing breakfast or from the television. We had ordered room service, and Josh had unlocked the door before he crawled back into bed. That's when I headed into the bathroom to take a shower. We. . .were going to have breakfast in bed that morning. . ."

"How very romantic," Jordan said sarcastically.

"You never heard a shot? Or any indication of a struggle or argument? Any voices coming from the room?" Holmes asked.

"No, nothing that sounded like a shot. My head was under the water, I suppose."

Jordan Gould took over as Geoffrey Holmes refilled Lori's coffee cup. "They probably had a silencer. No one else in the hotel testified to hearing a shot. And, as you are aware, the use of a silencer denotes premeditation." Gould continued pacing around the room.

Holmes turned to Lori. "Were you aware that Wheeler was on the run? Did he indicate to you that he was in any trouble?"

"On the run? No, not at all," she replied, shaking her head.

"She didn't need to hear it from him, Holmes," Jordan Gould said sharply. "It was all over the news." He turned to Lori. "Don't you listen to the news or read the newspapers or check the internet?"

Lori looked up, her face tight with anger. "Mister Gould, I was traveling all day from Phoenix to Chicago and then to London. I was very engrossed in a best-selling novel."

Gould broke in, looking Lori square in the eye. "You seem to be a bit on edge."

"For heaven's sake, Mister Gould, consider what I've been through!"

"I am, I am. Is there something you're not telling us, Mrs. Brill? Perhaps *you* are the one who shot Josh Wheeler."

Lori gasped, looking from Jordan Gould to Geoffrey Holmes.

Ignoring the question, Joseph quickly answered for Lori. "See here, my client is a seventy-year-old grandmother who suddenly finds herself in danger. Maybe there is something *you* aren't telling *us*. I find it interesting that someone from the FBI has traveled to England to investigate a murder when today, most things are handled over the Internet. What information are *you* withholding, Mister Gould?"

Jordan Gould paused his pacing and hesitated before responding. "I'm not the one being questioned here, Mister Lump."

"*Lunt.*"

"Is that right? But since you asked so nicely, I'll let you in on some information. Josh Wheeler has approximately fifty million dollars hidden somewhere. There are many people looking for it, the U.S. government, about two hundred investors who have lost their life savings, business partners from China who may be holding his Chinese girlfriend. Oh!" He turned and looked at Lori with a crooked smile. "You didn't know about the Chinese girlfriend? Maybe you found out in the hotel room that morning?"

Lori lifted her head and stared into Jordan's eyes. *Go ahead and try to tell me my life's story, Mr. Gould.*

"I trust you weren't put on the case, Mister Gould, to suss out Mister Wheeler's relationships. That's not exactly the FBI's field of concentration." Joseph crossed his arms over his chest, waiting for Jordan to give a better explanation of his involvement.

"Very well, Mister Lint, we. . ."

Joseph rolled his eyes and let out a sigh. "Some modicum of professionalism would be greatly appreciated right now, Mister Gould."

"What? What did I say?"

Geoffrey Holmes and Joseph both exclaimed at once, "*Lunt!*"

"I know, Mister Lunt. I was just making sure you were paying attention."

"I'm enrapt, Mister Gould."

"Excellent," Jordan continued. "We could put a hold on only half of the one-hundred million Wheeler managed to steal. That was in real estate. Besides the FBI and the many investors in Wheeler's schemes, I'm sure there are other adventurers hoping to find the missing fifty million.

Joseph looked grim. "This is not good news. Do you think someone is after my client?"

Jordan snorted and walked away from Joseph, mumbling under his breath. He didn't have time for dense. He knew he didn't like this guy from the get-go. Where did this guy get his degree, a Cracker Jack box?

Holmes watched Jordan move across the floor and chimed in. "My good man, be logical. Missus Brill is the last one who saw Mister Wheeler alive. The murderer or murderers are afraid she may have seen them, or they may suspect her to be an accomplice with Wheeler."

Lori took a sip of coffee while they were talking to each other. Her throat was dry, and her head throbbed. This was taking longer than she thought it would.

Gould continued. "Wheeler's girlfriends were all young and beautiful. Those who were after him wouldn't believe he was with Mrs. Brill unless she was helping him get away with the money."

Cate suddenly stood up and shook her fist in the direction of Jordan Gould.

"How *dare* you talk about my grandmother like that?" she shouted. "What kind of bullshit investigator *is* this guy?"

All eyes turned towards her.

Joseph quickly walked to the back of the room, took hold of Cate's arm, and, turning her towards the door, calmly said, "I think you better wait for us outside, my dear."

Embarrassed by her outburst, Cate looked away from the men's staring eyes as she left the room. She hadn't acted like a professional. After all, she was a lawyer, but she still couldn't forgive that Jordan Gould. What a hurtful thing to say about her grandmother. *Why that arrogant son of a bitch. Who the hell does he think he is? Why I could just kill him.*

Jordan couldn't guess at her thoughts, but he took a long, hard look at the young girl passing through the doorway, his gaze lingering on her tight little ass. *What a little firecracker*, he mused. She was lovely, no doubt about it. He hadn't been introduced to her, but from her outburst, he'd learned she was the old lady's granddaughter. One more piece of information to process.

Lori dismissed the scene with Cate from her mind and sank lower into her chair. She felt awful. The questions and allegations seemed endless as she continued to deny knowing anything about Josh's business problems, his reason for being in London, or any of his contacts in the last twenty-five years. Going over every detail of her stay at the hotel and Josh's murder was making her sick. Things like this happened to people in the news or on television, not to an old lady like herself.

Joseph addressed Geoffrey Holmes upon returning to the table. "You feel she is in danger."

Holmes nodded. "It's plausible. We can't rule out that possibility."

"Then we need protection for her."

Lori turned towards Inspector Holmes. She felt a kinship with him, some type of mutual understanding, maybe because he was closer to her age. He had told her he would retire next year at sixty-eight. His speech was slow and easy to understand, even though he clearly had a pronounced English accent. Jordan Gould from the FBI made her uncomfortable. Although American, she had a hard time understanding his fast, New York manner of speaking.

The other thing she disliked about Jordan Gould, besides his arrogance and rudeness, was that he was absolutely right.

Lori looked away from everyone, concentrating on her coffee cup. She was in conflict. She wanted to run, catch a taxi to the airport, hop on a plane, and get the hell out of England, taking Cate with her. She knew she was needed here in London for questioning to help find Josh's killer, a monster who had murdered her friend and had invaded her life. A part of her wanted to stay and help. She needed the police's protection, but there was Cate to think about. She silently prayed that the officers would allow her to go home, and then she and Cate would be out of the investigation and out of danger.

"Mrs. Brill, are you still with us?" Gould asked loudly after Lori didn't respond to his last question.

Lori turned towards Gould and blurted out, tears streaming down her face, "I want to go home to Arizona. I've put my children in harm's way."

"Mrs. Brill, we need you to stay here for a while. I'd rather it was on your honor, not at our insistence."

They are holding my passport, Lori told herself.

"We will put someone on the case to watch over you," continued Holmes, hoping to ease Lori's anxiety.

Gould shook his head in disbelief. "Come on, Holmes, this is ridiculous. There are millions riding on this. We need her to cooperate to find Wheeler's killer and the money he stole." Jordan Gould walked over to Lori and looked down at her, establishing direct eye contact. "Someone may contact you soon, someone who thinks Wheeler gave you something important."

"What on earth do they think I have?

"A safe deposit key and bank location, plus information for routing money. Something like that. If you should be contacted, act as you have it, and contact us immediately. Until then, carry on like nothing happened. We'll be watching."

Joseph spoke up. "It sounds like you're trying to put Mrs. Brill in harm's way for your own sake. I can't allow that, Mister Gould."

"Mister Lunt, I believe she has put *herself* in that position," Gould replied coolly.

Geoffrey Holmes held up his hand. "Stop this conversation immediately. We are definitely putting Mrs. Brill's safety first. She will have protection." He refrained from saying at this point that she was still a suspect and would be watched anyway.

Chapter Eight

Gould sat down across from Holmes after Lori and Joseph left the room. "Do you believe her?"

Holmes rubbed his chin, a habit he'd acquired since giving up his pipe. "I really think she is innocent." Looking Gould straight in the eye, he added, "And I must say, your interrogation technique embarrassed me."

Gould rose and walked around the desk. "My methods don't suit you, Holmes. I get it."

"Good."

"But it bothers me that she has been connected to Wheeler for so many years. Funny, her name never came up in the material on Wheeler that I went through before I was called to London."

"Jordan, she hasn't been in touch with him for over twenty years!"

"So she says. I was trained to suspect everyone. Maybe she killed him."

"Oh, Gould, that is such rubbish! She is a seventy-year-old grandmother, for heaven's sake."

"Come on, Geoffrey, do you *really* believe Wheeler would take an old lady like that to bed? I'm sure she may be charming to most men her age, but *not* Wheeler. He was a playboy! You should see his current girlfriend—or one of them, anyway. She's an Asian woman who did some modeling. She's now in her late thirties and still a real knockout." Jordan Gould smiled as he made his point.

Geoffrey thought that for a seventy-year-old, Lori Brill was extremely attractive. She was petite, probably only about five feet tall, with a nice figure at about one hundred pounds, striking silver hair, bright green eyes, and a pleasant smile when she wasn't upset. He looked at the young man before him. Gould had to be at least thirty years younger than he or Lori; thus, the different way of looking at things, he acknowledged.

"Still gorgeous at thirty?"

"Late thirties. Yes."

"Would you normally suggest women in their thirties be put out to pasture, Jordan?"

"I'm not saying it's what *I* believe. I'm putting myself in the mindset of Wheeler."

"Look, the coroner confirmed Wheeler was murdered approximately when Mrs. Brill said she was in the shower, which should confirm her story. We have much work to do on this case. How about a quick lunch before we get back to work?" Geoffrey suggested as he moved away from the desk and reached for his knit hat and trench coat.

"One minute," Jordan replied as he picked up his cell phone and called his office in the States. He spoke into the phone. "I need a complete profile on a Laura Weinberg Brill, Chicago, Scottsdale, Social Security number . . . ."

As the two men walked out of the station, Geoffrey turned to his companion. "Go easy on her, my good fellow. She is still under British jurisdiction, and her barrister is Sir Roger Lunt's son."

"So? Who the hell is that?"

"Sir Roger Lunt is a knighted member of Parliament. His family has been prominent in Britain for hundreds of years, and Mrs. Brill's granddaughter plans to marry his son."

Gould frowned. Born in New Jersey, he'd come from poor Jewish parents who'd struggled their entire lives to make ends meet. He'd pulled himself out of the slums using his brains and what his family called *chutzpah*. He'd managed, through hard work and strict dedication, to get into Harvard Law School and then into the FBI. At thirty-three years of age, he was very ambitious. This case had given him an opening to be in the spotlight, and he was going to pursue it, no matter who got in his way.

"Are you talking about that pretty American girl who yelled at me from the back of the room?" Jordan smiled. "How do you like that? I don't believe she's going to marry that stuffy Brit! No offense, Holmes."

"None taken. I'm not a stuffy Brit." Holmes shook his head as they walked two blocks to a small deli with a sandwich bar. They ate quickly, both thinking about how to proceed in the investigation. Afterward, they headed back to Scotland Yard but then went their separate ways—Geoffrey to the main office to deal with the press and Jordan to the computer and technology room.

By late afternoon, Geoffrey was starting to worry. The first forty-eight hours were crucial in solving a crime, and so far, all they had was Mrs. Brill. He had just gone over notes with his men, and nothing more had developed. Even their sources on the street had produced a blank. Though Wheeler was not a Brit, and had only been in the country less than twenty-four hours, the media pressed him for a statement. Maybe the Yank had come up with something.

Geoffrey left his office and walked to the computer room, a sort of database room at Scotland Yard. A few men were there, busy with cases of their own. He casually acknowledged them with a nod and walked over to Jordan, who was seated before a large, thin computer screen, shirt unbuttoned, tie thrown over a chair, and a large empty soda bottle by his hand.

"How are we coming along?"

Jordan had been sitting at his computer all afternoon. He looked up at Holmes and said, "This guy is a total prize. They filled me in somewhat back at home, but I learned a lot more about the man today. He was a scam artist of the highest degree, a real smooth talker who played a Ponzi scheme for years. Singularly or as a group, any of the investors cheated out of their life savings could have killed the bastard."

Geoffrey grinned as he walked over to refill his cup of tea. "You'll get as much information from the newspapers as from your FBI files. But you'd better watch out for yourself. I heard that a lot of the embezzled money came from small-time investors. The little guys are often more dangerous than the big money men."

"That may be so, but right now, I'm going through a list of his larger investors. A Chinese group is one of them."

Geoffrey stood with his cup of tea in hand. "What about Mrs. Brill? Have you found that she is an innocent bystander? I fancy she just got caught up in memories at the wrong time."

Jordan stood up and walked over to the coffee pot. He wasn't going to drink his coffee out of one of those dainty teacups, so he poured it into the only mug he could locate, a chipped souvenir of London.

Geoffrey shook his head. "How can you drink that stuff without any cream or sugar? Anyway, you didn't answer my question. She's innocent, right?"

"I'm not so sure about that. I haven't dug up much on her, except she did go to high school with Wheeler. But her husband's family wasn't so clean. Jerry Brill's brother was arrested for playing in a small-time Ponzi scheme, so there could be a connection." Jordan took a sip of his coffee, savoring the strong bitter taste.

"There's another odd thing with Mrs. Brill. Her mother spent time in a concentration camp during the Second World War, even though she came from a very wealthy and influential German family.

"Maybe Mrs. Brill is a spy," Geoffrey offered, joking.

"If so, she is not on our side," Jordan replied. "Nothing shows for a German investor. We do know that this Chinese company I just mentioned—Wu Industries—owns up to twenty-five percent of Wheeler's now-bankrupt company. Wheeler's girlfriend, Suzi Wu, introduced him to her family. Her maternal grandmother runs Wu's American division of their prostitution houses. That's where the majority of Wu Industries' wealth comes from. The sale of clothing is their legal front. By the way, that was a good point, Holmes. Could Mrs. Brill be a spy working for an anonymous German investor?"

Geoffrey Holmes was not happy to hear this. He had to admit to himself that he fancied Lori Brill, and he silently hoped she wasn't involved in anything untoward.

"Well, the investigation is still under my jurisdiction, so check with me before doing anything. Forensics hasn't come up with much. The bullet passed through his eye, producing massive brain damage and hemorrhage, along with immediate death. Fingerprints belonged to Wheeler, Brill, the housekeeping department, and the guard from security."

"Did you question everyone in the suites on the floor, especially the two families who helped Mrs. Brill?"

Geoffrey Holmes stroked his chin again.

Jordan stared at him. "Why do you always do that?" he asked, mimicking the investigator.

Geoffrey smiled. "Sorry, mate. Smoked a pipe for years. I can't seem to stop reaching for it. To answer your first question, yes, all of them. The occupants of the four suites, the housekeeping staff, the hotel security, the manager, the staff at reception, in the restaurant, and the pilot and flight attendants on the British Airways flight have all been questioned. Couldn't find the cab driver. Too many now, not like the old days."

Jordan paced slowly back and forth. "Strange, no one heard the shot or saw anyone suspicious. And you won't believe this, but the camera on that floor had been malfunctioning for a few days. I've got nothing substantial on film."

"Yes. That is rather odd, isn't it?" Geoffrey mused.

"Odd? To say the least," Jordan replied, bending toward the computer and clicking the mouse for a close-up view of the video. "See for yourself."

Geoffrey and Jordan both pulled up chairs and stared at the computer screen as Jordan pulled up surveillance images from the hotel hallway on the twenty-first floor. The image was not crisp, but it was clear enough to show a tall figure, with a cap and coat collar obscuring most of his face, walking down the hall near Josh's door. The film then jumped, and things went haywire.

"Strange. There is an obvious glitch in the film. Perhaps it's been tampered with?" Geoffrey offered.

"Perhaps. That's being looked into now, but it looks like a good, old-fashioned malfunction." Jordan leaned back in his chair and paused the film. "Are you sure there was no connecting room? The murderer couldn't have left through the window on the twenty-first floor."

Shaking his head, Geoffrey ruminated aloud. "Unless he rappelled down the face of the hotel. We've already gone over the room. The Italian couple at the end of the hall near the elevators thought they saw a large man getting on or off the elevator early in the morning when they opened their door to get their paper, and housekeeping thought they saw a large blond man on the floor the day before. We obtained descriptions of both. They were close to the same."

"Let's check those accounts with what we see here," Jordan said, moving toward the computer screen again. "Could be the same guy. He has the same build, but is he blond? Who knows?" Jordan blew up the image to better study the figure. "You know what? I think he has a stocking over his face."

"It would appear so, but . . . perhaps that is just the grain of the camera?"

Jordan raked his hands through his hair, exasperated. "This isn't enough to go on. And this guy just fucking vanishes into thin air? What the fuck! Sorry."

A few men who were also occupying the database room snickered.

Ignoring Jordan's outburst, Geoffrey replied, "My men did check everywhere, but I am open to suggestions. Besides, of course, the vanishing into thin air bit."

Jordan shook his head. "Holmes, do we have anything? Have we got anything at all regarding the structure of the rooms? We can't get a good ID from these images. Useless!" Jordan went back to fuming as he shoved the mouse across the desk. "We should have Lori Brill dead to rights. Nothing else makes sense!"

"No, we can't get much, I'm afraid, not from what I see here. The man kept his face well hidden. All we have is a figure, face obscured, gloved hands, gray overcoat. He isn't even seen entering the room. As for the room itself," Geoffrey said, rising out of his seat, "we'll have another look-see."

"Let me see the transcript from everyone you questioned that day. We need to go through the interviews systematically to make sure none of the occupants on the floor were connected to Wheeler or had invested in any of his deals. We're looking for a murderer connected to his Ponzi scheme, but it could have been anyone—maybe even the boy who brought in the room service breakfast or a former girlfriend or boyfriend. Remember, there was no forced entry."

Geoffrey and the other men laughed at that.

"It's entirely possible," Geoffrey replied to placate a humorless Jordan. "We . . . erm . . . we don't want to rule out any possibilities."

Jordan clenched his jaw and let out a long sigh before speaking. "Mrs. Brill said Wheeler was still in bed watching television when she went into the shower. Someone he trusted came into the room because Wheeler didn't attempt to get up. He let him in! He probably turned towards him, or her, and was shot instantly in the face."

Holmes resumed stroking his chin. "The feathers about the bed would suggest the mangled pillow was stuffed in Wheeler's face to prevent a blowback of brain matter when he was shot."

"Let's go over what the old lady said again."

Holmes rolled his eyes at Jordan's lack of decorum. "Well, Lori said the door had been left unlocked since Josh had ordered breakfast shortly before she went into the shower."

"Oh, yeah, the breakfast in bed bit. Boy, what a smooth bastard. Embezzling millions of dollars, then lounging around in bed with an old flame. He was still in bed when the intruder came in. Shot him from a closeup position."

"Yes, that sounds about right. I'll get those transcripts to you right away. I talked to forensics. Wheeler was left-handed, and the shot went into his left eye. They have not ruled out suicide, though they believe it would have been difficult lying down."

Jordan looked up, scowling, his thick dark eyebrows knit tightly together. "*Suicide?* No way. This guy liked himself too much. I've studied his profile. Anyway, the gun would be there if it was suicide. Maybe it's with Mrs. Brill."

"A woman constable searched her at the station."

"At the station, not at the hotel?" Jordan asked.

"The hotel was given a total sweep," confirmed Holmes.

Still, the weapon is missing, and there are no other suspects!"

* * *

Geoffrey Holmes had been on the force since he was twenty, working his way up from a lowly street constable to chief inspector of the MIT. Retirement was just around the corner. He really didn't need a case this involved now. His wife, Eloise, had died of cancer four years ago, and his son, daughter-in-law, and grandchildren had migrated to Australia. He knew he was assigned this case because he was even-tempered and a good mediator, something that was vital to London's Scotland Yard when working with the United States FBI.

While others in the department may have been upset by the intrusion of a Yank, Geoffrey Holmes didn't mind it. Actually, he was giving the Yank more freedom than he should, but it was an infamous American who had been killed. Arthur Isaacs and Milton Sanders, two detective inspectors he had put on the case, had complained earlier about taking orders from Jordan Gould, probably more so because he was only thirty-three and so full of energy and so full of himself while they were veteran old-timers.

Sanders, nearing fifty, had been in the computer room during the discussion between Holmes and Jordan. He'd watched Jordan stalk out of the room in a huff after the comment about the missing weapon. Now Sanders pushed his rimless glasses down from his forehead and addressed Geoffrey. "That chap is hard to. . .hard to understand, with that New York accent and his fast mode of speech."

"And your nasal words and constant repetition is very annoying, *very annoying*," Jordan announced mockingly as he re-entered the computer room, startling Sanders, who quickly turned away.

Geoffrey smiled and shook his head. *Like Eisenhower working with Montgomery!* he said to himself.

Chapter Nine

Lori, Joseph, and Cate left the station, slid into the Bentley, took a few turns through the bustling town, and made their way around the traffic circle. Within minutes, they were home in the quiet suburb of Mayfair.

While driving, Joseph turned to Lori and said, "You don't have to cooperate with the investigation. You are not under arrest. We need to think about this. We need to speak with my father. He will know what to do." Joseph tried to comfort Lori. He realized this could not be easy for an older woman, so far away from home, to have to deal with a murder investigation, especially the murder of someone close to her. In times like these, people need to be aware of the facts in order to not go overboard with needless worry.

Cate joined the conversation, addressing her boyfriend. "I think my grandmother should tell them to get lost. I don't trust Jordan Gould. What a bastard! Did you see how he treated her? He doesn't care if he exposes her to danger! I don't trust him, Joseph," she said as she angrily crossed her arms over her chest.

"Cate, for heaven's sake, calm down," Joseph said. "You very well know the type. He's just an American, of different culture. He's only doing what Americans *do*. They tend to be trigger-happy when we British address things and situations in a more cautious manner."

"Is my grandmother a *thing* or a *situation*? There you go again, making excuses, bringing up the American argument again. Need I remind you, Joseph, that I, *too*—"

"No, Cate, you *needn't*," Joseph replied, turning and scowling at Cate.

Cate fumed silently throughout the short trip while Lori looked out the window, ignoring their spat. She shifted her body nervously before she spoke.

"I think I need to cooperate because I need protection. According to that young FBI agent, someone may be after me for something I don't have or because they may believe I saw the murderer. I guess I am lucky to be alive." Lori leaned her head back against the seat, pressing her hand against her forehead in an effort to control a migraine that was forming.

They rode the rest of the way in silence, each deep in thought. Joseph hadn't realized how deep Cate's love for Lori was until now, or he would not have suggested to Cate that Lori stay at a hotel. That argument still hung in the air, coupled with his mistake of generalizing about Americans.

When they arrived at the flat, Lori ate a quick turkey sandwich and then retired to her bedroom. She'd had enough excitement for her first three days in London. She declined Cate's invitation to join them for dinner and stayed holed up in the room for that evening and the next day.

* * *

The stairs creaked from the quick bounce of heeled boots. Lori turned over and looked at the bright digital numbers on the clock—10:00 a.m. It did sound like Cate's footsteps, but Cate should be at school, she thought. The bedroom door slammed open. Tigger, arriving ahead of Cate, jumped on the bed and gently pawed Lori.

"Gram, you need to get out of the house and move again," said Cate from the doorway. "I've left you alone for three days. I've taken the day off and planned a day of shopping and sightseeing with you. I won't take no for an answer."

Lori had been the one to encourage Cate to speak out and be independent, something she wished she had been. She knew Cate would not take no for an answer, so she would try to move out of the house for her granddaughter's sake. Lori had pulled herself back together thirty years ago for her son's sake after her young daughter died of cancer; she would try to do the same for her granddaughter. Actually, half of her died with her daughter Julie; the other half was walking a tightrope now. A much older tightrope, too.

Yes, thought Lori to herself, *you've always been a good actress, pretending your husband wasn't an alcoholic, pretending nothing ever bothered you, making believe you were living a happily-ever-after life.*

"I'll try," she answered as she pushed herself out of bed and into the bathroom. It took her longer than usual to brush her teeth, shower, and dress. She finally walked downstairs, where a warm breakfast awaited her. She lowered herself onto one of the high-backed chairs and tried to enjoy the tasty cheese omelet Cate had made for her. But she'd had no appetite since the murder and simply played with her food while, in record time, Cate cleaned up the kitchen dishes, fed the cat, grabbed two raincoats, and told her grandmother to get going.

Lori waited outside near the colorful flowerbeds that adorned the front of the complex as Cate pulled Joseph's black Bentley out of the attached garage. Lori hesitated as she started to enter the passenger's door on the right side instead of the left. She would never be able to drive in England, but Cate wasn't having any trouble. She whipped the car out of the driveway while Lori was still buckling her seatbelt and sinking into the soft, warm luxury of the leather cushion.

Turning towards Lori, Cate laughed. "If the tushy warmer is too hot, let me know."

"Just right," Lori answered, glancing out the window.

The morning had been gray and foggy, but now the sun was peeking through the clouds, and the sounds of tractors and the smell of fresh-cut grass were in the air. The trusted umbrella, a trademark for anyone living in England, lay in the back seat. Mayfair was such a lovely, pretty little village with its perfect white stone English cottages surrounded by colorful clusters of daisies, lilies, and chrysanthemums circling small garden ponds. *The English have a way with gardens,* Lori thought to herself.

"Everything in England is so . . . so . . ." She searched for the right words.

Cate supplied them as they headed east toward Victoria Embankment/A3211 to drive along the Thames River to their first destination: the Tower of London.

"Tidy and proper, and sometimes it drives me crazy."

Lori smiled to herself. Like her grandmother, Cate possessed the soul of a gypsy and, sometimes, a mouth like Lori's late mother-in-law. *Cate is beginning to sound like London is no longer presenting a challenge to her, and my Cate needs tumult. Well, here I am!* Lori grinned.

"I thought we would visit the Tower of London, go see the Crown Jewels, though you have almost as much jewelry, and then do some shopping and an easy lunch. What do you say to that?"

Lori nodded. So far, this visit had concentrated on her. She needed to try to put Josh out of her mind for the day and concentrate on her granddaughter's life and plans.

"Tell me about Joseph, honey."

Without even turning her head in a matter-of-fact voice, Cate answered, "Joseph is wonderful. He's handsome, smart, rich, compassionate, a barrister with a good job ties to the Royal Family, and he wants to marry me."

"I hear a *'but'* in there and a lack of a very important concept. Do you *love* him, Cate?"

Cate turned towards Lori. "Gram, were you in love with Papa Jerry, or were you always in love with Wheeler and sorry that you let him get away?"

Lori took a moment to think before answering. "Cate, love is an emotion we can't control. When we are very young, we sometimes mix it up with infatuation. I was infatuated with Josh, but in love with your Papa. You didn't answer my question about Joseph."

"I'm not sure about Joseph. Anyway, he belongs to a different country, another religion, and another world."

"Elaborate."

"I would have to live in England, away from all my family and friends, deal with his stepmother, who thinks she's God, and reject my Jewish ancestry."

"Why on earth would you have to?" Lori asked again, "Do you love him?"

"Yes, I think so. He is so good to me, but there are so many problems."

Lori thought, *Like* Fiddler on the Roof: *a bird and a fish could love each other, but where would they live?* She shook her head, thinking, *The younger ones never know how lucky they are or what problems really are.*

"Honey, I can't tell you what to do, but if you love each other, those things can be worked out. Look at your mom and dad. They are from different religions, and they compromised."

"Not really, Gram. Mom gave in and raised me Jewish, even though her parents were devastated. You know Mom never converted. She kept going to church while she tried to celebrate Jewish holidays with us, which really left me confused. You're the one who made me aware of my Jewish heritage.

Lori hesitated before speaking, not sure of what her response should be. Then she decided to give her granddaughter an honest response.

"You're right. We left you confused. After my Julie died, I was so mad at God I quit observing. As for your father, he talked Judaism, but he didn't practice it beyond insisting that your mother not take you to church." They drove silently along the river, making their short trip to the Tower.

Yes, Lori thought, *there are problems, but not insurmountable ones.* She thought about her mother-in-law. It would be hard to find another as possessive and crazy as Shelly had been. Then she realized there had been no mention of Joseph's birth mother. She wondered, were his parents divorced or did his mother die?

"Cate, what happened to Joseph's mother?"

"She died when Joseph was seven. She wasn't English. She was German and, according to his stepmother, Lady Elizabeth, she came from the servant class. He never really talks about her. She had a crazy upbringing, came from a low-income family."

"How did Joseph's father end up marrying her? One would think back then he would have been required to marry in his class."

"I'm not really sure of the details, but Joseph's father met her while he was on business in Germany. They had a whirlwind romance and married against his family's wishes. Seven years later, she and Joseph's baby sister died in an automobile accident. It happened many years ago when Joseph was an infant. He is very stoic and wouldn't talk about it. He reminds me of my mom, who won't talk about anything emotional."

Lori shuddered as she thought of Lord Lunt and Joseph losing two family members in an accident. Lori knew what it was like to lose a child. Her daughter Julie had struggled with leukemia for over three years. Lori only came back to life when Cate was born. Memories of a time when she, her husband Jerry, and their best friends, Jim and Adele, drove through the narrow roads of the English countryside in an eighteen-passenger Hertz van made her smile. What fun they had, laughing all the way. They were all gone now, much too young. Jerry drank himself to death; Jim had a quick heart attack, and Adele, her best friend for life, died of breast cancer.

And now Josh.

Josh had been the golden boy of Chicago's North Shore in the early 1960s: football captain, prom king, smart, and handsome. How proud she had been when he made her his girlfriend and took her to her own prom. Everyone expected him to be successful. She had expected him to be hers forever, even though Adele and her father had warned her about not trusting him.

She was having a hard time keeping Josh in the present. It was as though someone else was murdered, and Josh, her seventeen-year-old sweetheart, was still alive.

"We're moving from Upper Thames to Lower Thames, Gram, so we'll be there any minute," Cate announced, acting like a tour guide as they drove on. "There's the London Bridge! It's only about a twenty-minute drive. See the Tower Bridge? Everything seems so close to each other," Cate said and then laughed. "Probably because you can drive so damn fast here, it takes no time at all to reach your destination."

Lori grew excited to see the Tower Bridge against a bright, clear morning sky. There sat the mighty bridge with its massive network of light blue suspension cables and two expansive, blue and white walkways that stretched high above the bridge, connecting its impressive gray towers. The bridge's bascules directly beneath the walkways were up, admitting a few boats to traverse the Thames River.

"I heard they closed the walkways many years ago because it attracted a less-than-desirable population to do its covert business there," Lori offered slyly.

"Uh, oh, what kind of business, Gram?" Cate asked, knowing her grandmother loved details of a salacious sort.

"Oh, the usual kind of business most people need privacy to conduct—prostitution and thievery."

"Where do you get this stuff?" Cate laughed and shook her head. "If you really want to see something naughty, take a look over there." Cate stretched her arm across Lori and pointed northeast. "See that greenish glass building? You can't miss it."

"Yes! Oh, that wasn't there last time I visited." Lori gazed at the large, modern glass building, seemingly striped black and green and oddly shaped like a giant bullet or a pickle.

Cate shook her head. "That was built in 2003 and opened in 2004. It's called. . . Well, it's got a few names. The Swiss Re, or Saint Mary Axe, located on the street of the same name." Cate grinned slyly. "You might enjoy its other name." She turned to her grandmother and laughed, "*The Towering Innuendo*."

"Really?" Lori asked, laughing.

"And that's the cleanest name I can give you besides the Gherkin." Cate threw back her head and laughed loudly.

Lori listened to Cate's description of the building, catching phrases like "first environmentally sustainable building" and "floor plan shaped like flowers," and envied her granddaughter's easy laugh. Would her heart ever be that light again? She knew if she were going to survive this latest ordeal, she would have to play along until she felt right again. "Fake it 'till you make it," Rain had told her once.

Lori laughed along with her granddaughter and continued gazing out the car window. "I should like to visit the walkways of the Tower Bridge if we have time. I'd like to see the exhibits there."

"Absolutely, Gram. You know, Joseph and I have an exclusive membership to the Gherkin, which means we have access to private dining there. You *have* to see the view of London from the very top of that building. It's breathtaking! So, that's another plan on the agenda. Oh! Thar she blows!" Cate announced in her best fake English accent, "'er Majesty's Royal Palace and Fortress—the Tower of London." Cate again stretched her arm out and pointed north toward the Tower as she made her way toward the Tower Bridge.

The fat and dominating medieval fortress sat right along the Thames River. At one time or another during its long history, the Tower had housed lords and their families, animals, prisoners, armor, a public records office, and the Crown Jewels. The English royals had also imprisoned rivals for the crown in the Tower, among them Anne Boleyn, mother of Queen Elizabeth I; the young princes Edward and Richard, sons of Edward IV; and Elizabeth I herself, before she was queen. This castle and its surroundings reflected the rich and oft-times dark history of England; it was a must-see attraction for anyone visiting London.

Lori could plainly see, beyond the castle's defensive walls, the four turrets of the White Tower, which housed the royal family as early as the 13th century. Tearing her gaze from the great stone keep, she did her best to relax and enjoy both the sun playing between fluffy white clouds and the warm breeze flowing through the open car window.

"It's really a lovely day. Before we go see the Royal Ravens, let's take a little walk," Lori suggested. "I could use a nice stroll, and we can catch up on things like your school, your boyfriend, and . . ."

"And anything other than, uh . . ."

Cate helped, nodding in understanding.

"Yes, *anything* other than. . . than poor Josh." Lori closed her eyes and faced the warm breeze, hoping it would blow away the image of her friend's body in the hotel bed.

Cate reached over and squeezed her grandmother's hand. "Anything you want, Gram."

Using a pass given to her by Lord Roger Lunt, Joseph's father, Cate pulled into a reserved parking area near the Tower. From there, the two women took a leisurely walk along the river to see London in all its past and current glory. Cate chattered non-stop about her life in London and also gave Lori a first-class tour, pointing out new and old structures that made the enchanting city of London a landmark. They sipped coffee while sitting in the sunshine alongside the riverbank, watching boats move lazily along the water in the shadow of the Tower Bridge. All the while, a voice in Lori's head kept repeating, *try, try, try for Cate's sake.*

After their brief rest, Cate and Lori headed for the Tower, where, thanks to Cate's special pass, they could slip in as VIPs, thus avoiding the long lines at the castle's tourist entrances. Their first stop was the west wing of the Waterloo Barracks, where the Crown Jewels had been kept since 1303 and where now sat the new Jewel House, built between 1992 and 1994.

"Listen to this, Gram," Cate said as she read from a tourist brochure. "Only once were the jewels ever moved from the Tower. That was during World War II when they were taken from England to be hidden in Canada."

The priceless jewels sparkled in their individual vaults. Lori and Cate marveled at their beauty and spent time just staring at the clarity and size of the diamonds, emeralds, and pearls. Cate dreamed of wearing the diamond tiara.

Lori smiled and turned to Cate. "Way back in the summer of 1981, my friend Adele and I stayed up all night watching the wedding of Charles and Diana. Oh, Cate, the jewels, the glass carriage, all the pomp and—"

Cate interrupted her. "Gram, what about the marriage of Kate and William in the spring of 2011? That one was really a fairy book tale. A commoner married a prince and is living happily ever after. After watching Kate and William's wedding, I decided to spend some time studying in London, and here I am."

They moved at a comfortable pace through the exhibit, stopping to view Queen Victoria's blue sapphire ring adorned with a red ruby cross. Lori scrunched her nose up at it and whispered, "Gaudy!"

At the heart of the display sat St. Edward's Crown. Made of solid gold and encrusted with four hundred and forty semi-precious stones, historically, it was worn only once, at the moment of a ruler's crowning during their coronation. It was the only crown ever used during a coronation besides Queen Victoria's Imperial State Crown, which was also used during Queen Elizabeth II's coronation in 1953.

Lori mused about being a woman in charge of a country, to actually living the life of a queen. *How different her world must be from ordinary women like myself*, Lori thought. Then again, there was murder and gore throughout the history of British royalty.

"Life is funny," she said to Cate. "I was in my mid-thirties when Diana married her prince, not too much older than you are now, and I still believed in the Cinderella story. In 2011, when Kate and Prince William married, I was old and disillusioned with that old *happily ever after* story. Didn't stay up all night. I just glanced at the reruns of the wedding."

Lori sat down on a bench to rest. "How about we leave here?" she asked, her mind now distracted and her feet tired. She eased off her right pointed-toe pump and rubbed her foot, thinking, *I'm getting too old to keep wearing these fancy, uncomfortable shoes.*

"Well, we need to do a fast run through the armor exhibit for Joseph's sake. He loves it and reminded me to take you there."

"I can't do a fast run anywhere, but we could glance at it. Can't we tell him we saw the Great Sword of State and be done with it?"

Seeing the look on Cate's face, Lori gave in and accompanied her granddaughter to the exhibit. They'd examined the swords for only a few moments when Cate turned from the display and tugged on Lori's arm. "Gram, there's a woman staring at you."

Lori turned around. A woman, maybe in her fifties or sixties (it was hard to tell) and dressed in a narrow black woolen skirt and boxy black blazer waved at Lori. Lori was stunned that anyone would recognize her so far away from home. She acted in a familiar manner, leading Lori to believe she couldn't be just someone who had recognized her from the newspaper. Was there even a picture of her in the paper? Who *was* this woman? Suddenly, Lori's face flushed pink.

"Let's get out of here."

When they reached the outside, Cate asked, "Do you know her?"

Lori gasped for breath from the pace she had been moving. She sat down on a bench just outside of the Tower. "I'm not sure, but I think she is one of the women who helped me after I discovered Josh's body, a Mrs. Sweetman or a Mrs. Putty. I don't know, something like that. Anyway," Lori said, stopping to take a breath and shaking her head, "for sure, I don't want to talk to her, even though I am grateful for her help."

Cate understood. Gram was trying to put all the ugliness, the horror of it all, behind her as best as possible. She watched her grandmother's face as she struggled with what could only be menacing images of her horrible ordeal. Gram hadn't told her much, but she would be there to listen when she was ready. Cate and Lori sat quietly on the bench, watching people and boats move along the river, Cate's hand protectively over Lori's.

"We'll get through this, Gram. You're not alone."

Lori fought back the sting of tears as she looked up gratefully into the eyes of her lovely granddaughter. She saw an inkling of her own daughter in Cate's sweet face, and instead of catching painfully in her heart, she found the similarity comforting, as though Julie was somehow comforting her through Cate across all these years. She smiled a half-smile; Rain would have hooted with joy to hear Lori's thoughts becoming so mystical. Rain's influence was growing on her, she had to admit. And she welcomed the new perspective.

* * *

Mrs. Sweeney stared off into the distance before turning to her friend. "Madge, look there. Up ahead. Wasn't that the poor woman who was involved in the to-doings at the Palace, the Wheeler murder? I can't get that scene out of my head, I simply can't. That wee little thing in absolute hysterics, and all the questions at Scotland Yard . . ." Mrs. Sweeney tsked. "Why, you would think *we* were suspects." Mrs. Sweeney waved and gave a weak smile. "Hello, dear girl," she said under her breath. "She sees us, I'm sure of it. Oh! Now, that is odd. Why ever would that woman be running from us? And all we did was be kind to her. You would think she would be grateful. No good deed goes unpunished, Madge, like I always say."

She put her hand down as she watched the diminutive woman give a furtive glance their way, turn her head quickly, grab hold of the young woman she was with, and disappear into the crowd. "Well! Maybe she *is* a tart. Anyway, I'm glad you suggested we move to a different hotel,

Madge. It was simply ghastly, remaining in such close quarters to that den of iniquity. Oh, the scandal of it all, and what a way to ruin a lovely . . ."

Margaret Putnam wished her friend would keep quiet. She was a dear friend, but she never knew when to close her mouth. Margaret stood and stared at the young girl with Mrs. Brill. She was a stunning girl, tall, slim, with long legs and high cheekbones. She so reminded Margaret of her own daughter. She was around the same age, some- where in her twenties. Tears came to Margaret's eyes as she thought about her only child. Celia had been such a happy, delightful child. She never had an enemy. Everyone was her friend. Where did they go wrong? Maybe they protected and shielded her too much.

Mrs. Sweeney shook Margaret. "Well, God, go with her is all I have to say. Let's be gone, Madge. Madge, stop staring. The men are waiting for us. Let's go."

* * *

"Okay, Gram, let's focus on our day together. Put that stuff behind you today, okay?" Lori embraced her grandmother and kissed her atop her head. "What would you like to see next?"

"Honey, I think we should forget the tourist attractions and go shop- ping. I need some things, and I'd like to buy you a pretty outfit." Lori forced a weak smile and rose from the bench. In truth, she had had it. Mingling among so many people was adding to her anxiety. She jumped when other tourists clawed their way past her in the lines, she gasped at the pungent smell of smoke from someone's cigarette or pipe, and she cringed when anyone looked in her direction. She felt like they all knew who she was and either gave her despising or curious stares.

She and Cate made their way to the car and settled in. They then zipped along the A3211, Lori watching the sunlight diamonds play atop the Thames as they headed west on their nearly three-mile trip to Trafalgar Square. Along the way, she saw the great London Eye observatory, which sat like a giant Ferris wheel on the river opposite the square. On arrival, they walked around the square, noting Nelson's column, and then stopped on the steps of the National Gallery to people-watch. They then moved on, ducking into quiet, clean, tree-lined streets, browsing the shop windows.

As much as she needed clothes, Lori couldn't manage to find anything but some underwear and a thick black sweater, which she figured would come in handy as clouds were building up and the weather was cooling. She moved on automatic but tried to remain upbeat. Cate fell in love with a black knit dress. Fitted with a large black leather belt around the waist, hitting just above the knees on Cate's slim body, the dress was a knockout. Lori promptly purchased it for her. In a men's shop, they found a Burberry cashmere scarf for Joseph.

Loaded with packages and exhausted from touring all morning, Cate and Lori headed for their car. The light breeze of early morning had become a gusty west wind, and gray clouds scudded across the sky, dimming the once brilliant sunlight and promising afternoon rain. Eager to avoid a drenching but hungry after the day's adventures, the two women decided on a short trip north of Trafalgar Square to famous chef Jamie Oliver's restaurant.

Lori marveled at how Cate had expertly maneuvered the Bentley out of the congested traffic circle and sped toward the restaurant. On arrival, they left their packages safely inside the car's boot, then made their way around a construction crew across the street and into the popular Jamie's Italian Restaurant.

"Cate, dear, you are distracting the street crew with your short dress and great figure," Lori said as she eyed the workers.

"Oh, Gram, those guys stop for anything in a skirt."

The place was crowded with tourists, and they were squeezed into a small table not far from the entrance. A busy young waitress handed them menus. "Tea, coffee, wine? It's Friday, the fish is on special," she said.

Lori put the menu down. She wasn't in the mood for decision-making. "Fish and chips will be fine," she told the waitress while Cate thumbed through the menu before settling on a small chicken Caesar salad and a glass of red wine.

Cate tried to keep the conversation light and avoided the topic of Josh, even though they did see his picture plastered all over the newspapers and tablets. In today's communications age, there is no place to hide from the topic. News of Josh Wheeler and his murder was on television, radio, the Internet, phones, and computers, besides magazines and newspapers.

Comments at court concerning Joseph's association with Lori had caused some dissension between Joseph and Cate. That morning, Joseph had said maybe Lori should stay elsewhere, and Cate had blown up, telling him that it was his fault for talking to everyone about the murder and her grandmother's involvement. She was hurt that Joseph would put his position before his fiancée's family. She was thinking about this when the woman sitting next to them pointed to the paper and, in a very loud voice, commented, "Why do the Yanks have to bring their criminals to our establishments? Bloody intolerable."

Cate, trying to ignore the woman, pushed loose hair from her forehead, leaned in towards Lori, and plunged right into the topic at hand. "You seem much better this afternoon, Gram. Do you want to talk about Josh Wheeler? I don't remember you ever mentioning that you were dating someone."

Lori dropped the piece of fish she was about to put into her mouth. She was at a loss for words; something new to her. She wondered how to explain a seventy-year-old's obsession with a man to a twenty-six-year-old. She was sure Cate had never thought of her grandmother and sex in the same sentence. Lori had been gray and thus old looking since the day Cate was born.

She needed a tissue and felt around the chair next to her where she had left her purse. She panicked. "Cate, my purse is gone!"

Cate got up and moved over to the chair. "Calm down, Gram. It must be here." She checked under the chair, crawled around the floor, and searched the area to no avail.

Lori's purse was missing, the purse the police had recently returned to her.

By now, they had gathered a crowd around them. The waitress asked Lori, "Are you sure you had it when you came into the restaurant?"

"Yes," Lori answered, though by now, she wasn't sure of anything. She frantically looked at the crowd, then over their heads in a futile attempt to see if anyone was running away from the scene, purse in hand.

"Let's check with some of the stores we were in," Cate suggested. She took out her wallet and paid for the lunch, then wrote down her cell phone number and address for the waitress in case they found Lori's purse.

They were out of the restaurant for only a few minutes when Cate's mobile rang. She held her dress receipt in one hand, ready to phone the boutique, but stopped and answered her mobile. It was the restaurant; they had found Lori's purse in the loo. Since Lori had never gone to the restroom there, she assumed someone had taken her money, credit cards, and cell and left the purse. That was not the case. Back at the restaurant, when she opened her purse, she found the contents of her wallet floating through the purse. She and Cate sat down at a table and took everything out, checking to see what was missing. All her credit cards, documents, three hundred dollars in pounds, and a lipstick were there. Nothing but the keys to her home in Arizona and Cate's flat was missing. The lining throughout the purse had been cut open. Whoever took her purse had worked fast. Lori went white. She looked at her granddaughter.

"Cate, we better go and check your place. I think this has something to do with Josh." They left in a hurry, driving to the apartment through a light drizzle of rain.

Lori's worst fears were confirmed when they arrived. Books, clothing, papers, and knickknacks scattered helter-skelter comprised the first scene that met their eyes as Cate flung the front door open. The flat, though in an old building, had been remodeled, with walls knocked down to give a wide-open feeling. Thus, they could see disarray throughout the flat. Expensive digital equipment that could have been pawned was searched but not taken. In the kitchen, copper pots and pans, silver knives and forks, and splintered drawers lay all over the shiny wood floors. A glob of yellow mustard dripped down the opened refrigerator door. Someone had even searched through the appliances.

Oblivious to the mess, Cate ran through the house, calling, "Tigger! Tigger!" Cate found Tigger under the bed, shaking. She picked her up, pulled her in close to her chest, and petted and kissed the frightened cat on the head. "They can take anything they want, I don't care as long as they didn't hurt my baby." Tigger purred in Cate's arms.

Lori crumbled into a chair. "Honey, I am so sorry." She began to cry. "All of this is my fault. Someone is looking for something they think I have, and I don't know what or why except it must have something to do with Josh. All I wanted was a nice vacation with my granddaughter."

Cate, shaking, took out her cell phone and called Joseph, who told her first off to remain calm, touch nothing, and leave the flat in case someone was still there, then once outside, call the police. He would be home as soon as he wrapped up what he was doing. Frowning, Cate hung up and called the police.

Cate was still holding Tigger, who didn't want to leave her arms when she ushered Lori out of the flat and toward the flat next door. They knocked on her neighbor's door. A ruddy-faced, stout gentleman somewhere in his eighties answered the door.

"George, can we stay with you until the police arrive?" Cate spoke rather loudly.

"Sure, me love, what's going on? Did you say the bobby?" George tugged on the suspenders holding up his baggy pants, and welcomed the two women inside.

"We've been robbed. Did you hear or see anything?"

George shook his head. "Never wear me hearing aid when I'm home. Did they take a lot? Haven't had a robbery in this area in years. Better start locking me doors."

"It doesn't look like they took anything, but they really made a mess."

George smiled at Tigger, who had made herself into a small little ball of fur in Cate's arms. "Aw, they scared you, didn't they, love?" George cooed as he stroked the cat's head. "What a sweet thing." He looked up at Cate. "Oh, your mister won't be liking this situation. I was just fixin' meself a nice hot toddy. Can I offer you ladies one as well? Calm the nerves, set things to right!" he offered enticingly.

Cate declined, but Lori eagerly accepted. A hot toddy sounded just like the thing for a chilly rainy day, and she figured it would calm her nerves, and make this ordeal easier to handle.

George smiled and pointed to his sofa. "Have a seat on the chesterfield, and I'll fix you the best hot rum toddy you've ever had! I got the kettle on." He rubbed his eyes before lowering his eyeglasses from the top of his head and heading toward the kitchen.

Lori smiled. Being close to his age, she understood he'd just realized where his glasses were hiding. She was sure Cate thought he was just eccentric.

She took a seat on the sofa, but Cate walked over and sat down on a chair near the living room windows where she could watch for the police. After a few minutes, George returned with two hot toddies.

"Catie, me love, you needn't be sitting by the window. You'll hear the panda car when it gets here."

He handed one toddy to Lori and kept the other for himself. Hitting Lori's mug with his, he uttered, "Cheers."

"What's a panda car?" Lori asked, taking the warm mug between her hands.

"The small police cars used in the village," Cate answered.

Shortly, a small, round car resembling a black panda pulled up to Cate's building. Cate rose from the chair, Tigger in arms, and took Lori by the hand, pulling her towards the door. Lori hurriedly took the last sip of her toddy, put down her mug, and thanked George before leaving the flat.

Three policemen clad in white shirts and black ties entered Cate's flat, weapons in their hands. They wouldn't let the women in until they cased the place for anyone hiding inside. Then two policemen went right to work, checking the house for fingerprints and clues, while a third, a tall, plump gentleman, questioned Cate.

"Do you have an alarm system?"

"No, not since we've been here."

"How long has that been?"

"We've lived here for about a year," Cate explained. "We've never had any trouble. This is a tranquil, safe neighborhood."

"Might be a good idea to think about one, and a safer front door lock should be installed. Looks like they either had keys or just jimmied the lock on the door. Are you sure nothing is missing? This place is really messed up. How long were you gone?"

Before Cate could answer, Lori broke in with, "Officer, the break-in was my fault. The criminals were looking for something they think I have, but I don't know what it is."

The officer scowled, giving Lori a skeptical look. "Who are *you*?"

Lori realized this was getting confusing. "Maybe you should call Scotland Yard?"

The police officer tersely answered, "Ma'am, this is a simple break-in in Mayfair, which is *my* jurisdiction. I'm certain we don't have to involve Scotland Ya—"

Cate interrupted, "Call Inspector Holmes at Scotland Yard. My grandmother was involved in the Josh Wheeler case."

The officer looked at Lori sideways, his big smile exposing a missing tooth as it stretched his full, rounded face. "The embezzler? *Well*, you don't say. Sure enough, I saw you on the *Fleet Street* news. You couldn't be the *girlfriend*," he said doubtfully. "Maybe the witness?"

Lori excused herself and retreated into the bathroom.

Cate immediately picked up the phone to call Scotland Yard. Why she had called the village police was beyond her. In a short time, Inspector Holmes was there with his men, and Joseph had arrived just in time, letting Lori back off from the interrogation.

Lori, Joseph, and Cate stayed at Joseph's father's apartment in London while Scotland Yard did a thorough sweep of their townhouse. When they were finally allowed to return, the three of them cautiously continued on with their lives.

By the second week's end, Joseph remarked, "Cate, you can stop double-checking the doors. I'm sure the burglary was just a random choice by a lot of young ruffians."

Lori was not that optimistic.

Chapter Ten

Lori turned over and blinked twice to make sure she was correctly reading the neon lights on the clock by her bedside. It said 11:00 a.m. She pulled the pillow tight around her head to block out the bright sun piercing the windowpane. She had slept through the night, actually almost through the day. Those sleeping pills definitely helped. Her nights without them were filled with terror, sleepiness, and nightmares. She just didn't want to become dependent on them.

Lately, she hated the mornings. Too many choices. Shower or bath, what to wear, and why am I here instead of in my home?

She readied herself for the day and dressed in a casual gray and pink jogging suit. The house was very quiet, except for Tigger's occasional meow. She made her way down to the kitchen, where she found a note from Cate next to the coffee pot. She smiled as she poured herself a cup of the freshly brewed coffee, thankful she didn't have to attempt to figure out how to make a pot of coffee from this highly specialized, complicated machine. Pot, water, heat; that's all she needed. She didn't need a coffee pot to tell the outside temperature and make one cup at a time. It was a perfect place to leave Lori a note; Cate knew Lori couldn't function in the morning without her caffeine fix.

She'd left her reading glasses upstairs, so she picked up the note and held it away from her face. That cataract surgery reversed her eyesight. Now she could see distances, but not close. Everything was falling apart since her seventieth birthday.

Gram, Joseph went to work, and I went back to school, but don't worry. True to his word, Inspector Holmes has a man outside watching the house.

Lori stopped reading, moved towards the windows, and pulled the curtain aside. Sure enough, there was an unidentified black car sitting across the street. She could not make out who was in it. She moved away from the window and continued to read the note.

The day is yours, but the night belongs to Joseph. He insists we dine with his father and stepmother at the Ritz, which means we must dress to the nines and be ready to leave the house by 7:00 p.m.

Cheerio!

"'Cheerio!' Dinner at the Ritz. What is wrong with them? Why are my kids trying to entertain me? I need this now like I need a *loch in kup.*" Lori said, referring to a hole in the head. *I'm hanging on by a twig;* she thought as she threw the note on the table. She sat heavily on a kitchen chair and put her hands on her head. A head that was beginning to throb.

Shaking off the headache, she stood up again and began to pace, then stopped in place and steadied herself. She reached for the cell phone in her pocket, called her friend Rain in Arizona, and talked and talked, ending with, "The only place I want to go is home."

"Lori dear, will the police let you come home?"

She laughed bitterly. "Of course not. I'm still a suspect. Oh, Rain! I don't know what to do. I feel so scared and lost. The last thing I feel like doing is dressing up and going to the Ritz. Help!"

"Okay, Lori. You need to get it together for Cate. You don't want to keep her from graduating from the prestigious London Law School or upset her relationship with Joseph. It may be good for you to go out on the town," Rain advised.

They hung up, and Lori thought about how life in Arizona's quiet retirement community left Lori out of practice to meet the challenges she was facing on this holiday. Holiday. . . What a joke! Oh, there had been many times in her life when every day was a battle. Anyone who had lived with an alcoholic husband could attest to that, but she was much younger than he. *Yes,* she thought, *the young are very good at denial.* To the world, the Brills had been a normal, upper-middle-class family of four living in a beautiful home in a North Shore suburb of Chicago. The best cars, the latest fashions, and tons of toys were part of the façade.

Behind that stunning carved oak door was hell: unpaid bills were thrown everywhere; mother and children cringing with fear at the screech of wheels stopping short of plowing through the garage wall into the family room; family members ready to run and hide if their dad/husband entered drunk, staggering, screaming, and throwing things, or heaving a sigh of relief if he actually entered sober and loving.

It was those few times he came home loving that kept them together. Grasping at straws, always believing things would get better—that was the young Lori Brill. The Lori Brill before her daughter died.

A question formed in Lori's mind: *Which Lori Brill will face this tragedy?*

She sat for a while, slowly sipping her coffee and staring into space. The morning seemed to last forever. She went into the parlor where Cate had left some books, but she couldn't concentrate. Her heart leaped in her throat each time her cell phone rang—and it rang all morning. But after checking the caller ID, she refused to answer the calls except the one from her son Barry and, of course, Rain. She couldn't bear to talk about Josh's death with anyone else. She forced herself to speak to her son only so he would not worry. He was such a stoic individual.

She tried the television but couldn't figure out how to work the new-fangled digital remote control, which was fine, as it probably would show news about Josh. Afraid to venture outside by herself or to stay in the house alone, she found herself checking the locks on the doors and the windows. The refrigerator cycling, the creak of wood settling, the hum of the overhead lights, the purr of the cat—everything sent her frayed nerves into a frenzy. Lori never had a pet while growing up. Her mother was afraid of dogs and cats. So Lori moved around Tigger cautiously, which only made Tigger more interested in Lori. The cat sniffed and rubbed against her all day until Lori finally picked her up and petted her on the head until the cat grew bored with that and gracefully jumped from Lori's lap and settled on the carpeted floor in the living room.

Hungry, Lori went back into the kitchen and opened the refrigerator. A chopped chicken salad had a note on it saying: *Gram.* It was very good, but she had a hard time eating it. Seemed with each swallow, food managed to get caught in her throat. She just couldn't relax, couldn't swallow, and or take a deep breath. She felt like a hand balled up into a fist. She tossed the uneaten part of her salad in the trash bin, poured herself another cup of coffee, and reached into the fridge and found a bag of bagels.

Lori nicked her finger while cutting a bagel in half and then froze at the sight of blood running down her hand. She had heard of post-traumatic stress disorder, an affliction some military personnel suffered after experiencing combat. The condition could also affect otherwise normal folks caught up in some kind of traumatic event, like an auto accident, abuse, or a violent crime. She was certain she was now in the throes of it.

Add mental illness to my list of things to get past, she thought bitterly as she left everything on the table, ran back upstairs, and popped some pills. She crawled into her bed, fought the painful, jarring images of Josh's dead and bloodied body on their hotel bed, and slept the afternoon away.

When she awoke a few hours later, the last thing she wanted to do was get dressed up and go to the Ritz. At least she wasn't made to deal with choices; there was only one suitable outfit among her things. She realized Joseph and Cate couldn't empathize with the ordeal she had been through. She thought about a story she had read years ago called *I Have No Mouth, and I Must Scream*. It fit her life now.

* * *

The flat came alive the moment Cate pushed the door open. One hand was busy texting on her mobile, the other reaching for cat food out of the cupboard while at the same time she issued orders. "Joseph, your tux is in the car. I've just picked it up from the dry cleaning establishment. Gram, we barely have forty minutes to get out of here. Do get upstairs and dress. Traffic today was horrendous. Where did I put that black beaded dress bag from her highness?"

At 7:00 p.m., they left the flat, pulling up in front of the Ritz about forty minutes later; they were only seventeen minutes late for their dinner with the senior Lunts. Lori felt more relaxed than usual. She found she enjoyed London at nightfall. She felt safer, anonymous, almost normal under the blanket of night.

The door attendant recognized Cate and Joseph and took their car while they followed another employee into the impressive, Neoclassical-style building. Built in the romantic Belle Époque of pre-World War I elegance, the Ritz Hotel opened in London in 1906 with fanfare. It had continued for over a hundred years to be the hotel for royalty and the finest in London society and the world. As soon as Lori walked into the lobby of the hotel with its opulent splendor and dapper butlers standing ready at your service, she felt she had stepped back in time. The ornate furnishings, the enormous sparkling chandeliers, the paintings, murals, and decorative staircases made her feel like they were in a private castle. A Tiffany stained glass lamp with blue birds in flight and bright-colored flowers sat on an expansive carved mahogany wood and marble lobby table.

The staff acted as if their job was to take care of each person individually. Lori was so engrossed in the furnishings and splendor of the Ritz dining room that she almost tripped when the butler stopped at a large table and pulled out an elaborate red velvet and gold brocade armchair for her to sit on. The table was set with gold and white dishes and linen napkins, surrounded by more silverware and crystal than Lori had ever seen on a table.

After Lori and Cate were seated, Joseph's father stood up and introduced himself and his wife. Lord Roger Lunt, a tall, comely man in his mid-sixties with dark brown hair, a round, high cheek-boned English face, and a prominent stomach, was dressed formally in a black tuxedo and an impeccably white starched tuxedo shirt.

Lady Elizabeth, to Lori's surprise, was much younger than she expected. She was a thin woman with a large head covered by a mane of pin-straight, bleached blonde hair. Lori estimated her age to be around forty or forty-five—or she was a master at getting face-lifts. Her lips were surely altered to be that exaggerated and overripe, and her features—long, aquiline nose, high, smooth cheekbones—seemed factory-made. She was a living Barbie doll, the quintessential trophy wife.

She was dressed to the hilt like a member of royalty in a full-length, deep emerald green designer gown and long black leather gloves. She held what could be readily recognized as a small, jewel-encrusted *minaudière,* or clutch purse, designed by the renowned "Bag Lady of Budapest," Judith Leiber. The clutch, shaped like a lady's Japanese fan but looking more like a stained glass work of Tiffany, was lavishly decorated with glass beads of blue, green, white, and bronze, along with precious and semiprecious stones, like lapis lazuli and jade. An enormous emerald stone clasp sat atop the glistening fan, while a thick, black-corded tassel served as the bag's strap.

Lady Elizabeth herself was extravagantly adorned with diamonds and emeralds dripping from her ears and neck, which almost outdid the room's opulent furnishings. Lori's black St. John knit and her gold necklace with matching gold earrings were no match for Lady Elizabeth's outfit. Lori doubted if anyone at the hotel had anything that matched this obnoxious display. For heaven's sake, it was dinner with future in-laws, not with Queen Elizabeth II. This was one Englishwoman who didn't adhere to their proper understated dress code.

Lady Elizabeth held out her gloved hand to Lori upon introduction. Her small brown eyes critically scanned Lori's outfit, and her bright red engorged lips opened on cue into a wide theatrical smile that sank into a stern grimace when a waiter bumped her arm.

Eyes flashing, she turned toward the waiter. "You bloody arse, do you know who I am?"

The poor man quickly apologized. *If not, she would have had his head*, thought Lori. By the way, she treated the waiter and her guests, Lori felt like Lady Elizabeth was no lady, just a fake trying to act as if she had class.

Lori looked at Cate with pride. She looked flawless in her new formfitting black dress adorned with Lori's long string of cultured pearls.

A full staff of waiters, porters, and kitchen helpers attended to them, appearing with trays of food obviously ordered ahead by Lord Lunt. The food was fantastic. They dined on caviar, canapé Diane, quail eggs, Cheshire cheese, and meat and fish dishes with rich sauces cooked to perfection. Rum cakes and summer puddings rested next to an elaborate antique silver tea and coffee server.

Early in the evening, Lord Lunt directed the conversation towards an account of Lori's activities and life in the States. "Mrs. Brill, Joseph tells me you are originally from Chicago. In my younger days, I did a grand tour of the States. I spent time with a banking family in an enormous apartment overlooking the lake in downtown Chicago. It was a marvelous city."

"It still is. I miss the city, but not the cold winters."

"Joseph chose a tour of Australia for his law school graduation gift. I'm sure he'll make it to the States sometime soon. Did your family travel much?"

"My father did, as he worked for the government." Lori smiled as she realized he was fishing out her lineage. "My early years were spent in a home in the northern suburbs of Chicago, but I've always loved our lakefront."

Surprising Lori, he avoided any mention of Josh Wheeler. After the main course was served, his wife took over the conversation; Cate sat looking bored, and Joseph stayed attentive but quiet.

The champagne and the wine kept flowing. After about an hour of Lady Elizabeth's bragging about Lunt's royal family and their titles, a slightly tipsy Lori decided she had had enough, especially since not one word of condolence was said to her about Josh.

Lori sat up straight in her armchair, took another sip of the expensive champagne, and smiled wickedly at Lady Elizabeth.

"Quite an elaborate list of ancestors the Lunts have. I believe you mentioned a Duke from Germany. My mother comes from German royalty. We may be related."

Lady Elizabeth curled her lips, lifted her square chin, and responded, "Highly unlikely, Ms. Brill. There are *no Jews* in our family line."

Alarmed, Joseph looked towards his father for help.

Aghast, Lord Lunt turned to his wife. "Elizabeth, my dear, please lower your voice and watch what you say. The bloody staff can hear every word."

Joseph sat up, a strained expression on his face. It wasn't exactly the help he was looking for, but maybe his stepmother would listen to his dad if she thought someone other than the family heard her.

"Oh, really, Roger," Lady Elizabeth said, looking around. "Do you honestly think any Jews are working as staff? At the *Ritz*?"

Lori burned, but she kept a calm exterior. Leaning in closer to Lady Elizabeth, she said, "One can never be sure! So many of us were forced to become secret converts. We could be anywhere, in any lineage." She then continued with her family tree narrative. "My mother's family owned many banks, and when they helped finance World War One, Kaiser Wilhelm the Second gave titles to the family. So we, too, are of royalty. How did you say your family obtained their titles?"

"Did your Jewish family also finance the second World War?" Lady Elizabeth raised a penciled eyebrow and allowed a crooked sneer to play upon her overripe lips.

Lori gasped and started to get up, but Sir Roger Lunt interrupted the women's cat-and-mouse game before it became a fist-fighting match. Moving forward in his chair, he turned to Lori, and with a big smile, he asked, "Pray, tell us, are you related to the Rothschilds? They are good friends of ours."

Cate pulled on Lori's arm and literally sat her back down. Leaning forward, Lori narrowed her eyes in anger, focusing on Elizabeth's smug face.

"No, Cate and I are related to the Brunes of Berlin and Munich, who I'm sure were friends of the Rothschilds. That is, before my family's fortune was stolen and my family exterminated in the camps."

Sir Roger Lunt's small black eyes opened wide. He dropped his champagne glass, turned white, and collapsed back in his chair. Hotel staff and his son Joseph quickly surrounded him and helped him out of the room. Lady Elizabeth followed, but not before shooting a withering glance Lori's way. Lori and Cate sat there silently for a moment before Cate spoke up.

"I hope he is all right. Do you think he had an attack over something I said?" Lori asked.

Cate raised her wine glass and took a long drink. "He probably drank too much. He does that frequently. He usually withers out slowly, though. Is she a dragon lady, or what?"

"Those aren't exactly the words I'd use to describe her. What a nasty, racist, arrogant bitch!"

"Yep, there are those words, too. Calm down, Gram. Don't let her get your goat."

"Get my goat? Honey, she is terrible! She grabbed the whole herd!"

"And I'm thinking of marrying into this family of arrogant sons of. . ."

Presently, Joseph returned. "Pardon me, ladies. I just wanted you to know Father is all right. I think he just had a bit too much to drink. Their chauffeur will take him home."

Lori was puzzled. She was sure Lord Lunt's upset was a response to her mention of the Brune name, not due to drink, but this was not the time to pursue it. Lori knew little about her mother's family history. By the time she found out she had an uncle who had survived the Holocaust and was living in Berlin, he was on his deathbed. It had been a family secret throughout her childhood. She would like to talk to someone who could untangle some of the remaining secrets.

Again they drove home in relative silence, though Joseph made somewhat of an attempt to apologize for his stepmother's rudeness. But the damage had been done, the insult hanging in the air like a mephitic fog. Cate gave Lori's hand a firm squeeze, and she smiled at her grand-mother sheepishly when helping her out of the car.

As for Lori, she was still feeling the effects of the alcohol, but she thought to herself, *Maybe I went too far with that horrid woman. Couldn't you just die over her comment about financing World War Two? The unmitigated gall.*

* * *

Joseph was clearly upset, having driven all the way home with his arms bent at an uncomfortable, stiff angle, his hands tightly grasping the steering wheel, and his jaw set firm and clenched. He had an irritat-ing habit of clearing his throat when upset. Cate feigned a headache, though before Joseph's father became ill, she enjoyed every minute of the exchange. She always found Sir Roger intimidating and his wife intolerable. She had wanted to match them wit for wit, but Joseph would have been horrified. She loved Gram's responses. Why, she was back to her old self tonight!

Cate did wonder what had set off Joseph's father. She had seen him drink tons more without getting sick. With a wife like his, who wouldn't use alcohol to excess?

Chapter Eleven

A rainbow spread out from the window across the ivory carpet. "Could it be a sunny day?" Lori asked aloud as she slid off the bed. To make sure, she pulled the curtains all the way back. Maybe spring was really appearing; after all, the days seemed longer, she thought. She brushed her teeth, swallowed her pills, and stared at the running water of the shower, thinking maybe she would take a bath instead. While contemplating this, Cate knocked on her door.

"Gram?" Cate and Tigger entered the room. Cate handed Lori the house phone while shrugging her shoulders, squishing her face into a question mark, and mouthing the words, "Joseph's father." Lori wasn't surprised.

"Heelllo, Mrs. Brill," said Lord Lunt. "It was an absolute pleasure meeting you last night. I'd be quite pleased if you would join me for lunch today."

Lori answered, turning off the shower water, "Sir Roger, I'm happy to hear you are feeling so much better, but I must decline. I am a bit under the weather today."

There was silence on the line, and then Lord Lunt, no longer friendly, said, "Mrs. Brill, it is imperative that we meet and discuss some family matters. My man Bly will pick you up in an hour." The phone went dead.

Lori hung up the phone and sat down on the bed, bewildered.

Cate asked, "Well, what was that about? Both he and his wife usually have very little to do with us, and for that, I am thrilled."

Lori related the conversation to Cate as the younger woman settled on the bed next to her grandmother, her eyebrows knit in consternation.

"Possibly, he wants to talk about Joseph's marriage to you?"

Cate cringed. "No, we're at a standstill, and Joseph would have told me. Do you think he knew your mother's family? Gram, please refresh me on our family history."

"Make some coffee, honey. I need to get dressed. We can talk in a few minutes."

Lori quickly showered and dressed in one of her finer outfits, a long-sleeved, cream-colored silk dress with matching heels. She took a few extra minutes to apply some makeup, just in case his wife was around. The alluring aroma of coffee instead of tea guided Lori down to the flat's kitchen, where Cate was pouring coffee and filling the creamer. When Cate saw Lori, she sat down across from her grand-mother, eager to hear about the family history. Lori took a gulp of cof-fee, bit into the cinnamon coffee cake Cate had made and sat back in her chair.

"Okay, I'll make this brief because Lunt's man Bly will be here soon. My mother came from a prominent German-Jewish banking fam-ily. They owned a mansion in Berlin and a country home in Munich, so she lived surrounded by all the trappings of the wealthy of her time: expensive crystal, china, silver, custom furnishings, and servants. She married a man named Alfred, and they had a son named Joseph. In 1943, my mother, *her* mother, father, and sister, and her husband Alfred and son Joseph were rounded up and sent to Auschwitz." Lori paused and watched her granddaughter's face turn from a look of concern to sadness and, finally, to anger. It was never easy to talk about this; harder still for people to hear it. "Her brother escaped to the under-ground. As far as we knew, just my mother and her brother lived through the war. Her brother and his family went to Israel, and my mother moved to Chicago with the American soldier who rescued her. That man was my father.

"My parents never told me any of this. I found out from relatives in Israel after my mother died. Nobody talked about the Holocaust when I was growing up. It was a secret. In fact, my mother's whole life was a big secret, a secret that has haunted me my whole life. She had a number from the camps tattooed on her arm, and I never saw it. That is how hidden it was. Ten years ago, I discovered my mother's son, Joseph, was alive. You were a teenager and probably didn't remember when I visited him in Berlin. Unfortunately, he was on his deathbed, so our reunion was brief. The money he left me helped put you through college. That is why you are one of the few who has graduated without owing your life to the government."

Lori became very quiet. The ache in her heart returned as she thought about her father's words, *"Don't judge her too harshly, Lori. Your mother has been through a terrible tragedy."*

Lori often wondered what could be worse than a mother who didn't love you and a father who was always gone. As an adult, she found out the answer—the death of a child.

"Gram, I remember you showing me your mother's letters. They were fascinating. In fact, after that, I read some of Elie Wiesel's books, and I checked different places on the Internet to learn more about the Holocaust."

Lori thought back to those letters she had translated from German to English. The ones she found right after her mother died, the ones she read over and over until she knew them by rote. One, in particular, came to mind.

> *March 25, 1945*
> *My dear brother Dov,*
> *I am finally feeling well enough to leave the hospital. I know you want me to join you in Palestine, but I have another interesting opportunity.*

The young American soldier who befriended me has asked me to marry him. He is seven years younger but a very capable young man. He comes from a Jewish family that has connections with the government, so I believe he will be able to get me into the United States.

Do I love him? You will ask. At this stage, I don't know what I feel; only that life must go on. He can never replace my beloved Alfred and little Joseph, but I must have been spared from death in the camps for a reason.

Your sister, Lillian

Lori also remembered some twenty years ago when she and her husband Jerry returned to Arizona from their son's wedding in Chicago. Her neighbor had told her some older man calling himself a baron had come around the house, and he had asked her if Lori had been born in Germany. Lori dismissed it as a mistaken identity, especially since she had more pressing problems. Jerry had started drinking again after years of being sober, and she had just given him a choice to either go back to rehab or she would leave him for good. Too bad she hadn't left.

Well, that was history now.

"What do you think this has to do with Lord Lunt?" Cate asked.

Lori looked up, startled. Cate's question had brought her back to the present. She heard the doorbell ring and answered, "I don't know, honey, but I will know soon. Lord Lunt's man is here."

Chapter Twelve

The sound of computers humming and the clicking of fingers on the table in the technology room of the station surprised Inspector Holmes. After all, it was almost noon on Saturday. He walked into the room. Sitting at the computer, pen in hand and coffee cup nearby, was Jordan Gould.

Holmes glanced at his watch. "What are you doing here?"

"Headquarters back home just sent transcripts of interviews with some of Wheeler's girlfriends and a list of others they are looking for. You need to see these."

"Come, let's have a bite to eat down the street, and you can tell me about it. I assume you haven't had lunch."

"Good assumption. Let's go."

The two men had put on their coats and hats and started out of the station when Holmes suddenly hesitated. "Good Lord, your intensity upsets me. I almost forgot why I'd come here. I left my briefcase in the office."

The phone rang as they walked into Holmes' office. Picking it up, the chief inspector listened and then handed it to Jordan.

After returning the phone, Jordan looked up. "We may have a breakthrough. My office has located the whereabouts of Wheeler's current girlfriend, Suzi Wu. She is in Shanghai, and it seems she's planning a trip to London. They have men watching her and will keep us informed. They have a few photographs of her with Wheeler from some charity events. They're e-mailing them to me now."

"Do you believe she has something to do with his murder?"

"My superiors do. As I told you the other day, Suzi is a member of the Wu family of Wu Industries, major investors in Wheeler's Ponzi scheme."

"Good to hear we may have a viable suspect in this case," the inspector said as they left the building and crossed the street. "I'm starting to get heat from my superiors." He raised his eyebrows while looking directly at Jordan. "They think I'm letting the Yank do too much, and I should be setting the machinery in motion."

Jordan smirked. "You won't be sorry I'm working with you. We'll crack this case. Your men are watching the house, right?"

"Yes, of course."

Holmes put a copy of *The New York Times* in Gould's hands. "It is mainly your press that's complaining."

A headline on the front page of the *Times* read: *Jilted Investors Anxious for News, Feel British Ignoring Wheeler Murder.* Jordan laughed.

"Geoffrey, you should look at the social network pages where everyone thinks they could be a better Sherlock Holmes than you." He didn't mention all the jokes and editorials about Wheeler and Mrs. Brill.

Holmes stopped in front of a pub called Hardcastle. The two men walked in through the large stained glass door. Inside, metal fans whirled above the room with its dark wood walls. Old beer steins adorned the shelves above the bar.

"Oh, there's a good spot," Jordan mumbled, and he was off in the direction of a deserted area of the pub.

"Evening, Inspector." A stout, ruddy-faced proprietor greeted Holmes. "Same table?"

Following Holmes' gaze, he said, "Ah. Got a Yank with you?"

After they were seated, Gould asked, "How did he know I was a Yank?"

Holmes just grinned at Jordan, who was dressed in khaki pants and an open shirt with the sleeves rolled up, thinking of how he had rushed to a table before the proprietor had a chance to greet him. *And then there is that accent.*

Approaching the table, the server smoothed back a piece of hair from her face and took out her pad and pen. "What will you have?"

Jordan said, "I'm not quite sure yet."

Holmes took the menu out of his hands. "They have the best-minced meat. And you must save room for a sweet. The lady bakes them herself." He looked at Jordan, who had turned his nose up at the mention of mincemeat, then said to the server, "Adrienne, give us the fish and chips with vinegar instead of the meat and two applejacks."

"Do ye want a starter?"

"No, just the meal will be fine." Holmes looked at Jordan. "Right?"

Jordan nodded his head in the affirmative, although he was not quite sure of the question, nor was he used to Holmes taking over as he was today.

Two friends of Holmes approached the table and greeted Geoffrey. One asked, "Heard you were the one on that Yank's murder. Anything new?"

Holmes smiled, "Scotland Yard always gets its man." He was happy when the server appeared with their food and drinks. "Ahhh, time to eat." He waved off his friends before digging into his meal. "Cheers! Take care." He stabbed a forkful of fish. Holding the fork in mid-air, Geoffrey glanced over at Jordan. "Okay, tell me about this guy's girlfriends."

"Wheeler was married and divorced twice. First wife comes from a prominent family, but she once lived on an Indian reservation in

Arizona. She calls herself Rain. Today she lives in the same retirement development as Lori Brill. I find that very interesting. His second wife died in an airplane crash several years ago. They had a son together, but apparently, he's been estranged from his father for most of his life. My department has talked to both the son and the first wife. They claim they haven't had contact with Wheeler in years.

"The younger Mister Wheeler is coming to London for questions and to pick up the body when we release it. I doubt he'll be helpful if he's telling the truth about not seeing his father since he was a child, but we'll see. No other relative that we can find. A lot of ex-friends that were investors are around. Surprisingly, some are not angry but sad that he was murdered."

"Sounds like you're on top of information on Wheeler. That chap must have had an interesting life."

Holmes took a hearty drink of his applejack before asking, "What do you think of the food?"

"Damn good. I could get hooked on this applejack stuff," Jordan said, smacking his lips. "Never heard of this in the States."

"By the way, did the FBI find anything of interest while investigating Wheeler's girlfriends?"

Gould smiled wickedly and reached into his briefcase, and took out a group of pictures.

"Interesting, oh yes. But pertinent to the case? No, except for the last girlfriend. The Chinese one they are trailing. Loads of fun stuff to find on the Internet. It's shameful, really, how it makes our jobs so much easier."

"Yes, and complicated at times."

"Well, there ain't nothing complicated about this. Take a gander," Jordan said, handing the photographs to Holmes.

Holmes's face turned crimson as his eyes fell on pictures of naked bodies, one of which was clearly Josh Wheeler. Wheeler lay entwined with at least three young women on a large bed in what may have been a hotel. Holmes quickly turned three of the pictures face down. He was still somewhat of a prude, even though he had seen much as a police officer.

"This chap fancied himself a Hugh Hefner? I hope the papers don't get hold of those pictures. How old did you say he was?"

"Around the same age as Lori Brill. And yes, the press would have a field day," Jordan said, sneering. "That Wheeler knew how to live, two or three girls at a time, and all of them young. My guys are trying to question his most recent friends and girlfriends. I'm sure we are missing many. I think he had one in every port."

Holmes looked up, resting his hand on his chin.

"I think I'll go out to have another talk with Mrs. Brill," Jordan said after taking another applejack drink.

Holmes held up his glass and grinned. "You know what I think? I think you fancy that girl, Cate. She gave you a proper tongue-lashing."

"Yeah, she got her panties in a bunch, as you Brits say."

"*Knickers in a twist*," Holmes corrected, smiling. "Still, I think you want to see her again. I saw you admiring her."

Jordan put down his glass, a frown wrinkling his forehead. "Yeah, well, what's not to admire? She is lovely, passionate, fiery. . ."

"Yes, she is very protective of her grandmother. And she is unavailable."

"Yeah, Lori mentioned Cate is engaged to that stuffy Lunt. No way that will happen as long as I'm around!"

Chapter Thirteen

After Lori left for the lunch meeting with Joseph's father, Cate took off on errands. It was Saturday, and she had the day off from school, though she did have a paper due on Monday. With everything going on, it was hard to concentrate on school. She couldn't wait to get her master's degree and return to work as a lawyer.

Cate pulled up to her flat a while later, parked the Bentley in the driveway, exited, and went to the boot to get her bags of groceries, shoving her keys into the slit pocket of her pin-straight black Capri pants. She was busy concentrating on the dinner she planned to make.

I think I'll bake the cod so the house won't smell of fish, then prepare the asparagus with cheese, she thought.

Cate didn't see him. Her peripheral vision detected something, but she paid no attention to it until suddenly, she was grabbed, lifted, and dragged away from the car towards the house.

"Get in the house now!"

Fear gripped her heart until she realized who it was. She turned around, furious.

"Get your hands off of me, Mr. Gould!"

"I have no time for this." He tightened his grip on her arm. "Get the keys out, and open the door. Quickly!" He pushed her towards the door, causing her to drop her bag of groceries. Ignoring the mess, he turned and drew his gun, shielding her body with his. He roughly slipped his thick fingers into the pocket of her Capris and, tugging at her pants, pulled out the keys and shook them before her. "Come on, come on, open the door."

"You son of a bitch! What the hell do you think you're doing?" Cate looked around and, in her periphery, saw a man rush into a black car across the street. She instinctively clutched her purse close to her chest.

"Would you just shut up and listen to me?" Gould eyed the man in the car, then turned to Cate and stared hard into her eyes. "Open. The. Fucking. Door!"

Cate fumbled with the keys but managed to get the door open. In an instant, Jordan had shoved her into the house and down onto the floor of the foyer. Keeping his hand on his gun, he watched the black car speed off down the street. He locked the door behind him.

"For fuck's sake, shut up and stay down."

Cate began yelling a string of obscenities at Jordan from her sprawled position.

Jordan rolled his eyes. "Yeah, yeah, you're welcome."

"Are you crazy? Am I supposed to be thanking you for something?" Cate rose from the floor and took a few swings at Jordan, who deflected her attack as best he could while securing the house. Following Jordan about the living room, she continued to hit and scratch him.

Jordan, having placed his gun safely in its holster, finally grabbed Cate's hands to stop her assault. "Will you keep quiet and let me explain?"

"You better have a good explanation, Mr. Gould!" Cate answered as he released her. She had become aware that her body had reacted to his touch, which irritated her. She moved as far away from him as possible.

Before explaining, he pulled the curtains back a fraction and looked out the window. *They're gone.* Then he turned to Cate, who stood with hands on her hips, her blue eyes narrowed in anger.

"There was supposed to be a car outside, watching your house all day. Did you see that guy? Running to his car?"

"Yes. He was parked across the street from my house. He was there when I left today."

"Did you talk to him?"

"No. I just nodded at him before I left for my errands. He stayed in his car. What is this about?"

"That wasn't our guy. I watched him for a while. Right before you drove up, he opened his car door and started walking towards you. When I showed up, he raced back into the car. He just drove away."

"You're really crazy," Cate answered with a smirk on her face. "That's the car from Scotland Yard, protecting us." Smoothing out her white shirt and her hair, Cate looked directly at him. "I intend to bring charges against you for assault." Then, in a flash, she moved towards him and slapped him across the face.

"Assault?!" He rubbed at his burning cheek with his palm. He faced her, and in a stern voice, he said, "Listen, I told you, I don't have time for your bullshit. Nice way to listen to an officer of the law, by the way. Good way to get yourself killed."

"I'm fine!"

Jordan made a quick call for backup and then turned to Cate.

"Yeah, you're fine. No thanks to your acting like a mad woman. Some lawyer you'll make."

"I'm not in the habit of listening to assailants who manhandle me and shove me to the ground!"

"I should say not," Jordan said, scowling. "You are in the habit of going off half-cocked, though. That's evident. You're a fucking pro at that. I assumed you'd had plenty of practice. Jesus, look at me!" He looked down at the bleeding scratches on his arms and shook his head.

"You are wasting my time, Mister Gould. You scared away the bad guy. Now, go!"

Jordan ignored her and continued inspecting his arms. "My men are watching the house from the side street, and . . ."

Standing up straighter and folding her arms across her chest, Cate stomped her foot and yelled, "I demand to know what is going on! I wish you would just leave us alone and keep my grandmother out of all this!"

"I tried to explain. The black Renault outside your house wasn't *our* car. Our car followed the car that picked up your grandmother, and I didn't put her in any of this trouble. She did! Wheeler's to blame for all this bullshit. Not me, these folks are tripping up our plans to keep an eye on you women. Well, somebody else is hard at work here, and your grandmother's boyfriend was in it up to his fucking—"

Before he could say another word, Cate flashed him a warning sign. "He wasn't her *boy*friend. And she's with Lord Lunt at his estate. You should know that. I thought you had a tracking device on her!"

"Yes, we put a tracking device on her cell phone. Could you check to make sure she took it and then call her? I'd really appreciate that," Jordan answered after taking a deep breath.

While Jordan went into the bathroom to wash off his arms and look for bandages for the deep cuts Cate caused with her nails, Cate went upstairs to check on Lori's cell phone. When she returned to the first floor, she approached the bathroom with a worried look on her face.

"She forgot her cell. It's still upstairs, attached to the charger. What's wrong with *you*?" Cate grimaced at the sight of Gould, although she was no longer angry with him.

Jordan scowled, glancing down at his arms as he scoured Cate's medicine cabinet. "You are a hellcat. That's what's wrong. Some of these cuts are deep."

"You'll be fine. It's my grandmother I'm worried about!"

"Help me find some bandages, please, and call Lord Lunt to make sure your grandmother made her lunch date. Hopefully, all is well," he said, trying to remain calm and not wanting to scare her.

Cate sneered wickedly as she reached into the cabinet and retrieved a box of bandages from a small drawer. "Next time, I'll send you to the hospital," she said, handing him the box.

Jordan had had enough of this woman's attitude. But he couldn't blame her; she didn't really know what was happening.

"Call Lord Lunt's house. Your grandmother could be in serious danger."

Cate rolled her eyes. She guessed her grandmother was with the Lunts, and Jordan Gould was being dramatic. If a car had followed Lunt's chauffeur, it would have probably gotten lost on the unfamiliar narrow winding country roads leading to Lord Lunt's estate. Bly was equipped with a mobile, so he could always call for help. Then again, she thought, if Jordan's men had followed Bly, he could have lost them, too.

Picking up her mobile, Cate rang the estate. "Hello, Julian," she said to Lord Lunt's private secretary. "Could I interrupt lunch and talk to my grandmother for a minute?" Cate turned white. "Julian, are you telling me my grandmother never reached the Lunts' estate?"

Jordan grabbed the phone out of Cate's hands. "This is Jordan Gould from the FBI and Scotland Yard. Get me Mr. Lunt."

Julian answered, "I'm sorry, sir, but my lord wishes not to be disturbed."

Jordan stamped his foot, and yelled into the phone, "Goddamn it, get the master of the house on the phone now! This is the FBI." Jordan, with a stunned expression on his face, stood absolutely still while holding the phone in his right hand. "The bastard hung up the phone! I'll have him arrested!"

94

Cate took the phone from Jordan. "The English do not like bloody asshole Americans."

"Cate," Jordan replied, exasperated, "I'm *not* an asshole. Your grandmother may have been kidnapped. Do you understand that much? We need to know if they heard from their chauffeur."

Panicked, Cate called back with shaking hands and managed to get Sir Roger Lunt on the line. She quickly handed the phone to Jordan.

"Mr. Lunt, we believe Lori and your driver may have been kidnapped. Have you heard from him?"

Sir Lunt answered, "Good gracious, this is serious. We haven't heard from him, nor does he answer his mobile phone. I just assumed they were detained by car trouble, perhaps a flat tire, which is why Bly couldn't answer when Julian called him."

"I'm sending a man to your house. We may have a dire situation." Jordan hung up with Lunt and speed-dialed another number. His expression grew grave when no one answered his call. "Detective Inspector Isaacs isn't answering his phone."

Shortly, there came a sharp knock at the door, followed by a curt, "Scotland Yard, sir!" Jordan opened the door, and two constables entered.

"Good." Jordan turned to Cate, who'd collapsed on a chair and sat nervously playing with the hem of her shirt. "I won't leave you alone."

"What is going on? Where is my grandmother? She can't be kidnapped." Cate wiped the palms of her hands on her pants. Her eyes were pleading with Jordan to tell her it wasn't so. Now she was having a difficult time accepting the dangerous events that had taken over her life in the last week. Things were happening to her family that she had only read about in books or had seen on the TV, Internet, or in the movies.

"When we know, we'll tell you." Jordan's expression matched Cate's deflated look as he thought, *Confident and strong during stress, attractive without makeup or fancy clothes . . . She is my match, hellcat or not. Pain in the ass . . .*

He opened the door to leave, stopped, glanced at his bandaged arms half-concealed by his long-sleeved shirt, and looked at the constables assigned to stay with Cate. "Be careful," he warned.

"I'll keep her safe, sir, no worries," one of the constables replied confidently.

"It's not her I'm worried about."

* * *

Jordan Gould acted cool, but he was actually in a panic. The possible murder of the Brill woman was the last thing he needed now. He had been surprised when, out of nine agents working on the Wheeler case, he had been chosen to work with Scotland Yard. This meant that for the first time in his seven years at the Hoover FBI office in Washington, D.C., he would be reporting directly to the office of the director of the FBI. It also meant that the men following Wheeler to London with orders to pick him up after he emptied his safe deposit boxes were now reporting directly to him. Unfortunately, when Wheeler changed plans and went to the Palace, they were just watching the hotel and were not on his floor. Too bad. It had all been set up; one agent was assigned to take the bellboy's place and deliver the breakfast tray. But Wheeler was murdered before that could take place. Someone was always one step ahead of them. He had to figure out who that someone was.

Now that Jordan was in London, he realized how different Scotland Yard and the FBI worked. He had to watch what he said and move more slowly than at home.

He checked out Lori's mobile, looking for any unusual calls. There were some new unknown ones that better be checked out, though he suspected they would turn out to be from a throwaway phone. Too bad the woman left the tracker phone on the charger. How could she be so careless? *Senior moment*, he thought wryly. He was concerned over the possible loss of Richard Townsend and Arthur Isaacs, the two men assigned to follow the car carrying Mrs. Brill. There was no reason, though, to jump to the conclusion that they had killed Mrs. Brill. If these men were in such hot pursuit to find something, killing everyone in sight would not help their search. Holmes' men just got in the way, that's all. *Damn it. Did they get too close?* His men watched the airport in case anyone connected to Wheeler was coming to or leaving London.

* * *

Roland stepped up to the black, nondescript car that held the bodies of Inspectors Arthur Isaacs and Richard Townsend. He paused to inspect his work; both officers had been shot in the head. Clean shots. Roland prided himself on good aim, but he felt incredibly proud of hitting moving targets. These were the perks of the job. The adrenaline rush he needed.

The two officers had been trailing the older woman and her driver, and it took nothing to overtake them, especially since they had slowed down upon gaining entrance to the estate grounds and had been oblivious to being followed. Roland had the curves in the road to thank for that.

After quickly maneuvering the unmarked police car into a secluded, wooded area, making sure it was not easily detected from the road, he returned to his car and slipped into the passenger side.

"Move," he commanded. A young man behind the wheel turned gloomily away from Roland and proceeded along the tree-lined road that led in a meandering manner through the Lunt estate, past bridges, babbling brooks, thick forests, rolling green knolls, and, finally, to the Lunt mansion.

Roland fished for his cigarette pack in his front shirt pocket and lit a cigarette, humming a jaunty tune as the car followed the black Rolls Royce at a safe distance. Extreme wealth and privilege gave one a false sense of security. He revealed, as he always did, in the feeling of being the predator in this scenario, with this old bird and old geezer being the prey as they took their time taking in the magnificent view while the luxury sedan wended its way through the picturesque scenery. Sometimes this job was too easy, and he bemoaned its lack of sport. He wanted more challenging opportunities than this thinning of the herd. But fun was fun, and soon this sport would be almost over. He had to think of ways to prolong the adventure. After all, if one didn't love his job, it ended up being a chore.

Chapter Fourteen

Lori settled back into the plush seat of the Rolls Royce. Though she was traveling in style on her way to a lord's country estate, uneasiness still encompassed her. Bly, dressed in a black chauffeur suit with a proper black cap covering a head of grey hair, had to be at least ten years older than Lori. He drove the car in a slow, steady manner as they traveled along narrow country roads.

"How long has Sir Lunt employed you?"

"Oh, since the lord was a young man, ma'am. Started when his father was still alive. You know, ma'am, my lord still is able to keep his estate intact while so many gents have sold out or turned their places into flats or tourist attractions."

"My granddaughter told me it was something to see. I guess it is four hundred years old or more, with a massive country home."

"Yes, ma'am, but the real charm is the grounds. Sir Jeffry Wyattville, a renowned architect, designed the gardens in 1810."

Lori looked out the window. Rain had begun falling in an even, rhythmic motion over the narrow winding road, which was partially hidden by enormous trees. The sun and the clouds were playing hide and seek, brightening and darkening the landscape. It seemed after they crossed a wooden bridge, they went from flat land inhabited by cows to a dark foggy forest.

"I guess you know these roads well."

"Don't be alarmed by the roads. I know them as well as the back of me hand. Even though we are on the estate, we still have a ways to go. Used to have foxhunts out this way. If you look out to the right, there is a large gray hawk in the tree, watching some animal intently. I can't make out what it is through the rain. He is hunting something."

Lori felt jumpy at the prospect of talking to someone who could unlock her family secrets, which had haunted her for seventy years. Josh's death even took a back seat. Lori sat there thinking about the many times her mother retreated into her room with a migraine whenever Lori asked her questions about her life in Germany. Lori's father protected and cared for her mother like she was a china doll that could break easily, and even a daughter's love could not penetrate this fragile, protected figure. Lori's childhood spent with an aloof and untouchable mother had been painful and puzzling. She leaned back in deep thought.

The black sedan flew around the curve and slammed directly into the front of the Rolls. It pushed it off the road right into a ditch, wedging the Rolls between the runaway car and the trees.

Bly, shaken but unharmed, turned back towards Lori and asked, "Are you okay, ma'am? Don't know why another car would be racing on the lordship's estate now. Must be visitors."

Before Lori could answer, the front car door opened, and she heard a loud blast. Lori saw Bly fall against the steering wheel. Blood ran down his face.

Lori felt a surge of panic take over her body. She screamed once and promptly blacked out.

Her car door opened. A huge man with massive hands slapped her face. "Wake up, and shut your bloody hole! Do as you are told." His voice was even-toned and quiet. A chill took over her whole body as her eyes gazed upon a cold steel gun pointed at her heart.

She looked at Bly's lifeless form slumped over the steering wheel, and her whole body began shaking. The man with the gun yanked her out of the car, leaving her coat and purse behind. She screamed, "No, no!" He grabbed her other arm and secured her hands behind her back with some kind of rope.

"One word out of you, and you'll be next to the geezer," he said as he pointed to Bly's body.

She froze and fought the darkness closing in on her. She desperately wanted to be awake. It would only be worse, unaware of where they were taking her. He pushed her into the back seat of the black sedan and slid in next to her, keeping the gun near her side.

"Move," he said to whoever was driving.

"What is happening?" Lori asked, her voice small and creaking. She shut her eyes tightly as she felt the cold steel up near her cheek.

"One more word out of you, and I'll tape your mouth shut, and one scream, and I'll blow you to bits."

The young man driving turned around, scowling at his partner. "Ye didn't have to kill the old guy. We're in deep *shite* enough as it is, killing those—"

"Shut it! Mind your tongue, you. So ye want witnesses? Are you *daft*?"

The driver answered, "What about the old bird? I thought you were going to blindfold her."

"You're right. Stop the car and help me. I can't be doing everything."

"Yeah, you've done plenty enough on yer own," the driver said under his breath as he stopped the car, fumbled in the glove compartment for a dark scarf, and handed it to the man guarding Lori. Lori detected alcohol on his breath. The driver held the gun on her while his companion, his face sporting a jagged three-inch scar, tied the scarf over her eyes. In a moment, all went black, sending her further into panic. Not able to move her hands and now unable to see a thing, she began breathing in shallow quick breaths.

In a hard cold voice, the man closest to her said, "I am goin' to frisk you for electronic devices. Be assured I have no other interest in an old goat."

At his mercy, she sat quietly, trying hard to keep from vibrating nervously while the man ran his large rough hands over her body. He snickered when Lori jumped as his hands now moved up her legs past the hem of her dress. He wrapped his hand around her diamond ring and gold bracelet. She was sure he would rip them off, but he left them on her arm. At a time like this, material things had no meaning.

She said, "Take my jewelry, but not my life."

He laughed softly, menacingly. "Aren't you generous? Well, neither are yours to give now. It's my choice. Hey, Tony, the old lady dressed up in her finest just for us," the man sitting beside her said.

Lori thought she was going to be sick. She swallowed hard and leaned back against the seat. *Do not faint.*

They drove for a long time before they stopped. She heard the door open before her arm was grabbed and tugged forward. "Get outta the car," her captor demanded.

Blinded, she had lost her sense of balance and nearly fell, stepping out of the sedan. The man pushed her up a flight of stairs and against a cold metal door with a metal handle. Then he shoved her into a building and through another door into a warmer place, probably an inside room. He thrust her down onto a hard wooden chair, untied her hands, and handcuffed them to the chair's arms.

She immediately screamed, "Help! Help!"

The only response to her cry was a sarcastic laugh and the click of a key in the door. Because of the blindfold and the handcuffs, she was afraid to move and wasn't sure if she was alone. The room felt cold and damp on her arms and legs. Either no light could get through the blindfold, or the room was totally dark.

She called out, "Is anyone in the room with me?" No answer, except for a creaking noise, which could be pipes or, God forbid, a small animal.

Short of breath and experiencing heart palpitations and cold hands, she knew she was panicking. *Think, think, and calm down,* she told herself.

If they planned to kill her, she guessed they would have done so back in the car when they shot Bly. Her mind was a mess as she tried to piece together what was happening and where she was.

She surmised they were in some type of warehouse or factory. She deduced this from the hum of a powerful electric motor and the reverberating echo when she called out. She also took note of having heard the echo of shoes clicking on the hard cement floor. Possibly the building was abandoned; it smelled of mildew.

If only I had remembered my cell phone with the government tracker, she thought dismally. Oh, what's the difference? It would be sitting in my purse in the limo anyway or taken away from me.

After a short time, she heard the door lock open, heard a chair being moved, and felt the presence of a person sitting directly across from her. She moved her head around awkwardly when he started speaking. She couldn't see him due to the blindfold, but his voice, cold and devoid of feeling, made her skin crawl. She knew it was the scarred man from the car.

"You're the Brill old goat, right?"

Lori didn't answer right away. The blindfold and her nerves left her confused. He hit her in the face. "You answer when I talk to you, do ye hear? Just hand over the safe deposit keys and the codes to the bank accounts, and we will return you to your granddaughter unharmed."

Lori flinched from the sting on her face. Her impulse was to touch her cheek, but her hands were secured to the chair. She had seen enough movies to know if she really had what they were looking for, they would take it and then kill her. Look what they did to Josh and to poor Bly, and to her now. Afraid to further provoke her interrogator, she tried to answer in a calm voice. "I have no idea what you are talking about."

"Don't play games with us. We know Wheeler intended to clean out his safety deposit boxes in London and then go on to Switzerland. We searched everything Mr. Wheeler had and then all of your and your granddaughter's things in the house."

She heard the chair's creak, and the voice grew closer to her ear, a soft, low whisper. She felt his giant hand on the top of her head. "Where did you hide the keys and codes?"

Lori was puzzled. "Why do you think Josh would give me those things?" she whispered conspiratorially.

"Why wouldn't he?" he asked, continuing his eerie, raspy pillow talk in her ear. "You were his traveling partner, after all. Hmm? Look." He began to play with her hair. "Stop playing games and just tell us what you've done with the items. They are of no use to you now. Remember, we know where your granddaughter is at every moment. Cate. . . is a tasty morsel. And I like to play with my food."

Lori cried out in anguish and fear. "I *don't have* any keys or whatever you are looking for! You are making a big mistake! You leave my granddaughter out of this! We've got nothing to do with this! Why won't you believe me?"

He sat back in his chair and stared at her coolly, silently. She sat, her head erect, her chest rising and falling rapidly from sobbing, her face half obscured by a blindfold. He surmised it would take her only a few hours to die if he beat her to death with his fists, keeping his blows central to her body for slow bleeding and maximum injury. This one was old, but she was fiery. Perhaps she would put up a better fight than he imagined. He hoped so. Time will tell.

"I'm going to give you some time to think about it."

The scraping of a chair against the concrete floor and the receding footsteps told Lori that her interrogator, with a monotone voice, was leaving the room. She soon discovered someone was to replace him.

She heard lighter footsteps approaching. She felt a cold chill down her spine. Instead of another interrogation, a different man fed her bread, soup, and water.

She would be fed the same way once every day during her captivity. She was given bathroom privileges twice a day and interrogated every morning by the same hard, raspy voice that sickened her as it grew tender in her ear, like the soft speech of a lover. She knew her interrogator was the same man who kidnapped her. She could detect the smell of Jack Daniel's anywhere. It had been her husband's drink of choice.

* * *

She guessed she had been there for four days already, though it was hard to distinguish day from night, and it was nearly impossible to sleep on the chair. In her lifetime, Lori had known emotional pain and fear but never had she experienced such physical pain. She longed to move her aching body, to lie down on a bed, to take a shower, to eat enough to keep from starving, and to scratch her back.

Minutes moved so slowly. She tried to pass the time by mentally putting herself elsewhere. She shut her eyes and pictured herself home in a suburb of Chicago laughing and smiling while playing with her beautiful young blonde daughter. The pleasurable memory only lasted a short time before she pictured her Julie lying in a blue coffin. She woke up with a start.

She wondered how her mother had endured two years in a concentration camp. Lori's bladder was about to burst as she sat there, still in her Sunday best, held together with an uncomfortable girdle, long-line bra, and pantyhose. *Here I am, fearing for my life, and the only thing I can think about is how miserable I am in this damn girdle or whatever they call them now!* She took a risk and asked for a bathroom break.

"Please, may I use the restroom?" She had addressed this person before, but he never responded to Lori or engaged her in conversation, although he went about dutifully tending to only her very basic needs.

"Yeah," her guard answered. She heard him move closer and walk behind the chair. "I'll remove the handcuffs, but remember, I still have the gun pointed at you, ma'am."

His fumbling hands while loosening the cuffs and the quiver of his voice made her believe he was younger than the other two and not a hardened criminal nor a murderer and gangster as the other ones were. For heaven's sake, he had called her "ma'am." She was slowly, over time, getting her guard to loosen up and talk a little. She could tell he was British—and scared. He had confirmed for her that she had been held captive for four days. It only seemed like an eternity.

"Thank you," Lori wearily answered as she rubbed at her wrists and rose from the chair. Her body was stiff from sitting in a cramped position for so long, and her wrists were numb and sore. She could barely walk. In the toilet, when she was certain she was alone, she lifted her blindfold, and she repeatedly blinked at the fracture of light that slipped through an open window, adjusting her vision until an open field of grass came into view. She leaned over the unclean sink for a while, hoping the cold water would ease the pain in her wrists. She cupped her hands and drank the tinny water from the faucet. She removed her girdle and stuffed it behind the pedestal sink. *What a pathetic clue that I was ever here*, she thought sadly. There was no escape route in this bathroom.

Her guard was somewhere behind the closed door, waiting for her to finish. When he heard nothing, he shuffled and cleared his throat to let her know of his presence. Relief overcame her embarrassment. She still felt the loss of her privacy.

Lori's bladder felt better, but her throat was still sore and dry. She desperately needed a drink. As she left the toilet, she asked in a rasping voice, "Could I possibly get something to eat and drink?"

Her guard, after securing her blindfold tighter, took her by the hand and led her to a different room, where she was handed a slice of sausage pizza and a bottle of beer. Normally, she wouldn't have touched either. Starving, she inhaled the smell of garlic and gobbled down the crunchy crust and smooth cheese topping. Even the foamed bottle of beer tasted good; for the last few days, she had been given only bread, something that passed for soup, and iron-tainted well water.

"Thank you," she said, relieved at having eaten. As they walked on, she suddenly felt his hand across her mouth. He made a *shushing* noise as they passed a room where she could hear her interrogator and another man talking.

"What should we do with 'er?"

"Maybe she doesn't have the stuff. She says she doesn't."

"Then we should just get rid of 'er."

"Our instructions are to wait for Suzi Wu."

"Who the hell is *she*?

"Suzi works for Wu Industries, the company that hired us. I was told she would represent her boss."

"Well, fuck it, I can't keep track of all these foreign names. So, where the bloody hell *is* she?"

"Don't get yer knickers in a twist. Her plane was late. She'll be here soon."

"It's your neck that's gonna be in a twist."

Lori flinched, and her heart pounded, filled with dread at the words *"get rid of her."* She had always thought she would accept death when the time came, why she could do nothing else in view of her seventeen-year-old daughter's bravery. But this was different; here, as a kidnap victim, she was not afraid of death but of the unknown and of the isolation from anyone who loved her. She found herself bargaining with God when the quote *there are no atheists in the foxholes* entered her mind. She was terrified of this game of not knowing what would happen next.

"God *damn* it!" she hollered, to the horror of her guard, who quickly pushed her back towards her prison room. She heard shouting in the hallway.

"What's all this?"

"I've got it. She's just scared, that's all."

"Keep her quiet."

"I've got it!"

Lori felt a glimmer of hope at the mention of Suzi. As her mind raced, she tried frantically to recall where she had heard or read the name, Suzi Wu. She figured it was somehow associated with Josh.

When they got into her prison room with the door closed, the guard's fine, thin hands grappled with the bindings as Lori allowed him to tie her hands behind her back to the hard wooden chair. She duly noted he had tried to be gentle when tying the ropes that held her, patting her hands when he was done.

In hushed tones, he said to her, "Ma'am, please keep quiet. I won't tie you again too tightly, but you *must* stay in the chair. I understand that you are scared. So am I, to be perfectly honest. But they won't be doing anything until that bird Suzi comes."

"Nate! What the hell is going on? What is she shouting about? Do I need to take over?" one of the captors hollered down the hallway.

"I've already told you everything is fine, Tony. She's tied up and settled in," Nate, Lori's guard, answered in a shaky voice.

"Do you want me to take over?" Another man's voice seemed closer to the door; this time, it was the man with the icy voice. It came in clear as the door to Lori's prison room opened wider.

"No, no. It's fine, Ro," Nate said again. "She is obviously upset and cried out. I got everything sussed out. She's just, you know, excitable. She's an old'un," Nate explained, sounding a bit meek. "Ease up on 'er," he said, shrugging nervously.

"Well, if you need to play nursemaid, do it. Just shut 'er gob. And keep 'er tied up."

"Roland. I've *got* it. I had to let her go to the loo."

"I don't give a toss if she pisses herself, got it? Just shut her up, Nate. Or I'll shut her up."

Lori could hardly breathe, much less move. This could not be a good sign, these men being so open about using their names in front of her. She knew her captor named Roland was capable of murder; the picture of Lunt's chauffeur, murdered in cold blood by him, never left her mind. A nightmare where Bly's dead face slowly turned into Josh's bloody face had startled her so that she had nearly fallen off the chair.

I've been kidnapped. My friend's face has been blown to bits. I could be tortured and killed. This doesn't happen to middle-class Jewish Americans. I must be in a nightmare. Oh God, let me wake up!

Chapter Fifteen

Restless, Cate tiptoed out of the bedroom, careful not to wake Joseph, more so for her benefit than his. She was upset at his calm attitude over the kidnapping, and she didn't want to deal with him. She'd hardly slept, tossing and turning while he was out like a light. Five days had passed, and still, her grandmother hadn't been found. Damn this police department!

Tigger followed Cate down to the kitchen as fast as her little legs could go. Cate pulled back the curtains from the window to check on their police protection. The street lamp cast a light that cut through the dark of night and rested upon the sleeping bobby in his sizeable black police car. As she watched him, he snorted, yawned, and shook himself awake, then drank from his thermos. She looked down the street. God knows who could be lurking about while he slept.

The digital clock on her stainless steel refrigerator read 5:03. She filled the teapot with water while Tigger, realizing there was no emergency, stretched out on one of the kitchen chairs and promptly fell back asleep. With a mug next to her, Cate went about warming up a plate of scones, then opened her computer to pictures, clicked on the family folder, and reminisced. She wished her mom and dad would hurry and get here already. She needed family around.

She turned off the large computer she and Joseph shared and turned to her private iPad, where she looked up any information she could find on FBI agent Jordan Gould. She told herself she wanted to check that the investigation was in good hands. After all, Gould and Scotland Yard had bungled the kidnapping.

There was nothing but praise for Jordan's time at Harvard and his work in the FBI. She was not surprised to see comments like he was brilliant, thorough, and exacting in his work, and she could surmise that he was also very competitive. She closed her iPad on his biography when she heard Joseph stirring in the upstairs bedroom. She would return to it at another time.

By the time Joseph came downstairs, dressed for work, Cate had worked herself into a state of anger and fear. He opened the front door and brought in the morning newspaper.

She snatched it from his hands. Her grandmother's picture was on the front page with the headline: *Wheeler's Girlfriend, Dead or Alive?*

Cate shouted, "Why are they so insensitive?"

Joseph put his arm around her, "They know nothing, darling. They are just trying to sell papers."

Quickly, she turned on him, brushing off his embrace. "You are no better. Joseph, I'm crazy with worry about my grandmother, and you could not give a damn. How could you go to work and leave me alone?"

He moved towards her again. "Cate, my dear, it can't be helped. I am a junior barrister, and we are in the middle of an important case. What could I do if I stayed home again? Scotland Yard is doing all they can." He reached for her shoulders to comfort her.

Again she pushed him away, dropping the paper on the floor. "God damn you. Get away from me!"

Ignoring her outburst, Joseph crossed his arms across his chest. "Cate, you ought to go back to school. You may not graduate at this rate."

"You don't understand. My grandmother could be dead by the time your bloody police department finds her. She has been gone five days already! How can you have no feelings for my family while you expect me to cater to your stuffy father and selfish, arrogant stepmother? They have expressed little to no concern over my grandmother! How insensitive can your family be? It's unnatural!"

Again he moved towards her. "Now, you know that isn't true. My father is doing what he can. I'm sorry, my dear. I will get a replacement at court and stay here with you. I understand you are upset."

Her voice rose to a scream. "You understand I'm *upset*," she mimicked. She turned away from him, her voice turning cold. "Get out of here. Constable Ascher will take care of me. I don't *need* you. Or your fucking family."

Before Joseph could fully realize the stinging Cate's words caused him, there was a knock at the door at the same time as the teapot screeched on the stove. Cate moved away from Joseph and opened the door, wiping the tears from her eyes. She greeted Constable Ascher, the bobby who she had spied napping in his car. She moved to the stove, turned off the gas, went to the counter, and poured the constable a cup of tea.

"Morning, all." Constable Ascher could sense the tension in the room and tried to make his greeting sound as upbeat as possible, given the circumstances.

"I see you have awakened from your catnap. Any news?" Cate asked as she ignored Joseph, who stood at the door, still wondering if he should leave.

Cate was still angry from the previous night when she lay awake worrying while he peacefully slept. Cate was not a patient soul. When a problem presented itself, Cate needed to solve it, and it was killing her just sitting and waiting. Powerlessness wasn't a feeling Cate was used to feeling. Joseph was happy to let the police do their job.

"Not as far as I know, but that Yank plans to come by and talk to you," Ascher said as he sat down, sipped his tea, and bit into a warm blueberry scone that Cate had placed before him on a plate. Ascher, a balding man of medium height with an angular nose and narrow face, was just a few years from retirement. He was good company but hardly an adequate guard. "I, eh, only dropped off for a few winks, ma'am. I've been up all night watching the window and all the phones. My superiors are concerned that there haven't been any ransoms demands."

At the mention of the Yank, Cate couldn't help but feel her heart leap. She closed her eyes, remembering his hands on her as he roughly grabbed her and brought her into the house, taking charge and protecting her. She shook her head to clear it, opened her eyes, and turned and looked straight at Joseph.

"Get out of here," she said, the ice in her tone still remaining. "The court waits for you."

Joseph watched her. A frown wrinkled her forehead, and she narrowed her eyes. He wasn't sure what he should do until Cate handed him his briefcase and softened her look with a half smile.

"Go, goodbye. I'll call if there is any news. Tell your father. . . Tell him I appreciate his help." Lord Lunt had pressured all law departments to speed up the search for Lori. So far, it had not helped.

She poured herself a mug of tea with a bit of milk and sat down at the kitchen table across from Constable Ascher.

"He just doesn't understand how special my Gram is to me. She is more than family. She's my best friend, the one who understands me better than my parents."

Ascher bit into his scone with the clotted cream and tried to listen to Cate, though she was really talking more to herself.

"Once, when I was nine years old, my parents canceled our spring vacation trip to Arizona because my dad was too busy to leave. They didn't understand why I was so upset since they had asked Gram to come to Chicago instead. Gram understood. Do you know what she did? She flew to Chicago, picked me up, and we flew back to Arizona the same day. Her friend Rain met us at the airport, and we went on an Indian retreat, sleeping in tents in the mountains with the coyotes howling. Another time, she took me to Vegas. When I was upset because I was too young to gamble, she brought some slot machines to our room."

Ascher asked, "What did your parents think about that?"

"Gram and I had a rule: what happened in Vegas, stayed in Vegas—and Arizona!"

"Did she fight your battles with your parents?"

"No, she said what happened in Chicago stayed in Chicago!"

"So, your Gram was boss in Arizona, and your parents were boss in Chicago?"

Cate sat back to think about it before answering. "Nobody was boss. Gram said she and my parents were like judges, and if I learned how to be a good lawyer, I could sway the judge my way."

"So that's why you became a lawyer?"

Cate's face broke into a smile. "I guess so! I always loved a challenge." She rose from her chair. "More tea?"

"No thanks," Ascher answered. "The scone was lovely. Much obliged."

Cate put the kettle down and turned towards the steps. "I'm going to change my clothes."

Upstairs in her bedroom, Cate put on something a little nicer than her old blue jeans. She picked out a blue cashmere sweater and a new pair of dark skinny jeans and then added a dab of lipstick. She eyed her running clothes with desire; her shorts, top, Nike shoes, and fanny pack had been retired by order of the police. They wouldn't let her out alone, fearing she, too, could be kidnapped.

On the way back down, Cate stopped at the guest bedroom. Her gaze darted to the bed where Tigger lay on a scrunched-up piece of material. Upon closer examination, she realized it was her grandmother's pink nylon nightgown. A tear trickled down her cheek as she remembered waking her grandmother just a few days ago. Grandma Lori had looked so petite and vulnerable in the flimsy garment as she took the phone from Cate. Suddenly the room felt cold and empty.

The loud hum of car engines pulled Cate's thoughts back to the present. She looked out the window and saw several news vans pull up to her flat. Eight days after the murder, publicity about Wheeler had slowed down to a crawl. Now, with the kidnapping the buzz throughout the city and across the ocean, press coverage was back to an all-time high. Amazing how people lived off of others' misfortunes.

She rushed down the stairs and found Constable Ascher standing by the open front door. As soon as she appeared, reporters holding mics, iPads, and pens crowded around her in the living room. They bombarded her with questions in several languages besides English.

"Who is Mrs. Brill to Wheeler?"

"Does she have the hidden money?"

"Did they find her?"

"Are you her granddaughter?"

"Sign here for an exclusive story, and we will pay you big time!"

"Sorry, Miss Cate. I thought it was Gould paying a visit!" Constable Ascher looked glum and guilty, but he did his best to push out the re-porters, more with his body than with his hands. "Move along; she isn't speaking with anyone. No questions, I'm sorry. Move along!"

"Get out!" Cate screamed as she pushed the news people out and tried to close the door. The e-mails, calls, and texts were easy to ignore, but an army of men and women wasn't. She really flipped when she saw herself on the television. Someone in the crowd was using instant digital equipment. She was beginning to think Joseph was smart for getting out of the house.

Jordan Gould suddenly walked through the door. With the help of two police officers, he could remove the interlopers from the house but not from the front lawn.

"Out, out! Inspector Holmes is the only one giving reports on the situation." Ascher was still trying to control the press as Jordan gently pushed Cate up the stairs toward the second floor. "After you," he said, pointing to her bedroom. When Cate resisted, he held up his arms. "Don't attack me. I'm trying to get you away from the press."

"No shoving," Cate warned, climbing the steps.

"Lesson learned. I'm not shoving. I'm merely urging you up the steps."

"Stop playing around."

"I'm not, honest."

Gould followed Cate into her bedroom. She shut the door and moved away from him. "Jordan, are you any closer to finding my grandmother?"

"Yes and no."

"What the hell kind of answer is that?"

"We have every reason to believe your grandmother is alive. Wheeler's girlfriend, Suzi Wu, works for Wheeler's Chinese investors. We found out she is on her way here from China, traveling on a passport identifying her as Suzanne Green. I, uh, I have a feeling she may not be traveling as the jet-set socialite she fancies herself to be. She may be disguised or, at the very least, dressed down.

"I received an e-mail from my research team identifying her as being born in Chicago to a Zi Wu and Steven Brill. Is she related to your family? Would you happen to have any photographs of her in her younger years, perhaps? Seems too much of a coincidence not to be related. If she is, your grandmother may be part of some plan to disappear with Wheeler's money. Maybe it's time for you to come clean." Jordan glanced at Cate's unmade bed and turned away.

Cate stood with her hands on her hips. "So, this has become another one of your interrogations, huh? *I* have to come clean." Cate guffawed and shook her head. "Unbelievable. Look, stop accusing me, stop accusing her, and go *find* her. I heard of Suzi Brill, sure. My uncle Steven was married several times, once to a Chinese girl. She was a very young prostitute. It's the family scandal. Suzi is Uncle Steve and the Chinese woman's daughter. Ol' Uncle Steve. He's since passed on. I can check my dad's Facebook page and go into his photo albums. He may have one of Suzi in there, I don't know. My dad is flying in today, so if you have more questions, ask him later. He knows more of the family history." She paused, then asked, "How did you know Suzi was coming to London?"

"Cate, I work for the FBI. We have our people watching Suzi. She definitely has something to hide now that Wheeler has been murdered. She's up to her neck in trouble and might feel threatened. Who knows who is after her now? She may very well need protection as well. Or she may be part of the kidnapping. Either way, we're figuring she will lead us to your grandmother. I'll be back later to question your dad, but I'd like you to check the photo albums now."

"It's not terribly convenient for me . . ."

"Please," Jordan stressed. "I will have more men on the house to ward off the press."

"My printer is up here, so you'll have to go into the kitchen and get my iPad. Please," mocked Cate, her arms crossed over her chest.

When he returned, Cate and Jordan sat down at a computer desk in the bedroom and pored over one of her father's Facebook photo albums until. . .

"There!" exclaimed Cate. "Here's a photo of them on vacation. That's her." Jordan sat close beside Cate as she turned the little computer for him to see. "That's Suzi, the model jet setter."

Jordan saw the photo of a pretty young woman wearing tiny wireframe glasses, short in stature, probably in her late teens, smiling and standing between her parents in front of a lake, her dark hair in long ponytails, and dressed in a thin green t-shirt with a yellow peace sign emblazoned on it and worn blue jeans.

"She looks like a kid!" Jordan scowled. Turning to Cate, he caught a whiff of her heady floral perfume and saw the curve and weight of her breasts against the thin fabric of her blue cashmere sweater. He closed his eyes and swallowed the lump in his throat.

"I think she was a kid. In her teens, anyway. That's the best I've got. She doesn't quite fit the jet set, Wheeler type, does she?" Cate asked, smirking. "But it's a good close-up of her face, so . . . Are you putting this photo through any database?" Cate went about copying and printing the color photo for Jordan as he glanced again at the bed, then at Cate, and tried to push thoughts of a more passionate nature out of his head.

"Well, we ran a check on her, and she doesn't have a record. We're going to use this to ID her."

"You're not using the MORIS, the iris scanning device?" Cate asked, wanting him to know he wasn't dealing with a slouch. She knew all the latest technology in criminology. "You know, where you take a photo of them, and it scans their iris, and then the MORIS system will analyze the special unique features of the iris, matching it up to . . ."

"It won't be necessary. She's not a criminal—yet. We've got ways of identifying her with this photo and information from the Internet."

"Sounds mysterious."

"It's not."

Taking the copied photo, he started to leave but then stopped to turn and face Cate. He put his hand gingerly upon her shoulder. "Cate, I'm really on *your* side. We had a bad start, and I'm sorry about that." He cautiously took her hand in his, and they stood there for a few seconds, reluctant to let go.

Cate pulled her hand away and said, "Find my grandmother. She has to be alive." Cate lived in the here and now. In her world, the thought that Lori could be dead was not a given.

As Jordan turned to leave, Cate's glance roamed over his long, lean, trim torso. She grinned.

He walked out of the house, carefully hiding the pictures as he tried to avoid the press who encircled him with questions. He waved his hands at them and speeded his movement towards the car.

"Come on, handsome. Give me some help. I'm from the USA," one nice-looking brunette said as she approached him. "What are you hiding in that envelope?"

Jordan remained quiet as he slid into his car and slowly moved it back from the crowded driveway and onto the road.

Actually, he didn't need the picture, but it was nice seeing Cate again. He had already hacked into the necessary computers. Her father might be helpful. Many things about this case were not adding up. There was no ransom note or other contact from the Brill kidnappers. No demands. There was no ransacking of the hotel room. If someone was looking for Wheeler's hidden money, why didn't they kidnap him instead of killing him? And most frustrating of all for him was not finding the Brill woman. After five days of no contact, kidnap victims are usually dead. Their only hope now was Wheeler's girlfriend.

Chapter Sixteen

Suzi stepped off the plane, exhausted. Not only had she flown economy, wedged next to a woman with a crying baby, but also the flight had been delayed by six hours. What a mess this had turned into. If Lori Brill hadn't turned up and got Josh all swept up in some bullshit reenactment of some stupid high school romance, she would have met Josh and walked off with his keys and Swiss numbers. Her employers would have paid her handsomely, and no one would have been killed. She wished she could just run away and hide, but she knew that wasn't possible now. Stealing money from thieves was okay in her book, but murder wasn't her game. The immigration officer looked at her passport before staring directly at her.

"Please take off that scarf. What is your name?"

"Suzanne Green."

"You are a citizen of the United States?"

"Yes."

"Why are you entering the United Kingdom?"

"Pleasure."

"How long are you staying?"

"One week."

"Where?"

"The Strand," she answered, naming a mediocre hotel. She stayed calm and courteous, though she almost wished the police would pick her up. She was more afraid of her Chinese employers and the men they hired than the authorities. They didn't care when they were reaping in a large share of Wheeler's money, but they went wild when things went belly-up, and Josh tried to run. What an arrogant ass he'd turned into. She did have a good run with him these last five years: Vegas, Paris, the Orient, jewelry, private parties, yachts . . . There was no limit to his spending or his sexual appetite. *I'm not gonna miss that*, Suzi mused.

She had met Josh while working as a model in L.A. When she had mentioned growing up in Chicago as a Brill, he had interrogated her about her family, admitting to knowing her aunt, Lori. Initially, she thought his concern had centered on her cousin, Lori's daughter, who died at seventeen. Now she was putting two and two together. Josh and her Aunt Lori had been lovers when they were young. What a crazy world. Aunt Lori had been the only person in the Brill family who was nice to her; she wouldn't let the kidnappers kill her.

Suzanne Green—in sneakers, blue jeans, sweatshirt hoodie, mousy brown hair in messy pigtails, and carrying a plastic purse from Wal-Mart—was no resemblance to Suzi the playgirl who traveled first class, with manicured nails, black hair coiffed just right, designer dressed, and met by an entourage the minute she stepped off the plane.

After the immigration employee concurred with another officer, Suzanne Green passed through immigration and was on her way out of the airport to her waiting driver.

* * *

FBI agent Jordan Gould's picture of Suzanne Brill from her teen years proved useful in identifying the woman with the Suzanne Green passport who had disembarked the Delta flight from Shanghai. His hunch had paid off. As this case progressed, Jordan's suspicion of Lori Brill's involvement looked more positive.

Too bad. He had to admit it. Holmes had correctly detected Jordan's feelings towards Cate. She turned him on. Oh, hell, whenever he was near her, he wanted to get into her pants. Being in close proximity to both her and her rumpled bed made the prospect all the more enticing.

He couldn't possibly picture her marrying that Englishman. She had too much passion, too much fire. And it wasn't just his regular attraction to sexy women, although he found her very attractive; this one was different. She needed someone in her life that could match her wit and brains, as well as her passion, and he did not think the barrister would be the one to do that.

Who was he kidding? He needed someone like that in his life. And she was causing more trouble in his life than anyone ever had. He could not stop thinking about her. He completely forgot Ginger, the young thing he had been hanging out with in D.C.

* * *

Scotland Yard, along with Jordan Gould and the FBI, were carefully watching and following Suzi Wu, hoping she was somehow on Wheeler's money trail. Her arrival also gave them hope that Lori was still alive.

When a young man in an orange Volkswagen bus picked up Suzi, the police made sure two different cars were tailing it. When they checked the license plates, they found the vehicle was registered to a seventeen-year-old, Nate Fillmore, living in London proper with his mother. Surprisingly, he had no record, rap sheet, or history of accidents.

* * *

Suzi got in the car and looked over at her driver. He was a tall, skinny kid with light brown wavy hair and small, rough-looking hands that showed signs of working outdoors. He sat quietly, waiting for her to speak or possibly waiting for orders from her. She needed him on her side. Sizing him up took only seconds. She would know how to win him over.

"You're just a kid. What's your name? How old are you?"

"Nate, and I'm seventeen. You aren't so old yourself."

"Twice your age."

"Fancy that," he said, shaking his head.

"Where did they get you?"

"They're staying in me family's warehouse."

"How is she?"

"You mean the lady they're holdin'?"

Suzy pulled her hair loose from the elastic ponytail holders, raked both hands through her knotted hair, and leaned back. "Yes, Mrs. Brill, the lady they are holding."

"I think poorly. I tried to smuggle some food to 'er, and I did loosen her ties. You know she's an old lady," Nate repeated, concerned.

Yes, I know, Suzi said to herself while turning her head away.

"One thing I gotta warn you about. It's Roland."

"What about him?" she asked.

"He's got a scar on his face. He's sensitive about it."

"I've spoken to him before. He doesn't seem the sensitive type."

"He's sensitive enough to bash your head in if you mention his fuckin' scar. You've been warned, is all."

"Thanks."

* * *

"We have the car in line, sir. Should we pick 'er up? Only a young driver in the car with her. It would be an easy pick-up," the constable said in his mobile call to Jordan.

123

Charlene Wexler

Damn, they're careless, Jordan thought. "NO! My God, you idiots, if you pick Suzi up, they will kill Mrs. Brill. Let them lead us to the hideout."

* * *

When they arrived at the warehouse, Nate directed Suzi to Roland's office. The sweet earth smell of pot permeated the room. Suzi realized she had to act tough and take control right at the start, so she stormed into the room and faced Roland, ignoring the long scar that ran from below his right eye down to the corner of his mouth.

In an angry voice, she said, "Well? What the hell went wrong here? Josh contacted me from O'Hare Airport, telling me he struck it lucky. An old friend was traveling with him, so he could hide the keys and codes to the Swiss bank in her things. He was supposed to meet me in Switzerland in two days."

"We found nothing in her things," Roland stated matter-of-factly.

Suzi ignored him and continued, "When plans changed, you were then directed by Wu to follow them and steal the items from the old lady's belongings, *not* to kill Wheeler and kidnap the old lady." Suzi paused long enough to glare at Roland, who sat silent, glaring at Suzi.

Who did this little monkey think she was, talking to him this way? Roland eyed the tiny woman, her worn jeans hugging her thin frame, her shapeless, dark blue sweatshirt covering what he knew would be two small, perfect breasts and a flat belly. He listened to her, musing how easy it would be to take her down with a well-paced backhanded smack across her stupid face. Another boring, easy target. Of course, he knew how to make this one more enjoyable.

"Wu, of course, is *not happy*. But he would forgive your terrible mishandling of the events if you could produce the items in question.

124

You were to give me the items and disappear. But Scotland Yard probably has all her shit now, and that's because one of you fucked up and went into that room and shot Wheeler! How stupid can you be? So, now I've been instructed to take over, and you can forget the rest of your money since you do not have the keys *or* the numbers. Eventually, they'll release her stuff, it will be back in her possession, and she'll be ready to tell us where the keys are. If she knows. She may not even know where he stashed the keys. If anything, you should have kidnapped her *after* she got her stuff back from Scotland Yard. She wasn't going to be a suspect long. Who's the hothead around here who called for this to take place? Was it you? *Bad move.*"

When Roland heard, "you can forget your money," his face clenched, and his hands rolled into fists. Only the sudden appearance of Tony stopped him.

Hand outstretched, the young Asian man turned to Suzi. "So . . . I finally get to meet the famous Suzi Wu. Ooh, lookit you, Suzi Wu. You look *different*."

Roland slipped out of the room as Suzi's attention turned to Tony.

"Yeah? Different than what?" Suzi made her way to the desk and sat down.

"Than your usual *Posh Spice* self. The one in all the pictures and videos.

"Huh. I had a long flight," Suzi replied dismissively as she grabbed her purse off the office desk, fished for a small hairbrush, and began smoothing out the knots still present in her long hair.

* * *

Nate returned to the room and completely untied Lori for no apparent reason. Fear seized her, and she began to shake. *They are done with me. It's over*, she thought.

"Nate, am I going to die now? Make it quick. Don't let Roland torture me."

Nate reached down and helped Lori get up. "It's okay, mum. The girl's here, and she wants to see ye."

Lori's legs went wobbly as she walked with Nate's help. Nothing could adequately describe what she felt when her blindfold was removed. At first, her eyes couldn't adjust to the light, and she quickly closed them. When she could focus, she saw a man walking out of the office. Lori eyed him carefully. Every time this man named Roland approached her, a feeling of panic took over. She recognized his cold deep voice and his enormous hands. She guessed he was Josh and Bly's murderer. She had made friends with Nate. He had smuggled food to her, but he panicked whenever Roland was around. The other one, they called Tony, also seemed afraid of Roland. She was glad the girl named Suzi was here. It had to be to her advantage to have a girl in charge.

Nate walked her toward the office and told her to sit down on the chair by the desk. Shocked by the appearance of the girl sitting across from her, she just stared while her mind made the connection. The Suzi Brill she last saw was a thin, gawky, bespectacled, coal-black-haired Chinese teenager with large, black, almond-shaped eyes and her father's dimpled cheeks. Could this be the same girl, her brother-in-law's estranged daughter? Tears of joy and fear flowed from her eyes.

"Is it really you?" she finally asked.

Suzi ignored her question and looked towards the guard at the door.

"Tony," Suzi said, snapping her fingers a few times, "bring some food and something to drink, and then leave me with Mrs. Brill."

"My orders are to guard her at all times."

"And this is how you've done it? Jesus, Tony, this poor woman looks like death warmed over. She doesn't need a guard. She needs a doctor. What good is she to us if she fucking dies, Tony? You think Scotland Yard's gonna hand over her shit to us in a tidy package?"

Suzi had a hard time recognizing Lori. The Lori she knew had been tough, taking no shit from the crazy Brill family, but now she looked old, small, and vulnerable in a wrinkled, soiled dress and torn stockings.

"No food in this place," Tony answered, shrugging.

Suzi's face hardened into a scowl. "Then go *get* some. There is a small store about a mile down the road. I remember passing it on the way here."

He stared at her with narrowed eyes and clenched mouth, all the while fingering the gun he held close to his side.

Suzi stood up and pointed towards the door. "What the hell are you standing there for? Gonna squint at me all day because I'm right and you're not? Get going! Go *now!*"

When he left, she turned to Lori, leaned in closer, and in a whisper said, "Just listen and do what you are told to do. I will try to get us out of here alive. Do you think Nate will help us?"

Lori couldn't help staring at the girl talking to her. Was this really Suzi Brill, her brother-in-law's daughter?

"Who are you?"

Suzi ignored the question and went to the window, standing there until she saw the car pull out of the driveway. Then she looked at Lori and said, "Yes, I am your niece. Believe me; I was forced to help the

Wus. They are my family, and they are furious with me for connecting them to Josh. Stay here. Let me see what is going on."

She would look for Nate to help them. He was young and dumb, and he never realized that they were being followed on their way from the airport, most likely by the law. If she could get Lori out alive, maybe the law would go easy on her and protect her from the Wus, who blamed her for their loss of millions. What a mess this had turned into. She had Josh thinking she would run away with him after he cleaned out his European accounts, while at the same time, she was being forced to double-cross him and lead Wu's men to Josh's hidden money. Once Lori Brill entered the picture, things changed. But even so, that was just a hiccup in the plans. Well, to Wu, it was a hell of a lot more than a hiccup. But still, Wu's men were supposed to go through Lori's stuff, no big deal. What in hell went wrong?

Lori sat in the room in shock. Things were moving like a scripted horror movie. What was Suzi doing here? Lori had heard Tony and Roland talking about their Chinese bosses, and Suzi's mother was Chinese. Lori shook her head in disbelief as flashes of the past went by in her mind. Almost forty years ago, her brother-in-law had divorced his wife of twenty-odd years to marry a very young Chinese prostitute. Suzi was the child of the young prostitute and her brother-in-law, Steve. She had not heard from nor seen the mother and daughter since Steve died years ago. How the hell did Suzi Brill get mixed up with Josh Wheeler? Maybe Suzi was thinking the same thing about Lori.

"Suzi, I don't have what you are looking for."

Suzi took a long hard look at the dehydrated, pitiful older woman in the soiled, torn dress. "I believe you, Lori. You wouldn't have held onto it this long, even if you did. Wu's men checked your home in Arizona and your granddaughter's flat, before they kidnapped you.

* * *

In a van, a half-mile from the barn, Jordan Gould and Inspector Reginald Tuttle kept the building under surveillance with telephoto lenses and up-to-date microphone devices while a few miles back, two officers in another car waited for instructions.

At around seven o'clock that night, a big black car pulled out of the driveway. The driver was male, possibly Asian, with dark hair. "Follow him and pick him up about a mile from the house," were the orders Inspector Sanders received, so he and his partner, Constable Ferris, took off.

At first, Tony was oblivious to the car following him. Normally, he would have looked around cautiously before pulling out, but he was angry about being first ordered around by Roland and then by a girl, a tiny Asian girl with a mouth that needed slapping. When he heard the sound of a car behind him, he looked over his shoulder and saw an unmarked police car. Instead of slowing down, he sped up, and the chase began around the narrow winding roads of the English countryside. By the time he reached the narrow wooden bridge, his car was moving over ninety miles per hour.

Tires skidded on the wet surface of the bridge, and the black Renault broke right through the wooden railings and plunged at least fifty feet down into the river. The car sunk quickly in the fifteen-foot-deep end of the water. Tony, not wearing his seat belt, was propelled head-first into the windshield upon impact, became unconscious, and drowned quickly. When the Scotland Yard divers arrived later, they pulled out of the black car a dead 5'10", 180-pound male with black hair. When the information on his driver's license was entered into the police car computer, he was identified as Anthony Hundai, a small-time criminal, arrested for possession of drugs twice and once for a DUI. He had a dual citizenship, English and Chinese. The car had been reported stolen from a Heathrow long-term parking lot only four days ago. It belonged to a dentist who couldn't find it after returning from a trip.

Jordan answered the phone and listened to Constable Sanders' report. "Do you know if he was on a mobile before the car went over the bridge?" he asked.

Jordan wanted to wait for an opportune time to have his men enter the warehouse, but now he couldn't be sure that the Hundai fellow hadn't alerted the others before his car went over the bridge. He knew his primary job was to get Mrs. Brill out alive, for the press and for Cate, though he was from the school that would concentrate on capturing the murderers first. He asked Holmes for permission to go in. Jordan was going over the evidence in his mind. This had turned into a mess. The FBI had been trailing Wheeler in anticipation that he would lead them to his hidden money. Lori Brill messed things up. He guessed Wheeler might have known the FBI and Wu's people were following him, so he used Lori to distract everyone. Now that Suzi was here, he could guess the Chinese hired the kidnappers. How would they prosecute the Chinese, and why would they kill Wheeler before getting the money? There were still a lot of loose ends.

Better to capture the other kidnappers alive to get some answers, Jordan thought, but not at the expense of the Brill woman's life. He had a very difficult decision to make.

Chapter Seventeen

Pounding footsteps echoing off the cold cement made Suzi think Tony had returned with the food. She left Lori alone in the office to look for the restroom.

"I'll be right back, Lori. Tony should be here any moment with some food. I think I heard him come in." She closed the door and made her way out of the room, then turned when she heard a voice behind her.

"Looking for someone?" Roland sneered. Suzi felt the hairs rise on her body at his sudden appearance. He quickly grabbed her around the neck and dragged her through the hallways and into the main floor of the warehouse. As soon as he loosened his grip, she spun around and kicked him under the chin. He dropped his hold long enough for her to take off.

Roland made a quick recovery. He ran after her across the warehouse floor, his eyes wild, his breath deep, running like a tiger after his prey. No woman would get the best of him, especially not this tiny little shit. He laughed gleefully, knowing the hunt was on. Finally, something fun to do!

Though Suzi was skilled in martial arts, Roland had a weapon and was so much larger. Her only defense against a monster like him was to run, and she did. He caught her by grabbing her long silky black hair. She screamed as he pulled her towards him.

"Gotcha!"

Smiling wickedly, he shoved Suzi to the ground. She reached up and dug her long nails into the tender pink flesh of his scar. Howling in pain and anger, he kneed her in the side, then grabbed her right arm and twisted it behind her. He pulled off her sweatshirt and ripped her shirt open, tore her bra off, and managed, despite a struggle, to pull down her jeans and panties.

With a smirk on his face, he unbuckled his belt and said, "Let's see who's going to be giving orders now." *This was so easy*, he thought, even though she did put up a good fight. She was such a tiny thing. He would break her in two. He didn't even need the gun he kept in the waistband of his jeans.

Through the sharp pain in her side, Suzi struggled to get up, digging her long fingernails into the skin of his arms. He held her down, though, by lodging his heavy boot on her leg while he lowered his pants.

"Gotcha," he said, panting into her face. "Now you'll get what you want."

Panicked by fear and pain, she screamed, "Wu will kill you!"

Roland stared at Suzi as the blood from his torn scar ran from his face onto hers. He watched how it fell in droplets onto her face, now twisted into a grimace, and how it caught up between the creases of her tiny neck. It looked like she had a thin red string choker around her neck.

"Pretty necklace," he cooed and laughed low as he maneuvered his body on top of her. She tried drawing her legs together, tried wiping his blood from her face, and attempting to push him off of her, which only enticed him. Tired of her flailing about, he held her arms down as she went for his gun, twisting them into an excruciating position. She attempted a couple of kicks to his groin, but he was already inside her. The movement of his enormous weight against her body left her helplessly pinned to the cement floor. He pressed his face to hers, smashing his bloodied wound against her cheek. She screamed in pain as his body violently pushed into her. Still pinning her wrists with one massive hand, he used the other to grip her head like a child's ball and slam it repeatedly against the concrete floor.

A cry like the scratching of chalk on a blackboard echoed thru the warehouse. Lori threw open the office door and stared in horror at the scene just a few feet away. On the open warehouse floor, Roland lay on top of Suzi. Without thinking of the consequences, Lori ran towards them, crying out, "Leave her alone!"

Roland jumped off Suzi and picked up his gun. He fired once at Lori. The bullet lodged deep in her hip, and she fell to the floor, clutching the wound. Her wide-open eyes registered shock at the pain and the sight of blood pouring through her fingers, spreading itself across the thin silk fabric of her dress.

Roland dropped his gun to the floor, straightened up, casually pulled up his pants, and secured his belt.

Nate, who had gone outside to wait for Tony's return, heard the cracking sound of a gunshot. He grabbed the gun Roland had given him and ran into the middle of the warehouse, where he immediately saw Suzi's still form on the floor and Lori writhing in agony nearby. He aimed his gun at Roland, crying out, "This ends now, Roland. You've got to stop!"

Roland walked up to the shaking young man. He smiled when he heard Lori's cries from behind him, then he moved closer to Nate and said calmly, "You wouldn't know how to shoot anyone, you little shit."

From behind Roland, a voice yelled out, "He may not, but *I* do. Police! Drop all weapons! Hands up!"

Nate immediately dropped his gun, but Roland bolted towards the exit. He butted heads with the policeman standing in the doorway, knocking him down. Jordan sprinted out of the building after him, gun ready to use even though he desperately needed Roland alive.

Roland was fast in spite of his weight. He dashed to his car and reached for the door handle. Jordan raised his weapon, aiming to stop him. A loud rattling bang echo through the area. Roland grabbed his left leg before shouting a stanza of obscenities. Three constables immediately surrounded the downed killer.

Nate had prostrated himself the moment the police entered the warehouse. Jordan ignored him and ran to Lori's aid while Tuttle went to help Suzi. Sanders left them to it and called for medical backup.

Jordan ripped off his shirt and pressed it against Lori's hip wound, which helped slow the bleeding. She was conscious, so he soothingly talked to her, assuring her that help was on the way. She didn't try to talk, but she thanked him with her eyes and a nod of her head.

It wasn't long before a medical helicopter landed in the open field near the warehouse. Jordan and his men stood back as the emergency crew loaded first Lori and then Suzi onto the aircraft. He listened as the emergency team wired the hospital. "Two patients coming in. One older woman, Caucasian, gunshot wound to her hip, blood loss, pulse weak, pressure 90/62, conscious. Chinese woman about thirty, bleeding head trauma, losing consciousness."

When the helicopter took off, Jordan called Cate on his mobile. Not wanting to alarm her, he made the conversation brief.

"Cate, we've rescued your grandmother. She is alive and on her way to London's Central Hospital."

While he was speaking to Cate, Roland McKeiffer was handcuffed and placed in a police car, where he waited for an ambulance. Sanders, overcome by anger and pain from the loss of his two police companions, wanted to blast him to bits, but he was a professional. He examined Roland's bloodied face and said, "Someone besides Jordan got you good. That's gonna leave quite a scar."

Roland spit into Inspector Sanders' face. It took much restrain on Sanders' part not to respond.

Nate Fillmore, shaking like a leaf, was thrilled to be rescued by the police. He had rented his family's unused warehouse and volunteered to help with odd jobs. He had no idea what he had gotten into. His dad had died in a car accident a few years back, and Nate and his mom had lost the import business; he was just trying to make some extra money. He felt sorry for the old lady.

He turned to Jordan, "Is the old lady gonna die?"

Chapter Eighteen

Joseph pushed aside his plate of stone crabs and looked across the table at his father.

"Dad, I don't understand why you've done such an about-face on Cate. I thought you had accepted her. I know your wife isn't thrilled with Cate's Jewish heritage, but to be perfectly honest, I find that attitude to be quite abhorrently racist. Where are we, in 1939 Berlin, for fuck's sake?"

"Manners at the table!" Lord Lunt spoke sharply, clutching his fork and knife.

"Manners, indeed. Did your wife show manners during the abominable, anti-Semitic conversation at dinner last week, when she . . ." Joseph paused and shook his head. "And what you consider to be Cate's common, middle-class status is not a hindrance in the twenty-first century. For heaven's sake, Dad, I believed all of this was worked out months ago."

Lord Lunt interlaced his long fingers and stared across the elegant English china on the table in his dining hall before repeating his request to his son: "Regardless of heritage or class, son, I strongly suggest you have nothing to do with the Brill family."

He pointed to the pile of newspapers and magazines he had set nearby on the table, their headlines concerning Josh Wheeler prominently displayed.

"After all, it would be in your best interest. That mess with her grandmother has put an unfavorable light on her family's status. For heaven's sake, Joseph, two men from Scotland Yard were murdered on the very grounds of this estate! And poor Bly . . ." He sighed. "She is bringing danger and scandal to our very doorstep. You know you've been groomed for a seat in Parliament. If you marry that girl, it will never happen."

"Father, Bly was murdered in cold blood by some crazed killer. Those men were killed in the line of duty, trying to protect Mrs. Brill, and—"

"That is enough, Joseph. You cannot defend this intolerable situation."

"Father, it's not Cate's fault!"

"The ghastly situation has stained our family name as far as I will allow. To say nothing of the fact that the girl has a quick tongue and is of the Jewish faith, which makes her unsuitable for the wife of a lord's son."

"I can't believe it! You *are* a bloody racist!"

"Now, Joseph . . . My wife . . ."

"Your wife," snarled Joseph, "can go *fuck* herself!"

Lunt paused to allow his son to vent his anger. He understood perfectly well he was breaking his son's heart, but there was absolutely nothing that could be done about it. Joseph was not going to marry Cate Brill; that was final.

"My wife knows a dozen young ladies who would be thrilled to be paired with you. Respected Protestant girls with class and station."

Joseph did not vent his outrage for long. He composed himself and regained his cool, thinking before speaking back to his father. Part of him understood what his father was saying; unpopular comment at court concerning his association with Lori had already caused dissension between him and his co-workers. There was no place to hide from the news in today's age of instant worldwide communication, but none of that mattered to him.

He refused to tell his father he would still marry Cate in a minute if she would consent, but, unfortunately, she was the one distancing herself from him.

"Dad, I love Cate very much, and I am totally confused by the change in your attitude. Cate is still the same person I've been living with for the last ten months."

Lord Lunt watched the hurt expression on his son's face. He dropped another lump of sugar into his teacup and motioned to the server standing by for some hot tea. He weighed his next move carefully. He felt sad that he had to be so harsh. He had used his wife's excuses because he didn't dare tell Joseph the real reason. If that family secret came out, Lunt would be destroyed, both financially and publicly. He had spent the last thirty-five years living a lie in order to protect his family's heritage, and he had kept up with the lie to keep his young wife from leaving him. And now that damned Brill woman who had invaded their lives could destroy all. He must make sure Joseph stayed away from the Brills. Time was of the essence. Too bad Baron Brune was dead. The baron knew how to take care of things.

"Joseph, things have changed."

"Well, Father, they haven't changed for me. I am very hurt by your attitude."

Joseph got up from the table, reached for his coat, and turned away from his father in order to keep him from seeing the pain on his face. Joseph was raised in the principles of the British gentry—chivalry, good manners, and, utmost, the fact that British boys do not cry. But this British man was feeling tears coming, tears he'd never let come when his mother and sister died.

In a quiet voice, Joseph said, "I need to leave."

Roger Lunt rose from his chair and followed Joseph to the door. He grabbed his son's arm to slow him down. He was a man in charge of a family dynasty, and he wasn't used to being disobeyed.

"Joseph, I need you to listen to me on this matter. It is so important that I would consider removing you from my will if you insist on marrying that girl."

Joseph left without looking at or responding to his father.

* * *

Utterly perplexed over the conversation at lunch, Joseph sat in his car outside his father's estate, unable to move. A tap on the window startled him. He rolled down his window. The new chauffeur looked in, smiling warmly.

"Pardon me for intruding," the young man said, "but I was wondering if you were having trouble with your vehicle."

"No," Joseph answered, totally at a loss for the new man's name. He missed the white-headed Bly, who had worked for them since Joseph was a young boy. It was hard to identify with someone else, especially someone close to his own age. Poor Bly got caught up in the Brill problems. As he started up the car, he had to admit to himself that since Cate's grandmother had arrived, his world had turned upside down. His life read like a soap opera: murder, constables, the press constantly hounding them, and now a kidnapping. Yes, admittedly, it would be tough for Cate to fit into his family's ordered life.

Startled out of his thoughts by the ringing of his mobile, he smiled when he heard Cate's excited voice.

"Joseph, Jordan did it! He found Gram, and she's alive! Meet me at London's Central Hospital." She hung up before he could respond.

Joseph made a turnaround and headed towards London. He was relieved that Cate's grandmother was found alive, but he was disturbed that Cate had only used the Yank's first name and had given him all the credit for the recovery. He turned on BBC Radio 5 and heard a report of Scotland Yard's successful breakthrough in the Wheeler case. Gould wasn't even mentioned.

* * *

Cate hung up with Joseph and tried her father's mobile, as he had not answered her home phone. When Barry answered, she yelled, "Daddy, Daddy, they found her! She's alive and on the way to London's Central Hospital. I'm leaving my classes and going there. Meet me. Oh, Daddy, I'm so happy you are here!"

Cate sped her car down the highway. Her mobile rang, and she pulled it out of her purse.

"Dad, what's wrong? Oh, you need the alarm code. It is Tigger. By the way, Dad, make sure that Tigger doesn't escape outside when you leave the house. She gets nervous around strangers. Don't worry. I'll get Joseph to pick up Mom at the airport. Just get to the hospital." It was at that point she realized how much she wanted to be back in the States where her family lived.

Cate pulled up to London's Central Hospital, parked her car, and ran to the entrance. She was so excited that her grandmother was found alive that she forgot Lori was in a hospital. Running down the corridor and throwing her arms around Jordan, who was walking down the hall towards the entrance, she shouted, "You did it! You got her out alive."

Jordan smiled as he pulled her closer to him. "If I knew I would get such a great greeting, I would have worked faster."

Cate pulled away, took a deep breath, and calmed down. She felt a sexual tension from his embrace that she shouldn't be feeling from him, especially at this time.

"Where is she?" she asked.

Jordan's face changed as he walked Cate away from the crowd of reporters. "Cate, she is alive, but she was shot. She is in surgery now."

Cate threw a horrified look on Jordan's way. "Shot? Is she going to live? Why didn't you tell me?"

"Calm down, please. She was hit in the hip, and the doctors feel she will pull through the surgery."

"Oh, God!" Cate screamed. "Take me to her." She started to run towards the elevator. Jordan had a hard time slowing her down. They got on the elevator, and he punched 3, the surgery floor. They exited quickly and entered the surgical waiting room, where, to Jordan's relief, Cate's dad was waiting for her. She folded into her father's arms.

Barry held his daughter tightly. "Cate, I know she will make it. You have no idea what she has endured in a lifetime. She may be petite and quiet, but she is tough."

Cate paced back and forth between the surgery desk and the coffee machine for over three hours while Doctor Quincy removed the bullet and worked to save Lori's life. Jordan stayed with her and her father. When Joseph arrived, Cate asked him to pick up her mother at the airport. As he left for the airport, he rested his eyes on Jordan, who was busy conversing with Cate's father.

Barry, Cate's father, spent time becoming acquainted with Jordan. Cate heard her dad say, "My father also came from poor immigrants from Russia. I was more fortunate than you. I wasn't saddled with student loans, but I worked through college. Now, Cate was a different story."

Cate was not happy with their conversation. She turned to them, "How can the two of you calmly talk about nothing while Gram's life is on the line?"

Barry answered, "Cate, honey, she is my mother, and I love her and care about her surviving, but I am a doctor too, and I know all we can do is stay calm and wait."

"Rubbish," Cate answered. "You are a man, and none of you men will let your emotions or real feelings out."

Jordan smiled and shook his head, thinking, *Too bad my dad is dead. He would have loved this girl.*

* * *

Lori wasn't sure where she was if she was alive, dead, or in the middle of a dream. First, she kept hearing voices screaming the word *code*, and she felt a sharp pain in her chest and a gasping for breath in her throat. The voices and the pain suddenly subsided, and she felt a very pleasant sensation of floating up and out of her body. In fact, she could see her still body lying on a cold hospital table when she felt forms swirling above her.

Voices, voices, soft, gentle, loud, steady. Voices from the past spoke to her, too, while forms similar to clouds that moved in and out of familiar shapes pushed her back down to the table.

Adele, her best friend who had died from breast cancer, appeared and, in a steady calm voice, told her, "You can't let Josh get you again."

Her father's gentle voice said, "My child, there are still jobs for you to accomplish."

Her late husband, Jerry's face, flashed in front of her, shouting, "Lori, I'm sober now!"

And the face of her daughter Julie, her beautiful blonde, blue-eyed seventeen-year-old daughter, flashed before her. "It's not your time, Mom. Cate still needs you."

Lori tried to reach out to them, and she thought she shouted, "Don't send me back; there is no pain here!" But the words seemed to be stuck in her mind. She believed they didn't hear her because they slowly faded away. Then, in their place stood one very clear form.

This form was not blurred like the others. As clear as could be, Lori could see her mother's full body. It wasn't the mother she remembered. This woman was young; she wore a sleeveless dress, her arms smooth, without any numbers from the days she spent in Auschwitz. In a very calm loving voice, her mother said, "My child, there is no life without pain."

Lori called out, "Mama, Mama, don't leave!" but her mother was gone, and the bright light that had surrounded her mother turned to pitch black. The next thing Lori heard was a foreign-sounding voice saying, "We got her back."

Then, Lori experienced waking up in excruciating pain in a room with all kinds of tubes and monitors attached to her and a nurse with coal-black hair moving around her. When she tried to move or speak, the pain increased, so she closed her eyes and tried to sleep.

* * *

At 7 p.m., Dr. Quincy—tall, bald, in his fifties, and exhausted, emerged from the surgical suite and met with the Brill family.

"We were sure we lost her. She totally flat-lined, but she came back to us. The bullet nicked the femoral artery, resulting in major blood loss and lowering her blood pressure while shattering the head of the femur, thus forcing me to perform a hip replacement. It will be a lengthy recovery.

Cate stepped forward. "Is she going to live? Please tell me the truth."

"I think she is over the worst of it, but we will know more in a few days," Dr. Quincy said as he put a large, strong hand on Cate's shoulder.

"May I see her?" Cate asked.

"Your grandmother is still in recovery. Then she will be in intensive care for a few days. Why don't you and your dad get something to eat? We will call you when she can be visited."

Jordan stood behind the exhausted doctor. He turned towards Cate. "Let me take you and your dad down to the cafeteria. I will tell James, Lori's guard, to phone me when you can see her."

Cate blurted out, "Why a guard? I thought you captured everyone. All over the television and the Internet, they're saying Gram's kidnappers and Josh Wheeler's killers have been arrested."

"Cate, we still aren't sure everyone connected with this case has been arrested. We need to be cautious." He looked at Barry and said, "See that she eats something." He gave them directions to the cafeteria. "I'm going to the station to sort things out. I'll be back in the morning."

Cate perked up at that comment. It sounded like Jordan was taking care of her. She had such contradictory feelings about him. Her dad shook Jordan's hand and watched him leave the room. Then Barry turned to Cate.

"That federal agent is a great guy. He went out of his way to be helpful. I believe he is concerned about my mom."

Her opinion of Jordan went back to being skeptical. Now she wondered why Gould was being extra nice to her dad.

She took her dad's hand and directed him towards the elevator and then down to the basement cafeteria, talking little as they were both emotionally drained. They walked through the old section of the hospital and into the new one.

The Royal London Hospital was founded in 1740, making it one of the oldest hospitals still running. In 2012, it was completely remodeled, with several new buildings added to the complex. Despite its modern equipment, cheerful paintings on its neutral-tone walls, and large windows that looked out onto typical London gardens with colorful flowers, to Cate, it was still an institution for the sick and dying, and she hated being in it.

As she walked along the cafeteria aisle picking up food, she thought, *What an irony. Dad a doctor, Mom a nurse, and their daughter a squeamish coward whenever she steps into a hospital.* Maybe it had something to do with her emergency appendectomy at six or her visits to the hospital to say goodbye to her Grandpa Jerry when she was almost eight. Her paternal grandfather, Jerry, was so much fun, always crazy, loud, silly, and loving. He told her to become a lawyer, like his brother, because she had the mind for it, and lawyers made good money. She still missed her Papa, even though she now knew much of his behavior was due to his alcoholism.

Cate paid for her tuna sandwich and cup of coffee before her dad made it to the cashier. She was still reminiscing when her dad finally sat down with his full plate of chicken, potatoes, and beans. She interrupted her father's eating with a startling question.

"Was Papa Jerry's brother, the lawyer, Suzi Wu's father?"

"Yes," her father answered as he put a fork full of beans into his mouth.

Cate continued with her questions. "Dad, he died while I was a baby, and anytime Papa Jerry started to talk about him, everyone hushed him, especially when I asked how he died. Now that Suzi may be back in our lives, I'd like to know the story."

Barry put down his fork and turned towards Cate. With a heavy sigh, he answered, "Honey, I'm not sure of everything. I know Uncle Steve divorced his wife, then bought and married a young prostitute from a place called The Enchanted Pussy." Barry shook his head and thought a moment before continuing. "Well, 'bought' doesn't sound right. He bought her freedom. She was bought from the madam."

Cate's eyes opened wide. "Wow, that is some name," she said, laughing. She looked at her dad quizzically. "Are you *sure* you got the name right?"

"Are you kidding?" Barry said, laughing. "I was a teenager then, so the name was the only thing that stuck in my mind!" Then he turned towards the cafeteria door, got up, and started to leave the table. "Mom's here."

Cate stopped him. "One quick question. How did Uncle Steve die?"

Barry turned back to Cate. "They found him dead in the trunk of his Lexus. No one was ever charged with the murder."

"Did he work for the mob?"

"Don't know. For, against, who knows?" Barry answered quickly as he greeted his wife, Anne.

Cate wore a snide grin on her face when she greeted Joseph and her mother. The thoughts behind that grin were, *Wouldn't Her Ladyship Lunt love that story about my uncle*? Cate hugged and kissed her mom, and she thanked Joseph with a slight kiss on the cheek.

He was upset at her lack of emotion towards him, but he didn't show it. He got himself a cup of tea and a beef sandwich and sat down to join them. Cate did most of the talking, explaining to her mom the sequence of events leading up to Lori's rescue.

Cate's mom was exhausted. Her plane had been forty-five minutes late, and then it sat on the runway at O'Hare for another thirty minutes before takeoff. Spring weather in Chicago could be nasty.

She sat next to Cate while Barry went into the cafeteria to purchase some food for her. Anne sipped at her coffee and played with her husband's plate of chicken while listening to Cate's account of Lori's condition. *London or Chicago, hospital food was all the same*, she thought.

When the call came that Lori was situated and awake in the intensive care unit, they hurried back up to the third floor.

Cate slowed her pace, allowing her mother to catch up to her before they quietly entered Lori's room. They were shocked by her appearance. In only four days of captivity, Lori had thinned out and shriveled up. Seeing her surrounded by the tubes and IVs holding bags of blood and fluid didn't help.

Barry sat down on the chair near his mother and gently took her hand in his. Cate stayed back for a minute, watching the tears flow down her dad's face. Her dad was not one to show emotion. He was the strong, silent type. After the surgery, Barry had conferred with Dr. Quincy professionally. In this room, he was a son afraid that his mother might die.

Cate realized for the first time the special relationship her father had with his mother. As an only child, Cate never felt the competition or jealousy of sharing. From the time she was a baby, Grandma Lori had belonged to her. She almost forgot that Lori was her father's mother. She looked at her own mother, who had stepped back from the bed. Her mother came from a family of four siblings, and she never understood the only-child syndrome, but she understood sharing and when to step back. This was something Cate needed to learn.

Lori's voice was so weak that she could barely talk. She glanced around the room. There was her son Barry, her daughter-in-law Anne,

Cate, Joseph, and some nurses. She had felt their love, but she had no strength to respond. She loved her living family, but they hardly needed her broken body and emotionally destroyed head. She was ready to go be with Julie. She closed her eyes and wondered why her dead friends and family had sent her back. Didn't they sense that she had no fight left in her?

Cate had to leave the room for a few moments to pull herself together. Outside in the hallway, she let the tears flow freely. Upon seeing her dad leave the room, she folded into his waiting arms; Joseph stood to the side, his arms crossed over his chest.

"Oh, Dad, she looks awful."

Barry looked down and gave her a half smile. "Cate, I know she will get through this. Mom is a fighter."

When Cate re-entered the hospital room, Lori held out a frail, shaking hand and summoned all her energy to look into Cate's face and smile. Lori had walked in Cate's shoes, caring for and worrying about sick and dying family and friends, but she had never been the victim. Lori had lived a life of good physical health. This was a new challenge.

Since Lori was in intensive care, she could not be seen after 8:00 p.m. Cate and her parents decided to stay at the hotel next to the hospital. Besides thanking Joseph for picking up her mother, Cate totally ignored him. Her mother talked to him while Cate clung to her father.

Joseph was beginning to feel like an outsider as he watched Cate walk out of the hospital arm in arm with her father and mother. He thought about his conversation with his father as he left for home without her.

Cate and her parents parted in the hotel lobby. She staying in one room, and they in another. The room at the Lyons Inn Hotel was small and sterile but clean and tidy, furnished simply with a chair, a desk, a bed, and a lamp. Their patrons were either sick and dying or visiting ill relatives or families. They needed little.

Exhausted, Cate dropped her bag on the bed. She'd begun to undress when she suddenly froze at the sight of a flashing red light on the phone. Her first thought was, *Oh, no, something has happened to Gram.* She reached for the message button and stopped. Her heart pounded. Slowly, she pushed the button.

"Cate, it's Joseph. I would like to come back and stay with you."

Irritated, she hit the erase button and swore, "Damn him. He scared the daylights out of me." She just wished Joseph would disappear. He just didn't fit in as part of her family, and she didn't fit in with him. The dinner at the Ritz was the last straw. She knew he was upset about his stepmother's behavior, but what about almighty Lord Lunt's behavior? How could anyone passively accept that kind of behavior? Well, she wasn't going to be passive about it. There was no way she wanted to be tied to a family with that kind of attitude toward Jews, toward other classes—toward anyone.

She recognized that the wealthy elite lived in a world of their own. Would she accept that kind of attitude coming from another lawyer or a college friend, or any boyfriend in the States? No way. But she knew—at least she thought she knew—Joseph wasn't like that. He wasn't like the snobbish Lord and Lady Lunt. And his kindness lately was complicating things. For months, even before Gram came to town, she had been questioning her feelings for him. She knew being comfortable with Joseph was not the same as being in love with him. She pursed her lips, uttered the word *fuck*, threw off her clothes, walked into the bathroom, and heaved a sigh of relief as she let the hot shower water run over her tired body.

Chapter Nineteen

A lump hardened in Cate's stomach as she neared her flat. She should be happy. Gram was doing well; in fact, she was alternating between the wheelchair and her cane, eating, and following orders in an effort to go home soon. Mom and Dad were talking about going home to the States, Cate's last days of school were practically behind her, and she had a new job waiting for her in America.

That lump grew larger as she pulled her car into the garage next to Joseph's. Joseph had been patient the last two weeks while her parents had been there, and Gram was recovering, but today was showdown day. She sat in the car for a few minutes, barely aware she was biting her nails, something she hadn't done in years. The fearless Cate Brill, who was always direct and truthful, was afraid to face her boyfriend. Bracing herself, she entered the flat.

Joseph greeted her at the door with a kiss. The only light illuminating the room came from two tall red candles in silver holders sitting next to a cut glass vase filled with roses atop a white linen tablecloth. Joseph helped Cate off with her coat and directed her to one of the chairs by the table.

"Cate, dear, I've purchased dinner at Bellissimo, your favorite Italian restaurant. To celebrate our first night alone in the last month." His hand brushed through her hair. "You look lovely tonight, Cate."

She sat there silently, watching his every move. She hadn't expected this. In the morning, before they both left the house, Cate had told Joseph she needed to have a serious talk with him tonight. He actually never answered, so she wasn't even sure if he would be there.

Joseph took the wine opener out of the drawer and applied it to a chilled bottle of Pinot Santa Margarita. She watched him pour the expensive white wine into the crystal goblets, open the boxed dinner, and gently spoon it onto the fine china he must have brought from his father's house.

Before he sat down on a chair next to Cate, he asked if he could get her anything. She shook her head.

She sank deeper into her chair with every one of his romantic attempts. First of all, she was so uncomfortable watching him trying to do her job. This was a poor rendition of dinner at his father's house without the servants, not dinner at their flat. Normally, she cooked or brought dinner home, and it was eaten on plastic plates with full light and in a hurry, as they were always busy; at least *she* was always busy with the next project. And most of all, he was so strange, like an actor trying to remember his lines.

Cate silently drank two glasses of the white wine. She'd begun nibbling at the Caesar salad and the vodka shrimp pasta when Joseph asked, "Is something wrong? You are very quiet."

She put down her fork and looked up. "Joseph, it's no good. I do care about you, but not enough to spend the rest of my life with you."

Joseph rose from the chair and went over to Cate. He took her hand.

"Cate, I don't understand. All was well before your grandmother came. Honest, Cate, I don't care about your family's scandals."

A smile flickered across Cate's face at a statement she knew came from his father. She wouldn't go into *his* family's scandalous attitudes and behavior; no, this was about their relationship. Leave family out of it. She couldn't prolong things; she had to be blunt and honest. She rose and walked away from him to stand by the kitchen counter.

"Joseph," Cate began, "you are a *wonderful* person, and you've put up with all my *mishigas* and have treated me like a lady, but I want to go home to the States. My love for you is more like a sister's. These feelings have been with me for a long time, but I talked myself into thinking with time, my love would grow and change. I hope we can be friends."

He stared at her with sad, wounded eyes.

"I'm sorry, Joseph." Her voice broke as she burst into tears, turned around, and left the room.

Joseph's six-foot frame crumbled onto his chair. He rested his head on his arms and began sobbing. Cate continued up the stairs to their bedroom, tears flowing down her face.

Fifteen minutes later, a composed Joseph came into their bedroom. He took out a suitcase and started packing his things. Cate stopped him.

"Joseph, don't. I'm leaving for the States in three weeks. I've accepted that job with Judge Pierce in Washington, D.C. You do not have to move out. I could stay in the guest room."

Joseph put the suitcase down, and in a calm, steady voice, he said, "Congratulations, Cate. A job with a federal judge is a great opportunity. Nice of you to tell me I can stay, but it won't work for me. I can move into Dad's townhouse close to the court."

"Whatever you feel is best." Cate went downstairs to the kitchen and cleaned the dinner dishes. Slowly, instead of her normal haste, she rinsed each dish and then stacked them in the dishwasher. She blew out the candles and turned on the lights. She listened to Joseph's footsteps moving around the second-floor bedroom. His footsteps seemed heavier than usual, to the point of making the wooden frame creak. Cate picked up the wine bottle, but instead of corking it, she took a big drink right out of the bottle. She wasn't sure why she felt so absolutely awful. She had been trying to break up for months.

Forty minutes later, Joseph came down with two suitcases.

"I'll pick up the rest of my things later in the week." He stopped at the door and turned around. "Cate, I'll always love you, even though I've known for quite a while that it isn't mutual." In a cold, tense voice, he asked, "Would you please answer one question for me?"

"What is the question?"

"Is it the Yank?"

Agitated, Cate burst out with, "No, I hate that arrogant . . . ."

Chapter Twenty

Lori tried to sit up in bed on her own, but her thigh was still painful, not excruciating as before, but still difficult to use. She reached into the drawer by her bedside and pulled out a mirror. Her face showed only a slight amount of brown bruising from her fall, but she appeared gaunt due to weight loss. She groaned as she hid the mirror back in the drawer. She knew she was lucky to be alive, but she was totally frightened by the experience. It made her realize how no one was immune and totally safe.

Of course, Lori would hide her fear from her family, who she knew would be visiting after her rehab session.

"Mrs. Brill, we need you to do a better job on your breakfast. You need your strength for therapy," Barbara said as she stood near the bed with Lori's wheelchair.

"I'm trying," Lori answered as she eased into the wheelchair that would take her to the physical therapy room.

Once there, she moved slowly between the bars, tolerating the pain the best she could. "Will I walk on my own?" she asked the therapist.

"You are a very determined lady. You will be walking again, probably with a cane for a while. We will be transferring you to a full rehab facility soon."

Lori had seen friends in her age group start out with bone injuries and end up in nursing homes. She was determined to make it back to her home in Arizona. She wasn't going to let this insanely mad world she had recently occupied get her down.

"I'll just think of it as just another one of Pauline's Perils," she said.

Her thirty-something therapist asked, "Excuse me. Either I didn't hear your comment correctly, or I misunderstood it."

Lori just smiled and shook her head. *Are they all so young, or am I just so old?*

* * *

Cate ran into Lori's hospital room. "How is she?"

Barry, who had just sat down next to his mother, turned around to face his excitable daughter. "Slow down, honey. Gram is sleeping. She had a full physical therapy session. Things are going so well. The doctor is planning to send her to a rehab center Wednesday morning."

"Great!" Cate almost shouted.

Her father gave her a stern look as he ushered her out of the room, repeating, "Gram is *sleeping*."

"Where's Mom?" Cate asked.

"Doing some shopping." He declined to say that his wife was out looking for a graduation present for Cate, but it did remind him to ask Cate a question. "Honey, do you think you could take care of Gram if Mom and I went home after your graduation next week?"

"Of course, Dad. I'll stay here until she can go back to the States with me. I better take off to class now. Today is my last day. I'll see her later." Reluctant to go, Cate stepped back into the room and took a long, loving look at her sleeping Gram, who finally was without tubes and IVs in her arms.

On Cate's way out, she literally bumped into Jordan, almost falling down.

"What are you doing here?" she asked as she bent down to pick up her fallen purse.

"I came by to see how your grandmother was doing, and if she's up to it, I need to ask her a few questions."

Cate immediately found herself going on the defense. "She is still recovering. You have no right to bother her now."

He put his hands up in surrender. "Okay, Cate, okay. Why are you always fighting me? It's clear I can't do anything right by you. You are like a tightly coiled spring waiting to unwind."

Her dad walked over to where they were standing. "Jordan, good to see you again. Mom is doing much better."

Cate left Barry and Jordan talking and continued on her way, keeping her mouth shut for a change.

Her heart plunged as she berated herself for always jumping to his bait. She turned around and eyed Jordan standing in jovial conversation with her dad. She sped up her pace in order to get out of the hospital before Jordan decided to join her.

At twenty-six, she would soon leave London with a master's degree in law. Why did she become a bumbling idiot every time she ran into Jordan Gould? Why couldn't they just be friends? He looked really handsome today with his crisp, white button-down shirt and black cotton trousers. She admonished herself for thinking like this. She just couldn't help it. Damn that, Jordan, complicating matters! She had to stay focused.

* * *

Jordan left, and Barry went back into the room to sit by his sleeping mother. He was anxious to talk to Lori about Cate. In many ways, his daughter was unlike him and Anne. Cate was smart, confident, and always looking for a challenge, yet she had a vulnerability, one that always showed up when she was near that Gould fellow.

He sighed, letting his body slump into the chair. Lori woke up and focused her eyes on her son. Alarmed at his posture, she asked, "Barry, you look worried. Is something wrong?"

"I'm not sure, Mom. Cate and that Gould fellow have a thing, but they won't acknowledge it. I don't think she is in love with Joseph."

Lori grinned. "So you've noticed."

Chapter Twenty-One

Chief Inspector Holmes called for a meeting of the team working on the Wheeler murder at nine o'clock on Thursday morning. Around the table sat Chief Inspector Holmes, Inspector Sanders, and Inspector Tuttle. They were waiting for the Yank from the FBI.

At 9:22, an irritable and hurried Jordan entered the meeting room. "Sorry, gentlemen, I stopped by the hospital to check on Mrs. Brill and possibly ask her a few questions, but her granddaughter wouldn't let me near her."

"Maybe her granddaughter is right," Holmes said. "We need to give the lady time to recover, to heal. I've been checking on her and Suzi Wu, too, but not to question them. Mrs. Brill, I believe, has told us everything she can, and unfortunately, the Wu girl is still in a coma."

Sanders, scowling, shrugged, "Are we ever going to start this meeting? I have work to do."

Jordan ignored the men's comments and poured himself a cup of coffee before speaking.

"The raid went well, considering the losses." He paused to acknowledge the gravity of his statement. The men of Scotland Yard shifted in their seats uneasily, each feeling the weight of the loss of Inspectors Townsend and Isaacs, who had shadowed Bly and Lori's car and were ambushed and murdered by Roland. It was never easy when officers were killed in the line of duty. It made the case more personal, no matter how objective they needed to be.

"Details regarding funeral services for Inspectors Richard Townsend and Arthur Isaacs will be discussed after Mr. Gould gives us the briefing," Holmes announced to the solemn group. Then he deferred to Jordan to continue.

Jordan turned his gaze on Milton Sanders, who sat glumly stirring the tea and cream in his cup. "Milton," Jordan said sharply to rouse him out of his stupor, "you are the one covering the Wu girl. I need to see the video of everyone who has visited her since she's been in a coma."

Realizing the room had turned silent as his companions focused on him, Sanders, a look of weariness in his eyes, took off his wire-rimmed glasses and looked sullenly around the table, then rose and left the room, mumbling to himself.

Jordan said, "Should we meet you in the computer room?"

"No. I'll set it up there, be back shortly," Sanders replied as he made his way down the hall.

Ten minutes later, Sanders reentered the meeting room with a metal cart upon which sat a television and video player. He was silent as he set up the video and turned on the screen. Jordan put his hand on his shoulder.

"You are the one who has identified and questioned Suzi's visitors. You need to stay and identify them for me."

Milton Sanders sat down and stared at Jordan. "So, you think now you're running England along with the colonies?"

Jordan laughed and patted him on the shoulder, trying to keep the mood light. He understood these men were under a lot of strain, but he needed work to continue.

"Hey, man, remember, we're on the same team."

The men at the meeting gathered around as the computer beeped and the video started. The first scene they looked at was of a small woman quietly entering Suzi's hospital room. Shuffling over to the bed, her back hunched, wearing baggy tan pants, sporting thin, cropped, yellow-gray hair, the older woman resembled a poor Chinese farmer from another time.

Jordan stopped the video and turned to Sanders. "Is *that* Suzi's mother?" he asked excitedly. "It can't be! This woman looks like she's in costume."

To think that Suzi came from Chinese peasants was almost too hard to believe. Didn't Cate tell him that Suzi's mother used to be a prostitute? Now she looked like a coolie. How was that possible?

"No, I don't think so. Through an interpreter, I learned she claims to be an aunt who came over from Chinatown in San Francisco when she heard about Suzi being in a coma."

"Did you check out her story?"

"We're not dumb here, Gould. Her passport is from California, and her residence address has been confirmed, though we couldn't confirm her relationship to the patient."

The next scene showed a tall, thin, blonde woman entering the room, arm-in-arm with a distinguished-looking older gentleman. Jordan recognized Cate immediately. His hands tightly clasped around his coffee cup until the man on the screen turned around, and Jordan realized Cate was with her father.

"Oh, yes, you should recognize these two," Sanders said slyly, then stopped the video. "Ah, yes. The lovely and cantankerous Miss Cate Brill and Dr. Barry Brill, Lori Brill's granddaughter and son, respectively."

"Okay, that is obvious. Now, what about the old woman?" Jordan asked, urging Milton to move on. He would have no part in whatever he was implying.

"The old woman sat by Suzi's bedside every day for a week and a half before returning to the United States. Cate and her father came by about once a week. Dr. Brill spent time talking with the doctor about the girl's condition. They were the only visitors, besides you, until a week ago. I will move the video forward."

Milton tried his best to be professional and not lash out at Jordan. After all, he had worked with him on the raid, and Jordan was no slouch in the field. He had heard rumors that the FBI was calling Jordan back to Washington. As far as he was concerned, the sooner, the better. Bloody Yank!

As the video moved forward, Milton narrated, "Two young women visited Suzi one day. When our man watching the room alerted me, I detained them and went down to the hospital to question them. Both . . ."

"Where were *you?*"

"I had taken my leave for an hour or so, and the room was watched while I was away."

Jordan simply nodded, prompting him to continue.

"Both women claimed to be models who worked with Suzi in Las Vegas." Milton checked his notes in a small notepad. "Their passport names were May Chung and Claire Todd."

Jordan and the men peered closer at the screen. Two leggy, paper-thin, thirty-year-olds toppled into the hospital room on five-inch heels. If Suzi was going to wake up, the clicking and clomping of those shoes would have done the job. The blonde's hair fell over her shoulders, and her red skirt barely covered her thighs. The Asian woman's dark hair was twisted and piled high into one of those beehive styles women wore back in the sixties, which only made her long black lashes more prom-inent. Her tight black dress reached to her knees, but it barely covered her breasts.

Jordan turned to the Inspector and smiled. "Must have been a tough job interviewing those two."

With a straight face, Milton answered, "Just doing me job."

The ice was broken, and the two of them laughed along with the other two men, but they were silenced as the screen showed a room empty of visitors, with only a petite, shriveled, silent patient attached to tubes and breathing machines.

"That's a tough break," Jordan said, shaking his head glumly. If they had only arrived sooner, Suzi's life might have been spared.

When the surveillance video was turned off, Jordan began his briefing.

"We rescued Mrs. Brill. Good job, Sanders," Jordan said, nodding to his partner. "We brought out Nate Fillmore and Roland McKeiffer alive, and we lost one of the kidnappers in a car chase. The press thinks we have the case solved, but we know better.

"Yes, there are still too many loose ends. None of the kidnappers' weapons matched the bullets in Wheeler, and none of their fingerprints matched the prints from Wheeler's room. The bullets in Bly definitely came from Roland's Smith and Wesson. And we know Roland was personally responsible for the deaths of our men on the force." Jordan stressed the *"our"* to emphasize his feelings of camaraderie with the men of Scotland Yard.

"Milton, go over the techs on Wheeler. We need to know how close the killer was to him so we can get an idea if he knew him or her or was surprised. In addition, we must go over the layout of everything in the room. We know he died immediately with one shot above his left eye. This was all confirmed by the autopsy."

"Will do."

Reginald Tuttle—short, stocky, thinning reddish-brown hair, bespectacled, rigid conformist, on the force twenty-two years—said, "I was the one interrogating Roland, the bastard. He is ready to take the rap for our men and Bly, with Brill there as a witness, but he says he had nothing to do with the Wheeler murder. Says by the time they got to the hotel to ransack Mrs. Brill's things, the chap was already dead, and the hotel was crowded with law enforcement officers. I don't believe him. I think he done him in." Tuttle scowled as he faced the others.

"You're a better man than I, Reggie," Milton Sanders spoke up. "I would have left him in a million pieces had I been the one interrogating him."

Reginald Tuttle shook his head and stared down at his hands; he'd clenched them in fists in an attempt to suppress his anger. "It took everything in me not to strangle the life out of that son of a bitch with my own bare hands. He was so cocky and smug . . ."

Chief Inspector Holmes rose from the table and poured himself some tea. He added his customary two lumps of sugar and some cream, took a sip, put his cup down, stroked his chin, and finally commented, "If we believe them, then we have to believe Josh Wheeler missed his connecting flight to Zurich just to stay with Mrs. Brill, not to throw people off his trail."

Jordan laughed and shook his head. "Sure, he stayed to fuck a seventy-year-old woman. It was a *plan*. His girlfriend wasn't scheduled to meet him for two days." Jordan then got up, poured himself another cup of coffee, and paced back and forth with the cup in his hand.

Sanders pushed his rimless glasses up to his forehead and shook his head in disgust. "How the hell did you get into the FBI? You're nothing like the Yanks we worked with before. Your family *knows* someone?"

The camaraderie, so tenuous to begin with, had dissipated with Sanders' rhetorical question.

Jordan stopped and stared at the British man who so openly offended him. "Don't fuck with me, *Milton*. I grew up in the Bronx; my dad was a peddler with six of us living in a small apartment. I worked every job possible and got into Harvard on brains, muscle, and *chutzpah*."

"No wonder you are so wired. You drink that stuff like it's water. Sit down, and for fuck sake, talk slower so we can . . . we can understand ye." He was in a foul mood, and Jordan Gould wasn't making it better.

Holmes, understanding tempers and emotions were high, jumped into the conversation before his team started to fight each other. It had been quite some time since they lost two officers. He also was distraught.

"We need to be working *together* for the common good. I'll have no more dissension or swear words here! Milton, perhaps you need to take a couple of days of leave. I know you and Arthur were close."

Milton Sanders shifted uneasily in his chair and stared glumly out the window. "When this case is closed, I'll do just that, sir. Until then . . ."

Jordan sat down and took a few deep breaths before resuming. "Roland McKeiffer is our prime suspect. He is forty-two, Irish, and quick to temper. When he was handcuffed and led out of the warehouse, he spit into Sanders' face. Obviously, he has no scruples when it comes to murder, but we still are not sure that he killed Wheeler.

"The other kidnapper, Nate Fillmore, he's a young kid. He was scared to death. He had rented his family's unused warehouse and got set up by Roland and his crowd. He had no idea what he had gotten into. The kid didn't know how to shoot a gun. He kept asking about the lady, how was the lady? Asking about her welfare. This kid's no criminal. He had a gun pointed at Roland to stop him, but I doubt he would have shot him. I'm sure he had nothing to do with the murder.

"The third kidnapper, Anthony Hundai, known as Tony, died in the car chase. He was a small-time crook hired by Roland. Roland raped and beat Wheeler's girlfriend unconscious. Suzi Wu may have the key to everything, but at the moment, as you know, she has not regained consciousness, so . . ."

"So it may have been Tony."

"Maybe."

"Did you find out about Suzi's connection to the Brill Family?" Sanders asked.

Jordan answered, "Lori Brill was able to tell me very little before going to the hospital. She told me Suzi's father, Steve, divorced Suzi's mother over twenty years ago, and mother and daughter went back to China. When they moved back to the States, we don't know. Lori has no knowledge of how Wheeler and Suzi got together. She hasn't seen her niece in twenty years, but she feels that because of the connection, she is still alive. Otherwise, she is sure Roland would have killed her. But seeing that in the end, he wound up shooting her, I have my doubts."

Jordan resumed his pacing and continued.

"Roland, after being interrogated," he said, giving a curt nod to Tuttle, "told us he and Tony were hired by someone named Chang, who represented a Wu in Shanghai. They met Chang in Chinatown, and he gave them five hundred pounds and promised them another three thousand pounds when they brought him some keys and codes that Wheeler had with him. They were told Wheeler was going straight to a bank safe deposit box from the airport. They planned to kidnap him after he left the bank. His detour to the Palace with Mrs. Brill made them change their plans. Seems they felt that Lori Brill may have been the mule in this scenario, that he would use her to plant the codes and such and make a clean getaway."

Jordan didn't volunteer that his own men from the FBI were also planning to pick up Wheeler after he left the bank. That would have made a wild party at one of London's major banks.

Tuttle interrupted. "He hasn't told us much about his plan change, only that he had been informed to thoroughly check Lori Brill's things, as the keys and code may have been planted on her. But he didn't have the chance to do that. Maybe Roland shot Wheeler because they didn't find anything, nor has he admitted to the Wheeler murder, and truthfully, there is nothing at the Palace to positively identify him as the murderer. Though the tape does show a very large man by Wheeler's room that morning."

"Wouldn't they have taken Lori then and there if they suspected her of carrying what they wanted?" Holmes asked.

"Good question. Anyone find out more about Chang and Wu?" Sanders asked.

Jordan looked down before answering. That slow, drawn-out voice of Sanders drove him crazy.

"We know all about Wu Industries. They invested with Wheeler. Trust me, to accuse them of anything will start an international political problem. I just wish I could talk to Suzi. She could shed some light on whether or not Roland is telling us the truth."

Ignoring Jordan and turning to Inspector Holmes, Sanders asked, "Do you agree?"

"What's in the boxes?" Tuttle asked before Holmes could respond.

Holmes got up and walked over to the table. "Forensics released everything they found in Wheeler's suite. I thought we could look through it again to make sure we haven't missed any clues. As we discussed, there were no fingerprints that could not be accounted for."

The men went over to the boxes. They each put on rubber gloves and looked through the evidence once more.

Tuttle shrugged as he went through Wheeler's wallet. "Funny, no money or photos were found on the man, just credit cards."

"Nobody uses cash anymore," Sanders answered. "Try giving one of the cashiers a pound, and they won't know how to make change."

"You are wrong, Milton," Jordan said. "There was no money in his wallet, but he had eight thousand pounds hidden in his carry-on. That Wheeler really knew how to live. Thousand-dollar handmade suits, diamond rings, Rolex diamond watches. Even his casual clothes ran in the hundreds. How did this get in the box?" Jordan asked, examining a plain wooden button.

"How do you know the price of his clothes?" Sanders asked as he pushed his rimless glasses down from his forehead.

"By the labels," Jordan responded flatly, putting the button back in the box. "You forget, I work in D.C., where the U.S. politicians live."

Jordan then spread the crime scene photos to both ends of the table. He pointed to a photograph of Wheeler's face, disfigured by the gunshot.

"Face shots are usually personal, where the killer wants to get even with the victim. Roland claims to be a hired killer. In all the people we've questioned, did anyone claim to know Josh Wheeler personally?"

"What Roland did to Suzi looked pretty up close and personal," Sanders offered.

"Fucking psychopath," Tuttle growled.

"So you are saying you wouldn't put it past Roland, a hired killer, to just walk up to Wheeler and shoot him in the face?" asked Jordan.

"The way that guy went off all half-cocked? Maybe Wheeler called him a name or swore at him. Jesus, anything would set off that bastard," Reginald Tuttle offered.

"I don't put it past him . . . past him, either," Milton Sanders said. "Look at what he did to Arthur and Richard. Close range. Headshots. That . . . *that* looked . . . personal."

"Okay, so this is your professional assessment of the suspect?" Jordan asked, sipping his coffee.

"Yes, it's my bloody professional assessment, Gould," spat Milton. "Look. Obviously, the murder of our men has upset me, which is only natural, but I am looking objectively at his behavior."

"And you, Reggie?" Holmes asked Tuttle.

Reginald Tuttle looked at Jordan, Milton, and Geoffrey before speaking.

"After spending some time with the suspect, I have to say he does bear the markings of a sociopath, taking pleasure in his predatory killings as well as his attitude of making a sport out of killing. Those are my professional observations. So, yes, I do not think the idea of Roland walking straight into Wheeler's room and shooting him point-blank is at all far-fetched. All we have to do is prove he did it."

"Or prove that he *didn't* do it," offered Jordan, who was met with such malevolent looks from both Milton and Reginald that he was caught off guard. Nonplussed, Jordan decided to move ahead, hoping things would settle down if he continued his train of thought. "Now, as I was saying, we have not come up with anyone who knew Wheeler personally besides Lori Brill and Suzi Wu. I've had passenger flight lists checked against his investors and girlfriends checked, and came up with zero."

"Interesting, Jordan. Can you get us a list of any British investors?" Holmes asked.

Jordan answered, "I'll have a list of everyone in your office in an hour."

"Everything here belongs to Wheeler or the hotel," Sanders said. "What about Mrs. Brill's things?"

"We went through everything when we brought her things back here, then gave everything back to her. The only thing in question is her suitcase. The hotel guard went into Wheeler's room before any of us got there. He brought the case to Mrs. Sweeney, who occupied the suite next door to the crime scene. She removed some clothes and gave them to Mrs. Brill, then the guard returned the suitcase to Wheeler's room. By the time we went through it, Sweeney's fingerprints were on it along with those of Mrs. Brill and the hotel guard."

"Are you saying our department botched it?" Sanders asked, bristling.

Holmes touched his chin, thinking for a moment before answering. "No, I don't think so. We should have been called right away to seal the room, but we weren't."

Gould pulled a piece of paper with phone numbers out of Wheeler's wallet. "Has anyone checked these? They may bring us closer to the money."

"Scotland Yard's main job is to solve a murder, and I thought we *did*. The money belongs to Chinese and American investors. Let them look for it," Sanders answered smugly.

Holmes felt compelled to, once again, admonish the group. "Everyone, stop bickering and sit down. We know Roland killed Bly and . . . our men, and he may be up for Suzi Wu's murder as well if the girl doesn't pull through, but we still are not sure about Wheeler. We need more evidence since Roland is not talking—well, he's certainly not giving us any more information about Wheeler. I think we should re-interview everyone who was on the twenty-first floor of the Palace as well as the help. Everyone should be shown a picture of Roland. We will meet back here Monday morning at nine. Meanwhile, I have a blasted news conference. Come with me, Jordan."

Holmes walked out of the meeting room, exasperated. This case was a hard one to crack. Wheeler, an infamous American with no London ties, left Scotland Yard with no informers to contact. That is why Holmes allowed Gould, the American, so much freedom. As chief inspector of the MIT, the international press was pressuring Holmes, and he needed someone else to share the spotlight.

The main part of the station was filled with reporters. You could hear whispers and loud chatter. The inflection of sounds represented the Brits, plus several international news people. Coffee cups were either held in hand or floating around every empty counter. Once Holmes entered the room, all heads turned towards him.

"Tell us about this Roland guy." "He killed everyone. Why?" "Who hired him?" "What is the connection with the Brill woman?" "Can we question her?" "What did Roland do with Wheeler's money?" "How did a big ape like Roland get to Wheeler and the two constables?"

Holmes, with Jordan at his side, calmly gave the press limited answers. He explained that he needed to make sure nothing was said that could endanger the case.

Jordan was upset. Obviously, everyone wanted to believe Roland killed Wheeler. They wanted to see this monster who had gunned down their colleagues, plus the chauffeur, fry over and over, but something was bothering him about it. Roland said he threw the gun into the Thames, which made things much harder. It could take forever to retrieve it.

He had learned from his training at the FBI that if something bothers you about someone else's investigation, check it out yourself. Instead of returning to his hotel room after the news conference, he headed by taxi towards central London and the Palace Hotel. He entered the lobby and went straight up to the twenty-first floor. He stood outside of the still-sealed suite, removed the yellow tape, and stuck the key in the door. Instead of opening, an alarm went off, and hotel security was upon him in less than four minutes.

"Damn it," he said as the guards approached, and he raised his hands. It took a few minutes, a phone call to Holmes, and a check of his badge before he was allowed into the crime site.

Inside, Jordan verified that the bathroom where Lori was taking a shower was on the right and just a few feet from the entrance. If someone came in that door, wouldn't Lori have heard it? Jordan spent fifteen more minutes checking the room for another entrance. He looked out the window. There was no ledge out the window of the twenty-first floor.

Outside the room, he approached the hotel guard and asked him, "We were told there are no connecting rooms on this floor. Is that true?"

The guard nodded, answering, "These rooms used to connect to each other, but after the remodeling two years ago, the connection was no longer accessible."

Jordan saw no extra door in the room, so he assumed the access door had been removed and a false wall put in its place. He walked around the room, knocking at intervals on the walls and listening for that distinct hollow sound of a false wall. Finding none, Jordan then moved to the large closet located on the wall opposite the bathroom.

Nearly covering the length of the wall, the closet was large enough for three or four people to stand in comfortably, about eight and a half feet in height and about seven feet in length. Perfect for visitors staying for an extended length of time. He thought it odd that Josh would choose this suite, as it was, really, only for the purpose of the one-night stand he would enjoy with Lori. Josh wanted to impress his high school sweetheart, that was certain. Jordan walked about the closet, inspecting the walls. His knocks were met with the solid thuds of sound, solid construction. Above his head sat a long shelf, probably where people placed their shoes or luggage. He wiggled the shelf; it did not give.

Moving toward the farthest, most remote corner of the closet, he got down on his hands and knees and found, next to a few small down feathers, a metal button, the kind a policeman or possibly a hotel guard would have on his uniform. He ran his hands over the wall and realized that in this section, the wall was not connected at the seams. He had found the connecting door. The closet and its shelving had been built over this small door, making access near impossible, if not nearly undetectable. A sliding door with a flush handle recessed in the wood, one that would have been used to gain access to the adjoining room, had just been blocked by shelving and locked, not completely sealed off. He figured the hotel must have figured no one would be the wiser, not with this door being so obscured and forgotten at the remote corner of the closet.

He didn't have time or authority to investigate it further but knew that the adjoining room had belonged to an elderly couple, an improbable pair of suspects. The small connecting door leading to their room was locked. Perhaps the perpetrator had snuck out of their room undetected. The compromised video, showing activity in the hallway, had not revealed any activity near or around the suite next door, nor had it shown anyone entering Wheeler's suite from the hallway. He dropped the button into his pocket, locked up the room, and noticed, as he left with the hotel security guard, that his uniform did not have this particular type of button. He still had a hard time believing that Lori heard nothing when the bathroom and the entrance were practically on top of each other. He figured he had better put his thoughts of interviewing her again on the shelf after his confrontation with Cate.

* * *

It wasn't that easy gathering the other eight people who were on the suite wing of the twenty-first floor the day of the shooting. The Bristol couple volunteered to be interviewed again, but on the Internet using Skype. They thought they recognized Roland as someone who ran down the steps in the early morning. They talked and talked to Tuttle, revealing very little of interest.

The two Italian men were unreachable. They had registered with false names, addresses, and phone numbers. They had paid with cash. Tuttle said he would pursue their identities, something that should have been done before they were allowed to leave, though he actually thought they were gay and trying to be discreet. Mrs. Putnam was burying her husband, so they left her alone until a later date; she'd had very little to say in her initial interview. Mrs. Sweeney, on the other hand, talked on and on about poor Lori, and Mr. Sweeney spoke about the chaos in the halls after Lori began screaming. The police had never received a statement from Mr. Putnam beyond the fact that he'd slept through the whole thing. Too bad; before he retired, he had been a hotel guard in London and in Manchester. If he had been awake, he might have noticed something the others missed. The laundry boy said he recognized the man in the paper and thought he saw him in the hotel the day before the murder. So far, the hotel video was no help except that the man or woman in it was tall and broad-shouldered, which matched Roland's description somewhat.

Monday morning, the investigators were back at the station to report their findings.

Milton Sanders, Holmes, and Gould sat in the large meeting room of the station. On the table was a stack of newspapers from England, the USA, and several other countries. The headlines all carried a version of Josh Wheeler's killer being captured and reported that Mrs. Brill was safe. Reginald Tuttle entered the room with the mail; letters from the prime minister and the president of the United States congratulated them on solving the case.

Holmes, with his everlasting cup of tea in his hand, pulled one paper out of the pile. Its headline read: *Killer Found, Money Still Missing.*

"Yes," replied Jordan. "The world is happy, but I'm not sure this case is solved."

Sanders leaned forward from his seated position at the large desk and pulled his eyeglasses to his forehead. "Jordan, you're never happy. Roland, from jail, called the press and strutted around his cell, bragging about how he had done the bastard in. The murder case now belongs to the prosecutors, not the police."

Jordan read over Roland's confession. He looked at the others in the room.

"I'm still not sure he actually murdered Wheeler. He knows he's a dead man for Bly and our men, so that he might be seeking publicity with Wheeler, and his story of Wheeler's murder has many holes in it. To start with, he denied murdering Wheeler, but confessed to Bly's murder and Suzi's rape, and the murder of our fellow officers. Why would he go in with the intention of killing Wheeler? He'd never get the code that way."

Jordan wanted to insist that they continue looking for the real murderer, but he had learned through trial and error that he must curb his feeling that he was always right. The murder trial was now under the prosecutor's jurisdiction.

"Once Suzi comes to, we'll know the answer," Sanders said as he plunged his hands into his pants pockets, fidgeting with some coins. Everyone knew that the longer Suzi was in a coma, the less her chances of recovering.

Holmes said, "Roland is getting his publicity. Two of the top criminal lawyers are offering free service to him. He has confessed. I've given a statement to the press. The prime minister has congratulated us, and the entire world is watching. My superiors have told me that our job is done. Thank you all."

Jordan was a very determined person, one who hated to be turned from his quest, but at this time in his career, he was subject to the will of his superiors. He walked over to the window, watching the steady raindrops falling against the small plate glass window. Justice, one way or another, was being served.

"Well, you don't have to worry about me anymore. I have been called back to the States. I leave in a few days. They want me to work on finding the money from home. But I found . . . I mean, I think someone here should pursue the strong possibility that the connecting doors between rooms at the Palace were not completely sealed off, just boarded up and—"

"How many times do we need to go over it?" Sanders asked in disgust. Nerves were still on edge because of the death of their two men. "Roland is guilty. He's a sociopath. He doesn't need a motive. Besides, he's confessed. Let him rot in jail for what he's done!"

Holmes raised his eyebrows and stroked his chin, ignoring Sanders' outburst. "Definitely something to look into. That would explain why no one saw or heard anyone enter or leave the room."

"But he was seen on that floor!" Sanders exclaimed.

"Must I repeat, it is over, out of our department. Roland Kiefer has confessed to all four murders and will be tried accordingly." Holmes emphasized his words with a determined look, thus ending the conversation.

Reginald Tuttle looked up from his papers and sighed in relief. He turned towards Jordan. "It's been an experience working with you. I still cannot understand how so many Yanks fell for Wheeler's Ponzi scheme. If one was to believe your newspapers and Internet, it seems many people gave him their life savings."

Jordan smiled. "Those kinds of schemes have been around for years, and people in every country have fallen for them, way before Charles Ponzi started swindling investors. But closer to home, isn't one of your elected officials being investigated for walking off with a considerable amount of money?"

Holmes quickly walked over to Jordan and stuck out his hand. "It's been a pleasure working with you, old chap. Let us know about the money recovery. Come back and visit."

Sanders and Tuttle stepped forward and shook Jordan's hand, the former more hesitantly than the latter.

Jordan gathered his things and walked out of the station when Geoffrey Holmes stopped him.

"Give me half an hour to tidy up some things, and then let's go over to the pub for a farewell dinner."

Chapter Twenty-Two

When Lori was up and around, and the doctors were making plans to transfer her to a rehab facility, Cate's parents started talking about going home. On one of those nights when Cate and her parents were visiting Lori, Joseph showed up. He was very gracious to her parents, not letting on about the rift in their relationship, and Cate appreciated that; after all, hadn't there been enough drama lately? Cate jumped at Joseph's suggestion to take her parents to London's modern Swiss Re Building—also fondly known as the Gherkin—at 30 St. Mary Axe, as they hadn't had a night out in all the time they had been in London. Lord Lunt had a membership to the private dining restaurant on the thirty-eighth floor, so Joseph had no trouble making a reservation. The plan was to dine there and then bring the folks up to the fortieth floor for drinks and a magnificent, panoramic view of the city of London through the domed glass overhead, known as the Lens.

Once they left the hospital, they arrived at Cate's flat, redressed, and started out in Joseph's black Bentley. Cate loaned her mother something dressy to wear, as one didn't go to the Swiss Re building in casual clothes; no one who would be dining at Lord Lunt's table, anyway. The black knit dress was a little tight on Anne, but it worked, as did her black, stacked, strappy heels. Cate looked gorgeous in a figure-hugging sparkling silver dress that draped down in a soft cowl just above her derriere, revealing her slender back. Her silver stiletto heels accentuated the length of her shapely legs, and her long beaded earrings glistened through her long straight yellow hair.

The Gherkin over East Central, a modern sky-rise of green and clear glass, cut a striking figure in the London skyline. While Joseph, dressed in a lovely, '60s-style, fitted, dark grey suit, checked in to the reception desk, Anne and Barry looked around in awe. Security was very tight. The group and all their belongings had to go through airport-style X-rays before entering the lifts to reach the thirty-eighth floor.

"Oh, my God, my ears are popping," Anne exclaimed. She barely had time to cover her ears when the doors of the first lift opened on floor thirty-four, as high as it would go. Next, they took another lift to the domed top, as Cate was anxious for her folks to see the best view in London.

She smiled as she watched her mom and dad step off the lift and take a look around. Her dad's outfit was much more casual than those around him, but it would pass as business casual in the States. He wore a pair of dark blue trousers and a button-down white shirt with a blue and grey tie. His matching suit coat was draped over his arm.

"All glass! Why I can see the moon through the roof," Barry said, awestruck.

"The moon over London," Anne said, sighing, taking her husband's hand in hers and gazing out at the twinkling city lights, the illuminated buildings, and the snaking traffic below. "Magical!"

After about ten minutes, Joseph nudged Cate. "We are running late with all this sightseeing."

Cate snapped back, "We came to show my parents the magic of this place."

"Fine, dear. You're right," he said as he stood back. He so hoped for reconciliation that anything Cate wanted was fine with him.

Cate, who had been there many times, was still taken by the expansive view. One could see all of London, from the ancient castles to the modern sky-rise buildings. She was happy that it was a clear, beautiful spring evening.

After returning to the dining floor, they were seated at Lord Lunt's favorite table, located in a corner away from others. In tune with the four glass walls and the glass ceiling, everything in the room was modern and sparkling.

The attendant approached. "Good to see you again, Mr. Lunt. Would you like to try your usual matching wine service and selection of starters?"

Joseph smiled, "That would be fine, William."

The full-bodied red wine was served in tall crystal glasses. They raised them in a toast. "To Lori's recovery."

While they waited for the starters, Anne leaned into Joseph and said, "Tell me about yourself."

Joseph faced her. "Not much to tell that you don't know. I'm a solicitor, the son of Lord Lunt, and . . . ."

Cate startled him with, "Joseph, stop. My mother knows your bio and that we are here because of your father. She wants to know what you are interested in besides sitting by the telly."

Anne was silent. She was a quiet, easygoing person who didn't like to get involved in controversy. She took a sip of the wine. Her daughter's disposition was more dramatic and less tolerable than hers.

Barry reached over and put his hand on Cate's arm. "Honey, you are being insulting."

William, the server, approached with their starters of caviar, red and black berries, tea crackers, smoked salmon, and a light white wine, just in time to save the day.

Joseph, ignoring Cate's rudeness, raised his glass after everyone's glass had been filled and repeated the toast. "To Lori's quick recovery!"

They clicked glasses as Barry said, "Amen. My mother will be fine. She is a tough one. Growing up, I thought my dad was the tough one. I was wrong. He was just loud."

Cate calmed down and smiled at her parents as she picked up a menu. "The food here is marvelous. Right, Joseph?"

"Yes, definitely. Make sure you keep room for dessert. I would recommend the monkfish as a main course."

William stood quietly until he was acknowledged and food was ordered. Joseph and Barry engaged in a political conversation while Cate let her mother catch her up on the news about family and friends in the States.

The main dishes were delicious, and their presentation was a delight. The twirls of color on the plates and the placement of the varied foods were definitely works of art. Both Cate and her mother had the fish with duchess potatoes and a vegetable cake, and the men had big, thick, juicy steaks. Being quite full of food and wine, Joseph suggested the cheese and fruit tray for dessert.

Anne, holding up a cracker loaded with cheese, commented, "I've always thought the cheese we get in Wisconsin, just over the Illinois border, was superb, but this continental blue just melts in my mouth." Turning to Cate, she said, "Honey, I think I'm going to bust out of your dress."

"I understand you will be returning to the States soon," Joseph said.

Barry answered, "Yes, as soon as Mom is transferred to rehab, we will leave her in Cate's and your capable hands. We both work in the hospital, and this was not a planned trip." Barry stopped and took a deep breath. "I really thought I was going to lose my mother this time. I live a calm, normal life, but my mother always manages to get involved in a tragedy or some craziness."

"Dad, this wasn't Gram's fault."

Barry smiled. "Cate and Lori are fifty years apart, but they are real soul mates. They understand and defend each other."

He took out his wallet and turned to Joseph. "This has been a delightful evening. Please let me treat you."

Joseph smiled and shook his head. "In here, the check is automatically put on the Lunt account. It has been *my* pleasure."

As they rose from their chairs to leave, Barry and Anne stayed a distance behind Joseph and Cate. They watched Joseph take hold of Cate's arm. They watched their daughter stiffen at his touch.

Anne leaned in towards Barry. "I have my doubts about a wedding in their future."

Barry looked at his wife and said, "Didn't Cate tell you she applied for an internship with a D.C. judge?"

* * *

Though Jordan had joked with Sanders over the prostitutes who had visited Suzi's room, it still bothered him that they had so little information about Suzi and the Chinese connection in the Wheeler murder. He decided to pay another visit to Lori now that she was on the mend and being prepared to move to a rehab facility.

He stopped by her hospital room late in the day after visiting hours, around nine-thirty in the evening. He entered the room carrying a box of chocolates. His Jewish mother always told him bakery goods were the way to everyone's heart.

He breathed a sigh of relief when he found Lori alone watching television. Approaching the bed, he handed her the candy and inquired about her health.

Lori accepted the candy while she eyed him with curiosity. "Very kind of you, Jordan, but I believe this is more than a friendly visit. What can I help you with?"

Jordan grinned as he looked down at the petite lady sitting in the large hospital bed.

"You're right. I'm troubled by Roland's confession to the murder. He seems to know so little about the Chinese who hired him, and it is impossible to ask Suzi, unfortunately. It seems Tony, the man who drowned during the car chase, was hired by the Wu family to follow Wheeler and abduct him to obtain his money from the safety deposit boxes. Tony hired Roland to help him with the job. Your appearance changed Wheeler's plans. Since you have some history with Suzi, I was hoping you could enlighten me."

Lori took a deep breath. "Could you please get me a glass of water and raise this bed up, so I am in a sitting position?"

When Jordan left the room to get Lori some water, her mind traveled back some thirty years or more to when she was young and married into the crazy Brill family.

Jordan handed her the water while she turned off the television and motioned for him to sit down in the lounge chair near her bed.

She turned towards him. "Back some forty years ago, I was young, naïve, and married into the Brill family. Now, you may already know some of this information from me, from Cate, but here it is. My brother-in-law, a lawyer, shocked everyone when he divorced his wife of twenty-nine years and married a prostitute named Zi. Zi was a young Chinese beauty who spoke no English. She was owned by a house in Cicero, Illinois, called—you're not going to believe this—The Enchanted Pussy. My brother-in-law had to buy her from the madam, who worked for people in China. I don't remember the name of her employers, but Wu sounds familiar. Huh, *employers*," Lori said, scrunching up her face in disapproval. "She was a sex slave, that poor woman, pure and simple."

Lori stopped and took a drink of water before opening the box of chocolates. She offered Jordan one, but he refused. Jordan had spent time arresting prostitutes and pimps while working his first job in New

York. It was frustrating to work because they could never catch the men who kidnapped the young girls in the Orient and brought them to the States to work as slaves in the prostitution houses.

He interrupted her. "Lori, how does Suzi fit into this picture?"

"Suzi is their daughter. She was a beautiful young girl. When my brother-in-law died, she and her mother left Chicago. My brother-in-law's children from his first marriage made sure Zi left penniless. They blamed Zi for their mother's suicide and threatened her with deportation if she took them to court."

"Do you know where Suzi and her mother went?" Jordan thought back to the woman at Suzi's bedside, incongruous with Suzi's lifestyle.

"Not really. I heard they settled in Chinatown in San Francisco. When she appeared at the warehouse, I was in shock."

Jordan clenched his fists together and shuffled his legs back and forth, but he stayed seated. It was sounding to him like Suzi ended up in the high rollers prostitution ring run by the Wu family. He wondered if that was Zi's payback for leaving the fold to marry Lori's brother-in-law. Wheeler was just one of her customers. Jordan had seen many politicians and businessmen worked by the girls hired by the Wu family. Somehow, Wheeler was able to turn the game around and get them to invest with him. Normally, the Wu family would be more interested in getting their money back than in killing Wheeler. Jordan would have to explore this theory.

Presently, a nurse entered the room. "Visiting hours are over. Mrs. Brill needs her medicine and her rest."

Jordan got up. "Thank you, Lori, for your help."

Lori grabbed his arm just as Jordan rose from his chair. "Is there any chance Suzi will come out of the coma?"

"It doesn't look good, I'm afraid, but one never knows with comas. There is a chance she may pull out of it. I'm not certain what condition she'd be in afterward, of course."

Lori dropped his arm and looked into his face. "Will you make sure that Cate or I am kept informed about Suzi's condition?"

"Yes," Jordan responded. Outside of the room, he stopped to reflect on Lori's last statement. Why did she tell him to keep Cate informed? He smiled a little grin as he left the hospital.

Chapter Twenty-Three

Jordan tossed and turned and finally got out of bed. It was still dark. Just a touch of moonlight streamed through the window, and the digital clock on his nightstand read 3:26 a.m. Last night he had gone to a noisy bar in Soho. He intended to have a last fling, but he had ended up giving a high-class call girl two hundred pounds for nothing more than a make-out session and some heavy petting. He tried to blame his unrest during his last two days in London on his uneasiness about Roland's confession, but in his heart, he knew his problems revolved around his feelings for Cate. He hated leaving London with so much business left unfinished.

From his visits to the hospital and then the rehab home to see Mrs. Brill, he'd learned Cate had graduated, and her parents had left for the States. Mrs. Brill had hinted that things were not good between Cate and the Englishman. He decided to give the girl one more chance. He waited until around 8:30 a.m. before driving out to Cate's flat. He didn't want to wake her, he just caught her before she left the house.

* * *

Cate had spent almost every day in the hospital with Lori, talking to the doctors, watching her, helping her sip liquid from a cup, eat her meals, and practice walking. Now that Lori was on the mend in a rehab facility and Cate's classes were over, she was able to start packing up her belongings.

She woke up early, somewhere around 7:00 a.m. The rainstorm outside made the room look dark and brooding. *A perfect day to work inside*, she thought. She showered, brushed her teeth, threw on a shirt and a pair of old shorts, and headed downstairs to start right in on her tasks. Two more weeks, and she would be on her way home to the States.

Busy tossing things into boxes and suitcases, she stopped to glance out the window at the water cascading down the panes. *I've had enough of this bloody weather*. She returned to the kitchen counter, picked up the teakettle, and threw it in the garbage can. *Gram's right. Enough of this abominable tea. I'm back on coffee.*

"We are done with tea, Tigger," she said aloud. Tigger lay sprawled out on the living room couch, purring and watching Cate go about her business, moving bags of garbage and give away things in and out of the flat.

He had only come up the steps when he caught sight of her. He stood in the doorway watching her hips swaying, the nice muscular legs showing through her shorts.

Cate suddenly became aware of someone standing in her doorway, and she gasped when she saw him. Her heart quickened in fear and excitement of seeing him smiling at her, but her excitement turned to anger, and she cried out, "What are you doing here? You scared me!"

"The door was open, so I walked in. I didn't mean to frighten you, Cate,"

Jordan said, apologizing.

"Well . . . What do you want?"

"I brought back your grandmother's travel bag."

"She is near the station at rehab. You could have dropped it there."

"I'm going back to the States, thought I would say goodbye. In person."

"Goodbye." Cate stuffed her hands inside the pockets of her shorts.

Jordan walked around the room. He picked up the teakettle from the trash bin. "Looks like you are going somewhere. Are you moving?"

Cate didn't look at him. "I've accepted a job in Washington D. C. Going home when Gram gets out of rehab."

Jordan tried to keep from smiling. "What happened to your stuffy Englishman?"

Cate turned around, faced him, and with hands on her hips, she declared, "Don't you belittle Joseph. He is twice the man you are. We . . . we just didn't fit." She walked towards the door, and opened it wider. "Thanks for stopping by. Goodbye."

Jordan started to walk out. "I'm stationed in D.C. Maybe we'll run into each other."

"Yes, maybe. Someday." She stood now with arms crossed against her chest.

The tension between them was thick. They both stood silent, staring at each for a few seconds. Then Jordan turned towards the door and quickly exited.

He jumped into his car and drove off, swearing to himself. "Damn, arrogant girl. Why did I belittle myself? There are plenty of girls in D.C. waiting for me to return."

The smell of exhaust permeated the flat as Jordan's car raced away. Cate lingered in the doorway a few minutes before closing it.

Why did he have to come here, and why did I have to be so mean? That man does something to me. I can't do anything right when he is around.

She sat down on the sofa in the living room next to Tigger, opened the curtains, and stared out the window, unable to go back to her packing.

About ten minutes later, she saw his car pull into her driveway. Her heartbeat quickened anew. She waited for the doorbell to ring.

Cate's previous sharp tones softened when she opened her door. "You're back!"

"Only to retrieve my cell phone. I think I dropped it in your flat."

"One way to find out," Cate said, as she pushed the front door shut and took her cell out of her pocket and dialed his number. "We'll see if it rings in here."

He didn't say a thing, though he was impressed that she had his number plugged into her mobile phone. A weird science fiction type of ring was heard very near to his body.

She moved close to him and, with a coy smile, she stuck her hand into his coat pocket. Laughing and looking him up and down, she whispered, "Um, I believe your pocket is ringing."

Jordan took hold of Cate's arm and pulled her close to him. He kissed her with a desire that was matched only by her own. His lips embraced hers, his tongue exploring every part of her mouth, savoring the sweet taste of cinnamon sugar scone.

He tore at her clothes, quickly undressing her. He wrapped his arms around her firm hips and pulled her towards his hardening groin. His heart raced as he felt her willing response, felt her fingers working the zipper of his trousers. They slid down on Lord Lunt's blue and green silk Oriental rug, which covered the living room floor. He lowered his trousers and paused to look into her eyes for any sign of resistance before entering her. Her moves were in perfect rhythm with his own, slow and deep at first, then quickening to hard and fast thrusts, and filled with just as much longing and fervor. Within minutes, it was over, and they lay there in each other's arms, panting and laughing until she rose and led him up to the bedroom.

"I'm not quite done with you."

"Fine by me. Lead on."

When they reached the bedroom, Jordan picked her up and gently tossed her onto the bed, where he disrobed her last piece of clothing, a half-opened cotton blouse. He slowly caressed her full lush breasts,

186

pulling each taut nipple between his lips, then working his hands and mouth down the full length of her body, stopping only to give special attention to the moist mound between her legs. He took pleasure in bringing her to another climax, hearing her hoarse cries of release, feeling her wetness increase as she clenched either side of his head with her thighs, her hands grabbing at his hair as he plunged his tongue deep inside her. To her joyful surprise, Jordan did not stop after she climaxed but continued his playful exploration of new territory until Cate came two more times. Afterwards, they lay back on the bed, arm in arm, completely spent. A short time later, Jordan awoke to the feeling of Cate's mouth hungrily working on his growing penis. Minutes later, with her mouth, tongue, and hands, she expertly brought him to a howling climax.

Jordan didn't know how long he slept, but when he awoke, the only one in the bed with him was a small black and white cat. He dressed and went downstairs. Cate, now fully dressed, was busy in the kitchen. She smiled sweetly when she saw him and motioned for him to sit on one of the kitchen chairs.

"I've made us some pasta for lunch," she said as she handed him a plate of spaghetti with a rich red sauce and a slice of garlic bread.

"I'm starving, and it looks delicious. Thanks," he said, placing his full plate on the kitchen table.

"Would you like a glass of wine?"

"Actually, Cate, a soda would be great."

"I'm from the Midwest. We have pop, but not soda," she answered with a mischievous grin.

Jordan broke out laughing. "Pop, soda! I guess you must feel we're becoming too nice to each other, out of character." He rose, walked over to her, and pulling her to him, kissed her on the neck while his hand moved up the back of her sweater. He inhaled the aroma of flowers on her long smooth neck. He tried to pinpoint her perfume choice with no luck and realized there were so many things he had to learn about her. His mind was already making that detailed list the FBI taught him to make, the one he tended to use on every one out of sheer habit.

Her manner was easy and flirtatious as she opened the refrigerator and took out a bowl of green grapes. She plucked one from the bunch and plopped it into his mouth. He held her hand, and they stood silent for a few seconds until Cate laughed and broke away.

She served them lunch and drinks, and they settled down to dining and talking about their past, present, and future.

Jordan grinned as he asked Cate, "So, my dear, I picture you as a Jewish princess, catered to by your quiet, easy-going, adoring parents, something like the famous Kate from *Taming of the Shrew*."

Instead of getting angry, Cate took a large sip of white wine straight from the bottle before she countered with, "Nice picture. But don't ever think you can tame me. Better men than you have tried."

Jordan leaned forward and rested his chin on his arm. "*Tame* you? I would never do that. I would, however, guess that while I was squeezed into a tiny flat, sharing a room with two siblings in the Bronx, working my ass off to get into Harvard, you probably had your own room in a massive, luxurious house, sailing through school on brains, wit, and connections."

Cate grinned at his words. Yes, she had a much more privileged life than Jordan. She was an only child, and her dad was a doctor, and her mom, though a nurse, was a stay-at-home mom, and her grandmother had connections with a famous federal judge, but she wasn't going to tell him all that now.

Instead, she answered, smiling, "And it's such a *fine* ass too. But no one gets into Harvard and London's esteemed law school without brains, Mister Gould, so, um, let's talk about something else."

"Speaking of fine asses," Jordan got up and moved toward her. Sliding his hand down her spine and cupping her rear end, he whispered in her ear, "Besides that stunning little heart-shaped birthmark on your spine, I love your sharp wit."

"That's not where I keep my wit."

"No? Is it . . . here?" Jordan slipped his hand down the front of Cate's pants and smiled as he found her panties rather damp.

"Uh, THAT's not where I keep my wit, either," Cate said, smiling, wrapping her arms around his neck.

"Hmm," Jordan said, kissing her neck, "We'll have to do more exploring, then."

The spell was broken when the fire alarm went off, and smoke poured out of the stove. Jordan turned the stove off, recovered the burnt piece of garlic bread, and opened a window as Cate reached for the phone and dialed the alarm company before the fire department appeared.

They opened a few windows and settled down on the sofa in the living room, congratulating each other for working together so well. Tigger hopped onto the window ledge and curled up before the screened window, welcoming the fresh air.

Soon, they settled into a normal conversation. Cate told him about her job offer with Federal Judge Pierce in D.C., who actually was a relative of her grandmother's best friend, Rain. He told her it would be a great opportunity for her and a chance for them to get to know each other better. He envied her connections to a federal judge, something he never had. They discussed his ambitions in the FBI, the differences between the British and American legal systems, and his doubts about the murder case being solved.

They discovered they had much in common besides their love of competition and sarcasm. They were runners, tennis players, game players, Harvard graduates, and Jewish lawyers. Once they discovered that they differed on politics, they quickly dropped the subject.

He insisted on helping her clean the kitchen, saying, "My mom worked, and we had to do chores. I would disappoint her if I left you with this mess."

Jordan left early that evening, knowing he would be heading for the States in two days and she would be following in two weeks. Before going, he held Cate close to him, once more exploring every part of her mouth as he kissed her goodbye. Cate reluctantly shut the door slowly as he left. Neither of them wanted their night to end.

Jordan grinned the smile of a Cheshire Cat as he turned the key in his car. That Cate is something else, self-possessed, someone he will never own. But what fun he will have trying!

* * *

Feeling like a high-school girl with a crush, Cate moved upstairs, taking two steps at a time, and settled under her nice warm comforter, smelling her sheets to breathe in the scent of their lovemaking. Tigger followed Cate onto the bed, only now, instead of sleeping at the foot of the bed, she occupied Joseph's former spot.

The next morning Cate woke up with a smile on her face. She lay in bed thinking about Jordan. She asked herself, *Why had I tried so hard to hate him?* They really fit together so well, physically and personality-wise. They were both smart, aggressive, ambitious, and fun-loving. She now allowed herself to admit that when she had accepted the job in D.C. with Judge Pierce, she was thinking of Jordan working there.

She made it to the bathroom, stepping over boxes, thinking, *Lots of work to do before picking up Gram.* Joseph had already moved back to his father's flat in town, which made things easier. Poor Joseph. He was such a good person, but as hard as she tried, she was never in love with him. Last night, things were so different with Jordan; there was chemistry there that was missing with Joseph. She wanted to do things to Jordan to get him excited, to make him crazy with desire; with Joseph, sex was nice, but . . . It seemed so proper, so obliging. Sex with Joseph was like coloring within the lines; sex with Jordan was like using a different medium altogether.

She stepped out of the shower, still daydreaming. She told herself to settle down and start working. Her flight back home to Chicago was only two weeks away, and her job in D.C. was to begin in three weeks.

Chapter Twenty-Four

Lori sat in the garden of Lyon's Rehab. The facility was an old country white stone building located in Chelsea with a beautiful English garden full of petunias, four o'clock marigolds, hollyhocks, and an interesting footpath along a meandering stream. Two ducks with heads tucked under their wings slept while another one swam aimlessly. A wind rippled the water's surface, but the sleeping ducks didn't stir, making Lori believe they were the older ones.

Lori was so happy to be out of the hospital. She hated hospitals. Every time she was forced to step into one, her eyes only saw pain and death, particularly the death from leukemia of a beautiful young teenage girl. She avoided the word *cancer* and hospitals like the plague, just as she avoided comparing Cate and Julie, even though they had many similarities. Both smart, beautiful, witty, and feisty. Stupid of her, but she had been so relieved when Barry passed seventeen, and then Cate passed seventeen, the age Julie died.

Lyon's Rehab was perfect for Lori now. She spent her days resting, eating, reading, and attending physical and emotional therapy. Her room and adjoining bathroom were decorated in old country English with toile-patterned wallpaper, oak dressers, wicker chairs, painted English plates, and flowers everywhere.

One day, while resting in her new favorite spot, the sun parlor, a heavyset, dark-haired woman dropped her newspaper in her ample lap, turned to Lori, and asked, "Have you been following the Wheeler case?"

Lori was about to get up and escape from the question when she glanced down at the paper. Today, the *London Times* article wasn't about Roland and the kidnapping or about the money lost to hundreds of investors; today's article was accompanied by a picture of a young high school football hero. Right there in the paper was a picture of the Josh Wheeler, a young, naïve Lori Brill was once in love with.

"Not a bad looker," the woman stated, glancing back at her paper, then up at Lori.

Lori smiled, remembering the tall, blue-eyed, blond, muscular boy she knew. *God,* she thought, *he put me through hell and heaven in those four years of high school.* She was his, but he wasn't hers. No matter how hard she tried, no matter how much she loved him. There, in the restorative warmth of the sun parlor, Lori recalled with painful accuracy the nights she cried her heart out because he didn't call or show up for the date he made with her or how she had refused to listen when friends spotted him with other girls, because he always came back.

When Josh came back to her, life was wonderful. She could fly through the air like a bird when he twirled her around the dance floor, with her petticoats and skirts swishing back and forth and everyone in the room watching them.

"Tea or coffee?" the server in the parlor room asked.

It jolted Lori back to the present. "Yes, please. Black coffee . . ." she started to say, then asked for some warm milk with it; she remembered Josh always drank his coffee with warm milk and a cigarette. She could picture him taking a gulp of coffee and then a deep drag on his Chesterfield cigarette. He was the one who taught her how to smoke, back when the world thought it was so cool and grown up to smoke. Who knew?

The woman with the newspaper said, more to herself now that she realized Lori was not engaging her in conversation, "They say he was so charming that he could sell sand to an Arab in the desert and make him believe he needed it!"

Lori stared at the paper in the woman's hand for a moment or two, thinking, *yes, he could sell you anything*. He charmed her into taking him back after fucking who knows how many high school girls; he charmed her out of her virginity at the age of eighteen, telling her she was the love of his life and they would always be together. Then he went off to college and disappeared. Only Adele knew how she almost killed herself when she thought she was pregnant. Thank God it was a false alarm.

A melancholy bitterness overcame her as she recalled their breakup; it was more like abandonment. She raised her coffee cup to her lips and took a sip of the warm liquid.

After her senior prom and their first night together at the Drake Hotel, Josh had flown back to Washington D.C., where he was attending college. She was floating on cloud nine until weeks and then months passed by without a word from him. Her letters and phone calls went unanswered. Finally, when he came home for Thanksgiving, she confronted him.

Shaking like a leaf, she had walked down the block and knocked on his front door. When he opened it, he was all charm, hugging her like a found puppy. "Lori!" He smiled that charmer's smile.

Then she accused him, "Josh, why haven't you called or written? I've been frantic with worry! I called your parents, and they said they heard from you, but—" Lori could not fight the tears flowing down her cheeks.

He'd moved away from her and responded, "Lori, I've been busy. School and studying. You know how it is, kiddo. But you do know how much I treasure our friendship." As he turned to her, his eyes twinkled, and he kept that brilliant smile plastered on his tan face.

Lori had cried out, "*Friendship*?! What the hell are you talking about, Josh? We're *friends* now? You told me you *loved* me, Josh! You

194

told me that we would always be together. I believed we would get married. What about our night at the Drake? Doesn't that mean anything to you? You left and never got back in touch with me! I gave up my virginity for you, Josh!"

His voice turned to ice as he gazed down at her, his smile gone; darkness had doused the light in his eyes.

"Jeeze Louise with the virginity thing again. Get *over* it. What is the big fucking deal, Lori? What's with you? Did you really believe me that we were gonna get married? I'm in college! Jeeze. You're nothing but a kid." He tousled her hair and smirked dismissively. "Go home."

He'd turned away from Lori and walked up the stairs. She'd run home in tears and shame.

Yes, Josh could be charming, and he could also be cruel. She must remember that, too.

Several people gathered around the paper. A stooping, bald-headed older man using a walker pointed at Lori and then at the picture. "I say, aren't you the Brill woman? Here, now, you seem to be a lovely lady. Why ever were you with that Wheeler bloke?"

Lori set her coffee cup down at a nearby table and rose from her chair, grabbing a hold of her silver walker that now accompanied her everywhere. She had had enough.

Before exiting the room, she turned to the old man and said, "Because fifty years later, I *still* believed him."

Lori's therapist Cassie, an Irish lass with emerald green eyes and ginger red hair, had the task of helping Lori deal with the murder of Josh and her kidnapping, a difficult task to accomplish in the few weeks Lori was scheduled to stay in the facility. They met for an hour daily. It took several sessions with Cassie, but slowly, Lori managed to pull herself together and begin the emotional healing.

"Lori, I'm so pleased with your progress. I even heard your appetite has returned."

"Hell, Cassie, anything would be better than that awful hospital food. I especially enjoy tea time here with those great sandwiches and cakes."

"I see you've exchanged your walker for a cane today. By the end of your stay, they will have you running in races."

"I doubt that. It's Joan who has encouraged all of us. She is a victim of multiple sclerosis at the young age of thirty-nine. Instead of giving up or being discouraged, she works like a dog at moving, and she pushes the rest of us. I so admire her."

"She is so full of life with all her problems. You know she's been here almost a year," Cassie said as she walked Lori out of the office. Lori meandered into the rec room, where a bingo game was in session.

Joan approached her. "Lori, you are too beautiful a woman to let yourself go. I'm going to schedule you an appointment with the beauty salon."

Lori hesitated. "Thanks, but I'm not ready for that."

Joan smiled. "Rubbish, you'll feel so much better when you look better."

Joan was right, Lori realized, after looking at herself in the beauty shop mirror. Yes, her whole being looked and felt better with a new haircut, some makeup, and soft hands with painted pink nails.

* * *

In the physical rehab room, Joan slowly maneuvered her legs with the use of hand braces. Though her movements were painful, she did not show it. On her face was a big smile, and her voice had a cheerful lilt to it.

"Good morning, everyone!" Joan called out. "Guess what? I was visited by a good fairy last night, and he told me we were all going to walk out of here straight and tall and happy!" Then she leaned on the chair and pointed one brace around the room. "That means you, Lori, and you, Nadine, and you, Jean. In addition, of course, me, so let's get to work! We can't disappoint, my good fairy."

They all laughed and started to work with their physical therapists. When movement became too painful for Lori, she looked over to Joan for inspiration and courage.

Lori had awakened this morning terrified. She had a nightmare where she was back in the barn struggling to escape, but she was chained to something and couldn't move. She woke up with a jolt. Sweat was pouring down her face as she had really struggled. It took her a while before she could calm down, shower and dress.

She decided to stay away from dealing with the kidnapping in therapy. Too many narrow death misses for her to confront now. Instead, during her sessions with Cassie, Lori spoke extensively about Julie, about their constant clashes until the age of fourteen when Julie was diagnosed with leukemia, and about the family banding together to fight to keep her alive. They lost the battle, and Julie died almost thirty years ago.

Cassie asked Lori, "How did the death of your daughter change your life? And did it prepare you to handle the kidnapping?"

Lori stopped and looked away for a while. "Cassie, my daughter came down with leukemia when I was in my late thirties, a time when one feels one can overcome everything and conquer the world. Most people, while scared of death, never really believe it will happen to them or their families until they are old. Parents are supposed to die before their children.

"You asked how it changed my life. I became a different person, a person with a permanent hole in my heart, a person with part of her mind shut down, a person who was again afraid to let love come in. Cate's birth provided the only healing spot in my life.

"How did it help me deal with the kidnapping? After you have lost a child, nothing really touches you deeply or totally surprises you. You have either gone crazy or let your heart turn hard." Lori turned towards Cassie and smiled. "Growing up, I hated my mother because she was cold and unloving towards me. Later, I learned in her former life in Germany, she had lost a son in the concentration camps."

"Did you forgive her then?" Cassie asked.

"The adult Lori did, but the child Lori couldn't."

Cassie stopped cold. "Lori, that one sentence covered a year of my schooling. I think you have done especially well, considering what you have gone through. My job was to help you deal with the kidnapping, but we've hardly touched on it."

"I remember reading Elizabeth Kübler-Ross's book about the stages of death. During the kidnapping, I never once thought I was going to die. I kept thinking, how did my mother and daughter tolerate the pain and fear? I guess I was in denial, or finally traveling in their shoes."

"We can't really deal with these dramatic events in your life in two short weeks. I know I can get you in touch with some wonderful therapists in Arizona, and I would be—"

Lori raised her hand to stop Cassie "Been there, done that. Too old to start again. I will be all right. I have a supportive family and some good friends. Thank you for your help."

* * *

Lori was sitting in the sun parlor reading a book when she heard someone approaching her chair from behind. Before turning around, she recognized the pleasant tone of voice with its full British accent.

"Mrs. Brill, I heard you were leaving London soon, and I wanted to give you a proper goodbye."

Lori looked up into Geoffrey Holmes' smiling face as he leaned over to see what she was reading. Her sweater fell off her shoulders, and he instantly picked it up and put it back over her arms. His touch quickened her heartbeat.

She patted the wicker chair next to her in a sign for him to sit down. "Geoffrey, what a surprise. How nice to see you!"

Geoffrey heaved a sigh of relief. The whole trip there, he had been anxious and uneasy like a schoolboy on his first date. He sat down on the wicker chair. "You are looking well."

Lori blushed. "Thank you for fibbing." She looked down at her thin body, covered by a common housedress, and realized she was wearing no makeup.

"Much better than you were in the hospital." Geoffrey, dressed in a herringbone blazer over a pair of dark brown pants, hair gray but nicely cut, smile wide, his eyes twinkling, asked, "If you can step out, I would like to take you to dinner."

"You mean this evening?"

"If possible, yes."

Lori felt flattered by the invitation. "That sounds very nice. I'm not a prisoner here, but I do need to sign out—and touch up a bit."

Geoffrey offered his arm and helped her up. He became aware of her limp due to the bullet wound, but he never referred to it, not even when she grabbed the slender cane she used to help her walk. Watching her go into her room, he thought, *What a sweet, elegant, petite little thing she is.* He compared her to his late wife, who was twice Lori's

199

size and very demanding, though he loved her dearly. Both he and his wife came from working-class London police families. His stomach twitched nervously at the prospect of having a relationship with Lori, someone of class.

Lori was excited about going out with Geoffrey. From the first day she met him, she found him to be kind and considerate, and she even liked his so very English Sherlock Holmes look. She quickly rummaged through her closet and pulled out a white silk blouse and a brown tweed skirt, took out her compact, powered her nose, and then applied a coral red lipstick. While inspecting herself in her room mirror, she said a silent blessing for Joan, as it was she who had convinced her to have herself made up, not to let herself go while she was at the facility. She then picked up the room phone and informed the front desk that she was going out with Chief Inspector Holmes.

Geoffrey's usual dining spots were London pubs, but tonight he was going to take Lori to a fancy restaurant in the theater district. He took her arm and helped her out of the rehab facility and into his car. For a change, it was a clear warm spring day.

"Have you seen any of our plays?" he asked. Geoffrey, contrary to the rest of his family, loved the theater. He probably would have pursued a career working behind the scenes, but all Holmes's family members were in the police department, and he was expected to follow.

Lori turned towards him, her lips pressed together, her neck and face tensing immediately. "Truthfully, I've been terrified of going where there are crowds."

Geoffrey smiled, looked down, and touched her hand. "Lori, you are in a police car with a chief inspector, so relax. If you are uncomfortable, we will go to a small, quiet restaurant."

Lori took a deep breath, relaxing her shoulders. "That sounds better, to be perfectly honest."

They drove for about ten minutes when Geoffrey stopped in front of a small, quaint restaurant called Sarah's Cafe. It was on a narrow road with few businesses around. The valet quickly came over and helped them out of the car. The restaurant proved to be just what he said it would be: comfortable and quiet, and only three tables were occupied.

"I love the red and white checkered tablecloth, and the melted candle looks like it's been here forever," Lori said as they were seated.

"Yes, this place has been here for years. One of my favorite spots."

Lori glanced at the old brick and plaster walls. The walls were mounted with photographs of gaslight London streets, men in top hats, and women with full floor-length frocks. The reference to years was much different in Europe than in the States.

The waiter inquired whether they wanted drinks. "Inspector, do you want your usual?" he asked. Geoffrey had his usual stout beer, and Lori had a glass of white wine. They ordered a good old-fashioned English meal of boiled potatoes, roast beef with horseradish, and popovers.

They fell into an easy conversation, telling each other about their homes and children. He told her about his family's long history with the police department.

"I've always wondered where the name Scotland Yard came from. Shouldn't it be called, London Yard? In the States, we name our police departments after the city they protect. You do know I am originally from that famous crime city called Chicago."

Holmes stopped to think for a few moments before answering. "The original headquarters was located on Great Scotland Yard, a street within Whitehall. It is believed that stagecoaches bound for Scotland once departed from that street. It goes back to the 17th century when the street became a site of government buildings. In 1890, Scotland Yard was moved to Victoria Embankment in Westminster, and in 1960, the new modern, twenty-story building was built on 10 Broadway in West-minster. Now, the term Scotland Yard is really used to refer to all of London's police force, and the building is called *New Scotland Yard*."

"You do know your history," Lori answered admiringly.

"I hope I haven't bored you. I can get carried away with details."

"No, of course not. I love to explore the history of the places I visit, though Scotland Yard and the hospital were not on my original itinerary when I left for London so many weeks ago."

They exchanged a knowing glance.

The waiter stopped at their table. "Dessert?"

"Just coffee, with a touch of milk," Lori answered, while Geoffrey asked for a hot kettle of tea with cream and sugar.

Geoffrey leaned forward. "What have you missed that you planned to do in London before disaster hit?"

"The theater, of course. London has the best theater and the most professional actors in the world," she answered enthusiastically.

"Perhaps I could take you to see a play some day next week before your flight home."

"That would be lovely," she answered.

"I will call your mobile when I get the tickets. Do you like mysteries?"

"I loved them before I came to London. Now I would be very happy never to see, read, or hear about a murder mystery again."

Geoffrey shook his head. "What a careless sod I've been."

Lori put her hand on his arm. "Don't worry about it. Actually, I used to take pride in solving the mystery before the play or book ended."

"How would you solve the murder of your friend Josh Wheeler? Do you believe Roland killed him?"

"Roland is very capable of the murder. He murdered that poor chauffeur in cold blood, and he threatened to murder my granddaughter and me. And what he did to poor Suzi . . ." Lori shook her head. "He killed a couple of your men, I hear. I am sorry, Geoffrey. He was cruel and brutal, but he never talked about murdering Josh, and he loved to brag about his brutal accomplishments. I think it would have been hard for him to quietly slip into the room, or especially *out* of the room."

"Interesting. The Yank agrees with you, and he has asked us to pursue some other evidence he's found. It could be, I have my suspicions, that someone above me wants to clear the case and is using Roland as the sacrificial lamb."

"Roland is hardly a lamb. He is more like the devil." Lori picked up her fork and continued to nibble on what was left of her dinner.

Geoffrey changed the subject. "Never been to Arizona, but when I retire next year, I would consider a trip to the States."

The waiter stopped at the table with a plate of tea cookies. "Complimentary for our chief."

Lori bit into a cookie and smiled at the waiter. She leaned in towards Geoffrey. "I would enjoy showing you around my home. It is very different from London and even from Chicago, my place of birth."

At one point, Geoffrey stopped and watched her intently, trying to decide if he should tackle the elephant in the room. Finally, he said, "Lori, you've been through a horrendous ordeal. Do not expect to get over it right away. It will take time."

Lori put her elbows on the table, folded her hands together, took a deep breath, pressed her lips together for a moment to collect her thoughts, and in a cracked voice, she answered, "I know. I've had to deal with tragedy before."

Geoffrey did not say anything, but his gaze was sympathetic, while Lori just sat there, quiet.

After a few seconds, she put her arms down and looked into Geoffrey's large brown eyes.

"I want you to know I am not a loose woman who falls into anyone's bed. In fact, in the last ten years since my husband died, I haven't been with anyone except for that one night with Josh. I must have been out of my mind when I went with him to the hotel. I acted like a teenager instead of an old lady of seventy."

"Lori," Geoffrey began, but she hushed him.

"Geoffrey, I want to finish. Josh Wheeler had a strange hold on me since I was a little girl, and—"

He stopped her. "Lori, you don't have to tell me anymore. From the first minute I met you, I knew you were a lady. I hope we can be good friends even though we will be miles apart."

Lori smiled. Geoffrey glanced up as the waiter, leaned down, and offered them a complimentary after-dinner drink. They declined and asked for the check. Geoffrey paid the check, helped Lori up, and they walked out together, arm in arm.

* * *

Lori had enjoyed her evening with Geoffrey. He was a kind person and a good listener. Throughout her life, she had known that friends in one's own age group made the best shrinks. She had missed that in London. Cate, the doctors, and the therapists had all tried hard to help her get through her ordeal, but it was hard for her to open up to souls so much younger than she was. Had she and Geoffrey lived closer together, their friendship might have had a chance to develop into something else.

Two days after her dinner with Inspector Holmes, Lori was packed and ready to leave Lyon's Rehab facility. Margaret was keeping her company until Cate arrived.

"Are you still experiencing the nightmares?" Cassie asked. "I could give you a prescription for more sleeping pills."

"No, thank you. Yes, sometimes during the night, I see a young Josh with his heart-stopping smile, and then I get a horrifying flash of his face blown apart. When my daughter died, I was hooked on pills for migraines, but I really used them to wipe out. I wouldn't go that route again." She told herself that she would not go the therapy route again, either. She was old and tough, and she could handle anything now. She remembered the motto they had at Children's Memorial Hospital: *Take one day at a time.*

Margaret gave Lori papers to sign her out of the clinic, plus some brochures on the care of her leg and lists of books concerning ways to deal with being a victim in a tragedy. If the nightmares continued, she told her to seek help in the States.

"You went through quite a lot between Wheeler's death and your kidnapping. You mentioned feeling your body floating during the surgery."

"Yes, I guess I went from stage one, denial, to the last stage, acceptance. I was ready to join my dead family and friends, but my mother would not let me go. She sent me back to the operating table." There was much Lori couldn't tell Cassie, who was trying so hard, but she was too young to counsel someone who had been through hell before and come back. There was an endless knot in her heart that wouldn't go away. She had come to terms with her cold mother and her alcoholic husband, she couldn't block out the death of her child, the witness of her friend being murdered and a relative being raped right in front of her, and her own kidnapping. She was afraid and paranoid all

205

the time, but thank God she was a good actress. There are some blessings with age. One is senility and loss of memory. It should help her survive!

Cassie called for someone to help with Lori's luggage. They moved outside into the warm spring weather and waited for Cate to come. A flock of bluebirds flew high over the tall ancient treetops, and a red squirrel ran close to their chairs. Lori inhaled the scents of jasmine and delphinium from the adjacent garden.

Cassie, still worried about Lori, kept her therapy going up to the last minute.

"Lori, are you coming back for the trial of the murderer?"

"Depends on which murder they are trying Roland on. I saw him murder Bly, so they would need me to testify." She shuddered as the memory re-surfaced. "If he confessed to the murder of Wheeler, they may try him on that one. I need to put everything here behind me. I never want to see Roland again. They have my testimony about Josh's murder, and I agreed to be interviewed by the Internet and to come back only if it is necessary. In addition, I am concerned about Suzi, though her Chinese family is here with her. Her chances of coming out of the coma are slim, but there is still hope, I suppose. I am really dreaming of sitting on my patio in Arizona, sipping lemonade and admiring the mountains."

She did not mention that it would be nice to see Geoffrey again, even though she thought about it. Life is all about timing.

Cate appeared, and Lori got up, and hugged Margaret. "Thank you for your help. You are a fine young therapist. This is not an easy place to work."

Cassie beamed upon hearing Lori's praise. Cate helped her grandmother into the car, put her suitcase in the boot, and started down the highway. She chattered excitable about everything, but mainly about going home in a week. Suddenly, she swerved the car around and into a parking space in front of a small Italian café while Lori hung on to the door for dear life.

"Gram, the apartment is a mess with all my packing. Let's stop for lunch here. It's one of the best Italian restaurants in all of London."

Cate led Lori out of the car and helped her sit down at one of the small wrought iron tables on the patio. The restaurant, situated in a quaint shopping center nestled among white stone buildings, was quiet, as it was an odd time of day between lunch and dinner. Schoolchildren walked by in their tidy white and navy uniforms. An older woman with a dachshund sat at the table next to them. She ordered lemonade for herself and water for the dog, who suddenly took off after a ball one of the schoolboys tossed down the road. Cate helped retrieve the dog.

Lori watched her run down the road. She looked like a young girl in her tight shirt and Capri pants, all bubbly and animated. *Something is going on with my granddaughter*, Lori thought.

Wearing a blue dress adorned with a long shell necklace, plump and pretty with a wide smile on her face, the server approached the table after Cate returned. "Anything to drink?"

"I'd like to see the wine menu. Gram, would you drink some red wine?"

Lori turned toward Cate. "Okay, honey, wine in the afternoon? What's up?"

"Oh, Gram," Cate sighed, "I'm so glad to be going home. It is time to put the last month behind us. Let's celebrate."

The waitress came back with a wine and regular menu. They ordered.

"Did you accept the job in Washington, where Jordan works?" Lori asked as she played with the brochettes appetizer.

"Yes," Cate answered with a wicked smile. "Besides Jordan being in D.C., the East Coast is where the action is, and I want to be a part of it. I'm not heartless. I didn't trade Joseph for Jordan. I kept putting off getting engaged to Joseph because something was missing—a spark, a chemical connection. Also, his way of life wasn't what I wanted. Gram, you were at the Lunt estate. Could you see me sitting in that castle, living in the shadow of my husband, Lord So-n-So? I want to achieve things on my own."

Lori smiled. She felt remote and old, wondering where her dreams and enthusiasm for life had gone. Was she too much into reality, too damaged by life? Right now, escaping into a castle and being waited on didn't seem so terrible. She understood that Cate came from the new woman's mold: educated, independent, and financially able to care for herself.

Lori then realized her granddaughter was waiting for a response from her. "Jordan has that missing ingredient?"

Cate grabbed Lori's hands. "Yes! I was fighting him all along. Then, a few days ago, we got together, and, well, it was wonderful. I'll take it slower this time, even though my heart throbs the minute Jordan is near me."

The glimmer in Cate's eyes and her lively conversation about Jordan sent Lori back to the days when she was young and in love. She remembered the longing, the anticipation, the pleasures and the pain of young love. She smiled, but inside she was worried. She thought about Josh, and she hoped Jordan would not end up hurting Cate. Then again, Cate was tough.

"Honey, I can't see you and Jordan doing anything at a slow pace!"

The server opened the wine, and Cate winked at Lori and took a long sip.

"Bellissimo!"

Chapter Twenty-Five

Lori had, once again, been invited to lunch with Joseph's father, Lord Lunt, but this time she refused to be picked up by his new chauffeur. Instead, Cate drove her out to their estate, which was about an hour's drive from London.

Cate planned to go into the village to do some shopping after she dropped Lori off at the Lunt estate. Since she and Joseph had broken up, she felt it would be better if she stayed clear of his family. Lori got out of Cate's car by the front door of Greyhall Manor, and Cate quickly drove on. About a quarter mile past the house, out by the open garden, Cate stopped the car and watched Lady Lunt's two young grandchildren playing croquet with their governess. Both were dressed like little princes, and they hardly moved. She shook her head, hit the gas pedal hard, and disappeared, thinking to herself, *Never could I have made myself live in that early nineteenth-century make-believe atmosphere.*

Lord Lunt, dressed in a brown tweed-riding outfit, greeted Lori with a warm hug.

"So thrilled am I to see you looking so wonderful. You do know how worried we all were about your welfare."

Lori ignored the comment and looked around at her surroundings. She stood still in awe of Greyhall Manor. It was a stately, three-story beige brick castle overlooking a massive garden with a river meandering throughout the property.

"Your home is amazing. Tell me its history."

"Come, let me give you a brief tour and history," he said. As Lord Lunt, in his very English stately manor, led her into the house, he started to give Lori a royal tour. "First of all, my home dates back to the 1200s, when eighteen-hundred acres and the original manor house were deeded to the Greyhall family by the monarchy. Kings and prime ministers have stayed here. In fact, we have an original oil of Lord Melbourne, who once stayed for several months. The Lamb family owned it for a short time before my ancestor, the first Lord Lunt, took over in 1745. The original manor had a fire around 1884. The present manor house was built then. Renovations, adding indoor plumbing to each bedroom and electricity throughout, were made at the turn of the century, and the whole manor was updated again in the fifties and in the eighties. The estate has been owned by a Lunt ever since, though my grandfather had to sell off one thousand acres, and I, as well as my contemporaries, have had difficulties maintaining such a large estate."

They walked down a white marble-floored hallway, one wall of which featured gilded framed oil paintings of Lunt's ancestors, some dressed in similar riding outfits to his. Most were in period costumes dating back hundreds of years. The hallway led to a room that appeared to be the same size as the Ritz's lobby.

A man wearing a bright black blazer with shiny gold buttons took her coat. Her shoes clicked on the Italian tile and sunk into the intricately woven blue, green, and gold Persian carpets as they passed Chippendale furniture, beautiful antiques, marble fireplaces, and original paintings. Lunt continued with the tour.

"My grounds have forests and rivers running throughout, which makes for great trout fishing and fox and pheasant hunting. Years ago, we had sixteen bedrooms with private baths, but I've recently closed off a wing, as just Elizabeth and her daughter's family and I live here. No need to engage extra servants."

She had to admit the place was meticulous, like a showplace. "It must cost a fortune to keep a place like this in such perfect order."

"Yes," he answered with a pleasing smile.

Lori noted there was no visible digital equipment, just an old television in a small den. Much different from the townhouse Cate and Joseph lived in. Actually, the Lunt castle seemed stuck in the 19th century, like one of the places in British history, though she hadn't been in the upstairs rooms.

He walked Lori through a carved, molded, heavy oak door into the billiards room. "This is my favorite room," he said.

Besides the large, elaborately decorated billiard table, the hall was adorned with an immense collection of hunting trophies and portraits of English prime ministers. He pointed to the one of Lord Melbourne.

"There is a family connection to his notorious wife, Lady Caroline Lamb. Do you know of her?" Lord Lunt did not wait for a response. "She had a notorious and, of course, scandalous affair with the author Lord Byron. She was a poet and an author."

"How wonderful for her—her writing career, I mean."

"Yes, a terrific scandal. Our family has weathered a few of those." He looked at Lori for a few moments. When Lori did not respond, he cleared his throat.

"Yes, well, I would imagine each family has its skeletons. Luckily, you have plenty of room to keep your skeletons safe from prying, yes," Lori said, laughing lightheartedly. "Of course, a historical scandal like Lady Lamb and Lord Byron can only be an asset."

Lori wasn't current enough on English history, but she did recognize the name Melbourne and a picture on the wall of Sir Winston Churchill.

He motioned for her to follow him out of the back of the house through white French doors to the patio. They launched in the English garden, where the flowers and plants ran wild in an orderly fashion, and the view reached across acres of manicured lawn. A butterfly flitted from flower to flower while a small sparrow scavenged the ground for seeds.

Prim and proper maidens adorned in white aprons over black uniforms served the meal, consisting of boiled fish, boiled potatoes, fresh green beans, and popovers. The gold-rimmed English china, lace tablecloths, sterling silverware, and crystal goblets enhanced the flavor of the food. The conversation was generic until the silver dessert tray consisting of fancy teacakes was served.

Lori finally asked, "Why were you so anxious to talk to me?"

Lunt sat back on his chair, crossed his arms over his rather large stomach, and remained silent for a short time. He then leaned forward and said, "I am acquainted with the Brune family. In fact, my first wife, Joseph's mother, was a Brune. Marie was a very young child during the Holocaust. She was hidden in the church orphanage and raised Catholic. Her first cousin, Baron Joseph Brune, found her after we were married. At her and my request, he kept the fact that she was Jewish a secret. He gave her and Joseph a generous sum of money, which I've kept in trust for Joseph. I didn't know if you were aware of it."

Lori burst out laughing. "I can just see your wife's reaction. By the way, are you aware that would technically make Joseph Jewish, and make him my blood relative, as his mother would be my first cousin/"

Joseph's father put his hands together in a plea motion. "You do understand what this would do to our family and Joseph's ambitions and why I needed to talk to you before Joseph and Cate married."

Lori smiled and moved her head from side to side. This was indeed the only highlight in this trip. "I think Joseph needs to know his rich heritage, but if my step-brother, Baron Brune, was willing to keep it a secret, I will keep it through your lifetime."

"You didn't know?"

"No."

He looked somewhat upset that he had revealed his secret to her, but being from nobility, he quickly covered his disappointment with a smile and a handshake. "Thank you, Lori. Now that we have family in common and a secret to share, I hope we can be friends."

"Lord Lunt, do you know of any other living Brune family members? My brother Joseph died shortly after we discovered each other."

"No, Lori. After the Baron died, I assumed all the Brunes were gone, and my secret about Joseph's mother was safe. That is why I was shocked when you said you were related to the Brune family."

He walked her out the French doors and to the front of the house.

"Thank you for an interesting lunch," she said as they shook hands.

* * *

Lori sat down on one of the white wicker chairs located on the front porch. She tried to clear her head a moment before taking out her cell phone and calling Cate to pick her up.

Within twenty minutes, Cate drove up, and Lori got into the car and buckled up, bracing herself for a fast ride through the narrow countryside. A month ago, she had been living a quiet, bored life in Arizona; now, every day brought a new crisis. She clenched the door handle as Cate sped on. *Time to fasten the seatbelts for another of life's bumpy rides*, she told herself, attempting to screw up more courage from her already compromised reserve.

Cate turned towards her grandmother. "That was a quick visit. I was doing a little shopping, so I was nearby. So, Gram, what was all that about?"

Lori took a deep breath; her heart was pounding, and her hands were cold and tingling. She was bursting to tell Cate about Joseph, but she had just promised to keep quiet, so she toned it down.

213

"He had a distant relative that was once married to a Brune, and he didn't know if I knew about it. I promised to keep it a secret, but I am bursting at the seams thinking about his wife."

Cate looked at her and started to laugh. "Oh, my God. I would love for her to find out. She is so anti-Semitic. They live in the past with their money, power, and religious snobbery. The world has changed, and the Lunts won't acknowledge it."

I so wish Cate was right, Lori thought.

"Who was it?"

"I've told you too much already." Lori smiled and shook her head.

"I love it. Okay, who?"

"Cate, I promised."

"Alright, for now, Gram. Oh, by the way, I have to move up our departure date by a few days as the judge wants me to start my job earlier."

Lori's face lost its smile.

"You look upset, Gram. Is something wrong?"

"Oh, nothing. I'm . . . just . . . I'm disappointed about something."

Curious, Cate sharply answered, "Spill it. What's wrong?"

Sheepishly, Lori answered, "Because I am leaving so fast, I will have to cancel my theater date with Geoffrey."

"Geoffrey, *who*?"

"Why, the chief inspector, Geoffrey Holmes."

The car nearly swerved off the road as Cate turned to face her grandmother. "Are you telling me you are dating Inspector Geoffrey Holmes from Scotland Yard?"

"Cate, watch where you are going! You nearly got us killed!"

"Oh, Gram, we're fine. We all drive like this. Now, don't change the subject. Tell me what's going on. Is this a *romance*?"

"Don't be ridiculous. Geoffrey and I are only friends. Why I'm seventy, and he is sixty-seven."

"Sure. I have to watch you like a hawk—First Wheeler, now Holmes. At least you've moved from criminal to chief inspector," Cate responded as she swerved the car into the garage.

As Lori exited the car, she turned to Cate, "You're not little Miss Innocence in the romance department."

They entered the flat arm in arm-and laughing, something they hadn't done in a long time.

* * *

Back at Cate's flat, Lori tried packing. She opened the closet door in the guest bedroom, where her clothes spent more time in the room than she did. St. John suits, well-designed dresses, and high-heeled shoes. She gave a short laugh as she dropped each perfect, unworn outfit back into the suitcase. Too bad she hadn't brought all her old sweats. She took the pair of Prada shoes she had worn during her kidnapping and threw them into the trash bin. She had even tossed out her intimates, as well. It was thoughtful of Cate to have them cleaned, but she never, ever, ever wanted to see them again.

Her lovely silk dress was missing, having been ruined not only by the bullet hole but also by bloodstains and the memory of her harrowing experience. She just assumed it had been thrown away at the hospital. Or perhaps it had been taken and wrapped in a paper bag as evidence. Good riddance, she tried to tell herself, but it spooked her to think of her tiny silk dress somewhere, hanging on a hanger or folded in a box in a paper bag as evidence in the vast building of Scotland Yard. Lori felt ill thinking how many bits and pieces of herself she would be leaving in this country. Would she ever feel whole again?

She had spent five days—*five days*— in the same clothes. A tight feeling in her stomach welled up as she stared gloomily at the trash bin. She silently admonished herself for becoming too morbid, remembering her dear therapist warning her against slipping too deeply into dark thoughts. She turned back to her suitcase and laughed when she saw Tigger busily exploring its contents, alternating between sniffing and rubbing against everything, leaving her scent everywhere. Lori was startled at first, then relieved to hear herself laugh. *I think I'm going to be all right after all.* Through this little cat, she realized the restorative, calming power of pets in one's life.

Downstairs, Cate was busy cooking. Lori had left her cutting beans and frying onions and garlic. The scent of Italian spices, garlic, and oregano floated up the steps, making Lori's mouth water. On the one hand, Cate was a health nut—running, doing yoga, exercising, filling her fridge with organics, whole grain breads, and alfalfa—and on the other hand, she was always cooking deliciously fattening foods. How she stayed so thin was beyond Lori. For Lori, it had been a struggle her whole life. It was only in the last twenty years, when she moved to Arizona, that she had been able to remain small and petite. Her friend Rain, with all the hiking and walking and healthy eating they did back at home, would not let her gain an ounce. Well, she was going to come home much thinner than she was when she left.

Suddenly, Lori heard a tremendous crash, a meow, and then a barrage of swear words. Lori left the room in disarray and hurried down the stairs. Cate looked up from the floor, where she was cleaning up pieces of crockery intermixed with pasta and sauce.

"I was in a hurry. It was too hot, and I dropped it. I'm sorry, Gram."

Lori smiled, "Forget it, honey. I have an idea. Let's go out for dinner and let someone else do the dishes."

Lori finished packing while Cate cleaned the kitchen. Then they dined at Bellissimo's, Cate's favorite Italian Restaurant, just a few miles down the road from the flat.

Carlos greeted Cate with a hardy handshake and hug. He turned towards Lori. "Now, who is this lovely lady?"

Cate laughed. "My grandmother, Lori."

"Welcome to Cate's, abuela." He opened his arms to her, but Lori just gave him a nod.

Before the murder and kidnapping, Lori had a tendency to talk to everyone—the taxi driver, the man on the street, and the waitress. It had bothered Cate, but now she missed it.

Lori skipped the wine and ate a light shrimp salad while Cate enjoyed their special mushroom cream ravioli and a glass of Merlot. They lingered in the restaurant enjoying each other in lively conversation. The waitress refilled their coffee cups, and inquired whether they wanted dessert. Refusing, Lori slipped on a small pair of reading glasses in order to survey the check and pay with her new American Express credit card. All her cards had to be changed after her purse had been floating around everywhere.

Home close to midnight, Lori excused herself as she walked upstairs. "Cate honey, I'm beat. I plan to sleep in tomorrow morning."

Chapter Twenty-Six

Sunday morning, Cate woke up to the ringing of her cell phone. She yawned and squinted at the clock. She had stayed up most of the night packing and was unhappy about being awakened at seven-thirty.

"Hello?"

When she heard Jordan's low, warm voice over the phone, her mood changed. She hadn't expected to see him in London again, so she was delighted to accept his invitation to play a game of tennis on his last day in the city.

"Are you *sure* that's what you want to do today on your last day here?" she asked.

"Sure, but that's only part of the plan."

"You have a plan, huh?"

"Well . . . Let's just say I have a good feeling about how the day will play out, how's that?"

She quickly dressed, left Gram a note, and packed her tennis clothes in a bag. Since Gram came to town, she hadn't played tennis, so she was hoping to get to the club a little early to practice some, but Jordan was already at the Standard Health Club when she got there, probably thinking of doing the same thing. They were both very competitive people, and as soon as they got on the court, they engaged in a heated tennis competition, with Jordan outscoring Cate by one shot. Exhilarated and dripping with sweat, they headed to the club's dressing rooms, showered, dressed, and met in the club's restaurant for a quick lunch.

Cate swirled her fork around her salad while Jordan bit into his Club sandwich and gulped down his coffee. As with their game, their conversation took on a passionate discourse. Jordan soon realized that no matter what subject he brought up, politics—philosophy, sports, art, or business—Cate was truly knowledgeable. He enjoyed how she punctuated her opinions and stated facts by prefacing them with, "What you must understand, Jordan, is . . ."

He liked it when she called him by his name. It was very personal and intimate, and he felt himself drawing closer and closer to her as though she were mesmerizing him, seducing him, even when they were discussing something as banal as grocery shopping.

"What you must understand, Jordan, is I hate grocery shopping. Well, I love it, but I wish I had the place to myself because I must buy my own ingredients. I love cooking! As soon as the ingredients are united, something magical happens. It's like alchemy. It's a heady experience where all your senses are engaged, and one that you can have more than three times a day—if you're lucky, if you live right. No matter how busy I am, I won't deny myself the pleasure of a good meal, whether I'm the one making it or they're making it over there at Bellissimo's. Oh, what am I gonna do without my Italian restaurant?"

"I'm sure we can find a few good ones in Washington," Jordan replied, smiling.

"You have to find one, Jordan. Well, I better pick it out. I'm not sure you know good Italian food," she teased.

"Uh, I grew up in the frikkin' Bronx, Cate. I know my way around a good brasciole or a plate of homemade gnocchi."

"You are a man of many talents," Cate cooed, popping a grape into her mouth.

She was taking over his psyche on all levels. When his eyes focused on her short black skirt that showed off her smooth, shapely legs, he leaned closer to her across the small table and inhaled her perfume. He felt the familiar stirring in his loins, and he was no longer interested in his sandwich.

"Let's get out of here."

He paid the check, picked up his and Cate's bags, and walked with her to the parking lot.

"As you know, I'm leaving tonight, so I must pull out of my suite in a few hours." He stopped and smiled warmly at Cate. "Meet me there. It's the Wingate, just a short ride from here."

"Sounds like a plan," Cate answered as he reached up and touched her face, and gave her a slow kiss. She returned his kiss in kind, and she fought the urge to throw him into the back of her car and ravage him right then and there.

As he walked down to where his car was parked, he heard a shrill female voice declare, "Cate Brill, this is a bloody surprise! Did I really see you kissing that American detective, the one that you despise?"

He would have loved to hear Cate's response. Grinning with satisfaction, Jordan entered his car and drove on.

He lingered outside the hotel and watched as Cate arrived, dressed in her sexy little black skirt that barely skimmed her thighs and her fitted white blouse she had buttoned haphazardly, leaving most of it unbuttoned.

Cate walked slightly behind Jordan through the hotel lobby to the elevator and eyed his wide, sculpted shoulders, slim hips, and muscular legs. She smiled to herself as she thought; *This guy's ass was made to be in those jeans.* Inside the elevator, they spoke of her grandmother, how things were going well with the move, and how they liked the gym.

She inhaled the musky scent of his aftershave as they exited the elevator arm-in-arm and entered his room. She had dodged her friend's remark with a well-placed, "I simply changed my mind!" because she no longer despised Jordan. In fact, she was crazy about him now. Joseph, as sweet and loving as he could be, did not stir her passions the way Jordan did. Every time she saw him, she wanted to screw his brains out. It made everyday chores quite difficult. She looked at his face now and anticipated the fun to come.

Upon entering his room, Cate turned towards Jordan and, with a mischievous smile, she said, "I've been thinking about it. You shouldn't have won that tennis match. That ball was out of—"

He didn't give her time to finish. He put a thick finger to her lips, and with a light kiss, he silenced her. "Let's not talk about that." Moving her towards the bed, he embraced her tightly, kissing her neck, nuzzling her collarbone, making her squeal with delight.

On the bed, Jordan looked deeply into her eyes while slowly undressing her. He unbuttoned her fitted shirt first so he could fondle her perfectly shaped round breasts and kiss her smooth belly. Their first encounter a few days ago had been fast and hungry. Now, they took their time exploring each other, slowly removing articles of clothing, taking time to taste, touch, smell, and see one another completely. Jordan's oral talents surpassed anything she had experienced, and she moaned with delight as his tongue worked its magic.

She spread her legs wide to allow him further access, and he lovingly cupped her rear end with his strong hands, tilting her pelvis forward so his tongue could enter her more deeply.

Cate was further aroused by Jordan's own moans of desire as he pleasured her.

With Joseph, Cate had used sex to have power over him. Joseph quite liked to be in the submissive position, allowing Cate to take over, to make demands, to orchestrate the act. With Jordan, she only had control over her responses, as she had barely any control over what Jordan would do next, which she found exciting. He wasn't taking control from her; it felt more like she was letting him celebrate every inch of her. It was evident in his actions that Jordan was there to please his woman, and it was apparent he got off on that, as well. The more pleasure Cate derived from Jordan, the more desirable he became.

Nothing is quite as sexy as a man who wants nothing more than to please his partner.

When Cate felt close to orgasm, she pulled Jordan up by his shoulders, and he climbed on top of her. She kissed him passionately, slipping her tongue deep into his mouth, shocked at her own taste, and she grasped his erect penis and guided it inside her. Jordan's eyes closed, and his mouth grew slack as he moaned and bit at Cate's lower lip.

"Jesus, Cate, I don't know how long I can . . ."

Cate hungrily bit at Jordan's neck as he anchored his hips into hers, thrusting himself deep inside her.

Soon they were moving in tandem, groaning and laughing out their pleasure and losing themselves completely in one another.

True to his word, Jordan came first, growling out his release, his face buried in her neck, holding her so tightly she thought he would break her ribs. Cate followed soon after, the room resounding with her shuddering cries of successive orgasms.

Afterward, completely spent, they fell into a deep sleep, entangled in each other's arms and legs. When Cate awoke, she was alone in the room. There was a suitcase and a travel bag by the door. Cate dressed hastily and scanned the small kitchen for a quick coffee or a piece of bread, but alas, there was nothing. She was famished, and the place had been cleared out of all food. She wasn't sure of Jordan's flight time. Maybe they could go for an early dinner.

The door opened, and Jordan literally ran in.

"Where were you?" Cate asked.

"On a last run along the Thames."

"Are you fucking kidding me?" she laughed. "Who could run after that? Who would want to?"

"Well . . ."

He had left Cate for a run because he needed to think, and running had become his outlet. Jordan had used expressions of love to many women before, just to get them into bed. He couldn't do that to Cate because he believed he was really falling in love with her, and it was scaring him to no end.

"Why didn't you tell me?" she asked.

Jordan moved toward the bed. "Tell you? Tell you what?" Had she read his mind?

"Why didn't you tell me you were going? Maybe I would have liked to come, too. Or at least, maybe I would have been able to talk you out of going." She playfully stuck out her leg from under the bed sheet and touched his groin gently with her foot.

"Cate, I hate to do this," Jordan said as he gently lifted her pretty foot to his lips and kissed her toes, "but . . . there's no time to talk. I must throw you out and get to the airport. My plane leaves in less than three hours." He kissed her quickly on the forehead, then turned and went to the bathroom.

"I don't think so, Jordan."

Twenty minutes later, they both came out of the bath, showered, and squeaky clean.

He came out fully dressed; Cate emerged in an oversized white towel.

"Now, *there's* a proper sendoff, Mr. Gould," Cate said, raising an eyebrow as she watched him straighten out his shirt.

"I appreciate your efforts, my love, and now I'm completely spent."

"Sleep on the plane."

"I'd rather sleep on you." Jordan smiled at his girlfriend and pulled her towards him. He delivered a sensual kiss, savoring her sweet taste and her warm, scented skin, knowing, with a sharp twinge of longing, that they may not be together again for weeks.

Soon, Cate was dressed, and they were off, racing down the stairs to their cars.

As he got into his rented car, he leaned out the window and shouted, "I beat you fair and square. You weren't fast enough to get the ball!"

Cate stood by her car door with her mouth open, about to respond, but Jordan was gone.

Chapter Twenty-Seven

On June 12, 2013, six weeks after arriving in England, Lori was finally going home. She looked at herself in the mirror. She was much thinner, by at least ten pounds, not by choice, and she walked with a limp, and she knew there were a few extra lines on her face, but she was alive. Her silver grey hair was lying on her neck like the old days when she was young, though then it had been coal black. She would check Cate's reaction before cutting it short again.

Their taxi arrived. Cate checked the house, left a note to thank Joseph for letting her stay, and put a reluctant Tigger in her cat carrier.

Cate and Lori hurried along to their American Airlines flight to the States. As they were walking through Heathrow airport, a brittle noise jolted Lori, and she quickly turned around.

A tall Englishman stared at her before he commented, "Terribly sorry, I dropped my keys. Aren't you . . .?"

Cate grabbed Lori's arm and literally pulled her along, out of the man's path, until Lori made her stop long enough to rest her leg.

Cate said, "I keep telling you to take a wheelchair, but you are stubborn."

Lori shook her head and smiled. "It must run in the family. Besides, we can stretch our legs in first class, Miss Big Shot!"

They made it to their flight just a few minutes before the doors closed.

Once they were seated on the plane, Cate whispered, "I must tell you a secret. Jordan contacted me from the States. He told me Holmes followed a lead Jordan had found before going home, and Holmes believes it has led them to Wheeler's real killer. No arrests have been made so that Jordan couldn't tell me anymore for now."

Lori's body stiffened as she realized she had actually put the murder out of her mind the last day or two while preparing to go home. She had doubted that Roland was Josh's murderer, but she also knew he was capable of anything.

"Wine?" the flight attendant asked, and they both quickly answered, "Yes."

They talked for most of the flight, with Lori doing most of the talking, revealing more details about her kidnapping. Lori kept the secret of Joseph Lunt's birth for now.

Cate opened the U.S. newspaper. The front page was filled with shock waves over the bombing at the Boston Marathon. Shaking her head and throwing up her hands, Cate turned to her grandmother. "Gram, I can't understand this world. Why do so many bad things happen to good people?"

"I don't know, Cate. The older I get, the harder it is to understand. I once read a quote by a Shari Barr that summed up my thinking: 'Expecting life to treat you well because you are a good person is like expecting an angry bull not to charge because you are a vegetarian.'"

"That one is great. I'll have to remember it." Cate gave her grandmother a kiss and put down her tray for the flight attendant to serve her meal, a turkey sandwich with fruit and chips, while Lori tried the roast chicken and pasta.

People will forget about Josh now that there is a new crisis, Lori thought. She felt guilt and relief when this thought entered her mind. She had been worried about-facing friends and everyone else back in the states. She anticipated questions and questions.

After dinner, Cate and Lori put back their seats and napped while the plane flew over the Atlantic Ocean. Lori woke up first. She opened the shade on the window and watched the bright orange sunrise over the white, billowy clouds. She had been in Europe for only four weeks, but it felt like another lifetime.

She looked over to her darling granddaughter and thought about what it would be like to be young and innocent again. She realized she didn't want to be young again, but she did want to laugh again. Then she thought about Geoffrey and how they had laughed together over their inability to remember the names in the Sherlock Holmes stories, and when he asked if he could give her a kiss goodbye and they bumped noses. She hadn't been able to let another man into her life after being hurt by her alcoholic husband.

Cate stretched out her arms and legs and slowly sat up. "Morning already." She looked under her seat to check on Tigger, who promptly scratched at her cage and started to meow. The sedative the vet had given her had finally worn off. The meow was answered by a soft bark coming from somewhere in the back of the plane.

The stewardess approached their aisle. "We will be landing in less than an hour. We have a cheese omelet or cereal for breakfast."

A few minutes later, Lori put her spoon down. The cereal was cold. She took a gulp of coffee and turned towards Cate. "Tell me about your new job in D.C."

"I accepted this job with Judge Norman Pierce because D.C. is where the action is. I am determined to work for the government, possibly as a trial lawyer. Jordan and I are very similar. We both know what we want, and we are willing to fight for it. Oh, there will be problems, as we both have to be in charge, but life will never be boring."

Lori asked, "Are you planning to move in with him?"

"No, not right away. We need some time to get to know each other. When we get to D.C., I will look for an apartment, check out the job, and then go home to Chicago to see everyone."

"Cate, a wise man once said, 'Learn from the past, prepare for the future, but live in the present.' I try hard to remember that saying and live it."

As soon as the plane landed, Cate pulled out her iPad and checked her e-mail. Lori glanced at it.

"I'm sending you an iPad. It's time for you to get hep," Cate said.

Lori patted Cate affectionately. "Not yet, honey. I've been hep enough this last month."

Cate grinned as she helped Lori off the plane and through immigration in D.C. Cate stopped in the bookstore and came out laughing, a caged, restless Tigger in hand.

"Hey, Gram, I just asked the clerk where the *loo* was, and she looked at me like I was crazy! I've been in London too long. I have to learn American English again."

"Honey, while you're relearning the language, I'm going to pee in my pants."

"Good thing you're wearing a dress!"

They both laughed their way to the nearest restroom. When they exited, Cate kissed Lori goodbye, and they embraced for a long time before parting. Tigger meowed when Lori tried to pet her through the carrier.

Lori made her way down to collect her luggage. Cate was now at her destination, while Lori had another five-hour flight to Phoenix, Arizona. Lori watched her granddaughter's brisk walk down the corridor. Cate's thick, honey blonde, chin-length hair looked much better than the conservative bob she wore when Lori first arrived in London. So did Cate's multi-colored embroidered shirt over her slim-legged jeans and tan knee-length boots. Cate had a Bohemian look. Lori guessed that style of dress had made a comeback.

Lori remembered the 1980s, when she dressed like that. Oh, those were the days when she was trying to keep up with the North Shore crowd in Chicago's suburbs and at the same time keep the family secret. Her rich, cool husband—who had provided her with two wonderful children, a beautiful home, clothes, jewelry, and trips—was really an abusive, blazing alcoholic lunatic who was bankrupting them.

Lori said to herself, *Remember, and learn from the past.*

She walked to her gate for her flight to Phoenix. Lori stopped at a magazine stand to pick up an American paper. The sales clerk stared mutely at her as they completed their transaction and Lori collected the paper.

On the second page, there was a large article with the headline: *Wheeler's Body Released. Son Plans a Private Memorial in L.A. Investors Still Hope to Retrieve Their Money.*

Rest in peace, Josh, Lori thought, putting the paper down. She couldn't manage to read it. She wondered if she would ever find peace while alive, or would she always be haunted by her connection to Josh's murder and by the picture of Josh's mutilated face? She wondered if she would ever be able to remember and find someone to talk to about the Josh she had loved all those years, not the scoundrel everyone remembered. Maybe one day she would look up his son and tell him about the father who went out of his way to bring a dying girl an autographed photo of Bruce Springsteen. The last time she saw Josh before this trip was when he made her daughter so happy with that photograph.

Lori ducked into a restroom to wash the tears off of her face, and then she went over to Starbucks, ordered a latte, and sat down at one of the tables. She sat quietly, sipping her coffee, staring into space. She had some time before her plane connection left for Phoenix. The woman sitting across from her looked vaguely familiar. Coal-black shoulder length hair covered what must have been a recent facelift, as she was still swollen and puffy. She was probably in her middle fifties and was expensively dressed, in a conservative way. She kept checking her watch and looking around.

Shortly, another woman approached the table. This one was blonde and chic; Prada, Channel, and Gucci dripped from her every limb. These two looked like they were straight out of the old *Dynasty* series. Blondie dropped the newspaper on the table and pointed to the picture on the front page.

"You know," the blonde woman said quietly, "I actually miss the bastard. They still don't know who killed him."

Lori instantly knew they were talking about Josh. She didn't run away, but she did turn her head to keep from being recognized. She slowly sipped her drink while concentrating on their conversation.

Facelift tried to laugh, but it didn't really materialize; she just made a strange clucking noise at the back of her throat. "You must be kidding. He walked off with a million dollars. Of *your* money!"

"He was so much fun and such a good lay, it was worth it. Stop being so innocent," Blondie playfully admonished. "Wasn't it your husband Max who brought him into our group? *The Golden Boy from Illinois*, the one with those gorgeous blue eyes, the one related to a federal judge, the real estate tycoon. What a line!" The woman laughed wryly, more to herself than with her friend.

"Oh, you're right, Muriel. We all believed the bullshit he handed out, and we were foolish enough to invest our money with him. Yes, he was fun to have around, always coming up with something exotic to do. Remember when he flew us to Paris for lunch on his private plane?"

The blonde woman known as Muriel laughed, while holding her coffee cup in the air. "Here's to the Mile High Club!"

"Ah, yes, plenty of good times on that plane. His private plane financed with *our* money. Oh, he was good. Too bad the pyramid tumbled on him. You think he had that bed cleaned, or do ya think he just had it burned and bought another one?" Facelift asked.

"Do you have those pictures? I wonder what they are worth."

"You think we're the only ones with pictures of that playboy's naked ass?" Facelift managed to crack a smile without tearing her skin while continuing to cluck.

"Who do you think killed him?"

"It had to be someone's boyfriend or husband. Maybe *mine*," Facelift grinned. "Can't you see Max pounding him to death with his walker?"

Lori knew she should leave, but she had a hard time pulling herself away from the conversation. She wanted to tell them she too had pictures, pictures of a young innocent boy before his chest was covered with curly blond hair, and before his mind was full of devious schemes. They were talking about the Josh she had lost track of. Finally, she got up and proceeded towards her gate. She would miss him too. She smiled as she pictured a hotel suite full of flowers and champagne.

On the Phoenix flight, Lori accepted the airplane attendant's offer of wine with a dish of assorted snacks. She thought, *By the time I get home, I will be an alcoholic. My husband Jerry was right; it helps dull the nerves and memory.* After resting, thumbing through some magazines, and eating her dinner of pasta and a salad, Lori leaned back and fell asleep.

On arrival, Lori pulled her luggage through Phoenix Airport until she found her friend Rain's smooth, tanned, smiling face and welcoming open arms. Rain—the tan-skinned, sharp-looking, coal-black-haired woman in boot-cut brown jeans, wearing a turquoise embroidered shirt and enough silver jewelry to open a mine—greeted Lori at the gate. Lori shook her head before giving her friend a big hug.

"Tell me, Rain, why do you always look like a thirty-year-old instead of someone in her late sixties?"

Rain bellowed out one of her loud deep laughs.

"No husband, no kids!" she answered. Then she held Lori away from her and looked at her up and down.

"First, we have to get that God-awful prim and proper dress off of you." Next, Rain grabbed Lori around the waist. "Hell, woman, there is nothing left of you. What did they feed you?" She turned and began walking. "Okay, let's get you out of here!"

Lori, shorter, thinner, and frailer, tried to keep up with her tall, muscular friend, but it was a losing proposition. Finally, she stopped cold and called out in a breathless, cracked voice, "Rain, I can't keep going at this pace."

Rain turned around and surveyed her friend. She realized that hearing about someone's ordeal is much different than seeing the effect it had on that person. "Okay, what's with the cane? Temporary, I hope."

"I know I need it now, so slow down, girl."

Rain brought Lori over to a chair. "Honey, you sit right there, and I will get the car and meet you in front of exit three in ten minutes." She squeezed Lori's hand affectionately before she took off with Lori's suitcase and travel bag. Only three years younger, Rain was still in great shape.

Lori took her time getting to the exit. Stepping outside, she scanned the clear blue Arizona sky. Taking off her sweater, she basked in the eighty-five degree temperature. "It's *so* good to be home."

When Rain pulled up in her black Jeep, Lori struggled to get over the high step. She carefully loaded herself down in the passenger seat of Rain's Jeep.

As soon as Rain entered the car, she handed Lori a bottle of water. "You're home in the desert, drink up. There's, uh, some good stuff under the seat, if you can handle it," Rain said with a wink.

Lori smiled. "Not now, maybe later," she answered as she dug into her purse for sunglasses. Already she was squinting.

When Rain turned the key in the ignition, the car speakers blasted out with *Cathy's Clown*, an old sixties tune by the Everly Brothers. Lori smiled as she thought back to the sixties, when she and Rain were on the opposite sides of the poles. Lori, the establishment, and Rain, the wild hippie protester. Now they were the best of friends.

Home. Finally. Lori sank back in the car seat and watched the scenery along Highway 101—the paint-blue sky, russet and purple mountains, open expanses of land peppered with giant cacti—passed before her in a welcoming slideshow, as, bit by bit, she absorbed the fact that she was back home, back in familiar surroundings, and hopefully, given time, back to normal. She closed her eyes to rest for a few moments.

* * *

"Hey, Lori," Rain asked, gently nudging her friend with her elbow, "are you hungry?" She had let Lori doze for about half an hour before speaking. She knew her friend had been through the wringer. "We could stop for something to eat, and you can tell me about your adventure."

Lori awoke and stretched her arms and legs. "Sounds good, but let's stop at a fast food place, as this jet lag is really doing a number on me, and I might fall asleep at the table."

"You just might. You already fell asleep."

"I did? How long have I been out?"

"Oh, about half an hour. I let you sleep. Looks like you needed it."

Lori checked herself in the sun visor mirror and combed her fingers through her short hair.

"Jeeze, they must have slipped me a Mickey on the plane. If I had known they were serving those, hell, I'd have asked for more!"

Rain bellowed out one of her hearty laughs as she pulled off the expressway at Camelback Boulevard and pulled into the Cheesecake Factory restaurant. She opened the car door and helped Lori out. Rain stared at her friend as she walked behind her towards the restaurant.

"We have to do something about that limp, lady. You know you are signed up to do the rain dance in next month's Indian festival."

"Oh, Rain, how I missed you, my direct and witty friend." Lori turned and gazed upon her friend's tanned face, her slim figure adorned with its embroidered blouse and tons of turquoise jewelry. Renee, alias Rain, the daughter of a federal judge who had given up luxury and safety for life on an Indian reservation, was Lori's savior in Arizona.

Lori stopped in front of the restaurant and inhaled the scent of the flowering cactus by the front door. She watched the patrons' calm, quiet, easygoing pace as they walked in and out of the establishment, politely allowing her to move in front of them.

After she and Rain were seated in a cozy corner booth by the window, Rain ordered a bottle of Merlot. Lori sipped the wine while Rain took a full swig from her glass. She smiled at Lori and said, "So tell me about your vacation—er . . . Well, I guess we can call it a vacation, right?"

Lori took a deep breath and shook her head from side to side.

"I don't know what to call it. Or where to begin; besides saying the fact that I am alive is an achievement of luck and the help of many special people. I think I can say that I finally topped your adventures at Woodstock."

Rain answered with a reminiscent smile and thought of the dragon lady tattoo on her ankle. "If you were wiped out on some of the drugs I was on then, your horrors in England would have been a lot easier. In fact, trying a little pot now would help you to forget."

Lori, who grew up straight and narrow, never engaging in anything not kosher except for her nights with Josh, didn't respond to Rain's comment on her drug use. Instead, she started her story. "I've told you most of what happened with Josh and the kidnapping."

The waitress approached them to take their order.

Rain ordered a veggie burger and a small salad, while Lori, too tired to look at the menu, said, "Santa Fe salad, if you still have it, and some coffee too."

"Decaf or regular?"

"Regular, black," Lori answered.

"Before you tell me about the investigation, tell me about Cate," Rain said.

Lori was all smiles as she told Rain about Cate, her stylish clothes, her ultramodern condo, her graduation, and her breakup with Joseph. The food arrived as Lori regaled Rain with tales of Joseph's insufferable stepmother.

"Oh, my god, she sounds like an absolute nightmare!" Rain exclaimed, taking a stab at her mixed greens salad.

"She was an expensive, obnoxious, gaudy nightmare. Your head would have been spinning, Rain, I just know it."

While they ate, Lori told Rain about Cate's new job and her bonding with FBI agent Jordan.

"I get the feeling you're not that fond of Jordan," Rain said, as she took a bite of her veggie burger.

Lori swished her fork around her salad, turned towards the window, and stared at the tiny red and black bird standing half in and half out of

235

an opening in the large Saguaro cactus before turning back in Rain's direction.

"It's not that I dislike him . . . I just am afraid he will break Cate's heart."

"Cate's tough, Lori."

"He reminds me of Josh." Lori said, as she leaned her chin on her arm.

Rain, who had been married to Josh for a short time, opened her dark eyes wide and pressed her lips together. "That's not good! In what way?"

"He's cocky. Self-assured. I mean, confidence is as asset, but . . . You know what I mean."

"Yeah," Rain snorted, "if he's *too* cocky, then he may very well feel he has the right to take advantage of her—and anyone else who crosses his path. I get it, Lori. But Cate, from what you have told me, has a good head on her shoulders. She won't take any shit from any man."

"Not like I did," Lori grumbled.

"Don't linger in the past, Lori. It serves no good." Rain reached across the table and affectionately grabbed her friend's thin arm. "Oooh, eat some bread! We have to get some meat on those bones!"

Dessert normally was one of the perks at the Cheesecake Factory, but after a few more minutes of conversation and eating, Lori looked at her watch, and, without having to apologize to her friend, she said, "I'm wiped out. Let's go home."

Without another word, Rain paid the check, helped Lori back to the car, and headed north on 101 towards Ventura, their retirement community which was next to Desert Mountain. Lori leaned back and rested, and Rain kept quiet even though she had a million questions she wanted to ask.

They pulled through the gates. Ventura Retirement Community, one of the relatively new retirement communities, was well stocked with happy and active retirees, several swimming pools, a couple of fine dining and casual dining restaurants, and a large community center. They stopped in front of Lori's two-bedroom, beige stucco, ranch-style home. It was one of the few homes that were butted right up against the large Desert Mountain.

"You're home! How does it feel?"

Lori stood for a while, admiring the clean, neat cactus garden with hearty shrubbery that decoratively flanked her flagstone walkway. She fished out her keys and headed toward her red door.

"It looks like home. Things look perfect. Just like I left it. Seems months and months ago."

Rain, sensing Lori's weariness, followed her inside. "I stocked your fridge last night, just in case you were too tired to shop. All you have to do now is relax."

"Everything looks great." Lori paused and sighed a deep heavy sigh before turning to her friend. "Oh, Rain, thanks so much for . . . for . . ."

Rain could see Lori was going to get emotional, so she nipped it in the bud. Her friend needed sleep more than anything, not an emotional breakdown. There would be time for that later.

"No need, no need, my friend. Rest up and enjoy. Call me if you need anything," she said, embracing her friend and feeling her frailty. "My God, you're going to enjoy yourself putting some flesh back on those bones! Good thing I stocked the fridge, huh?" Rain winked and kissed Lori goodbye. "See you tomorrow."

Lori listened as the glass door slid closed. Her friend had realized how much Lori needed some time home alone. She walked around smiling as she basked in the comforts of her own possessions from the pastel Indian painting on the wall to the out of place family Victorian chair. She remembered a quote Rain had told her many years ago, when Lori's life was in turmoil.

Life isn't about waiting for the storm to pass. It's about learning how to dance in the rain.

She had danced in the rain this past month for certain—and also for a good part of her seventy years.

Chapter Twenty-Eight

It was past noon when Lori woke up. The time difference between London and Arizona, along with her new aches and pains from her surgery, had played havoc with her body over the past several days, but now that she had been back a while, she was falling into her old pattern. But last night she'd had a tough time sleeping, and she found herself rising late today. Josh had crept into her dreams after a weeklong absence, and as always, the dream left Lori awake in the middle of the night, processing her ordeal once again.

They say it can take days before one's body re-adjusts to transatlantic flights. Lori decided that, in light of her harrowing experiences, she would be gentle on herself, allowing extra time before things got back to normal—or what Lori called her "new normal."

She stepped from the shower and looked at her skinny frame in the mirror and thought how, in her youth, she dreamed about being skinny. *Better watch what you wish for*, she told herself. Now she was too skinny, despite Rain's efforts to fatten her up by taking her out to lunches and dinners. That scoundrel Roland had starved her in just five days. Until the kidnapping, she had used the word *starving*, but she had never really understood it.

The sun shone in through the large windows, and her whole house lit up. Lemons and oranges ripened on the trees outside, low pink and cream-colored buildings spread across her development. She smiled to herself and thought, *It is good to be home.*

She threw on a pair of white shorts and a thin, pink short-sleeve t-shirt, and went into the kitchen to toast a bagel. Once the bagel was ready, she poured herself a tall glass of lemonade and sat at her kitchen table, enjoying her cream cheese bagel in the afternoon silence. She decided to leave the unpleasant job of unpacking and washing clothes to later in the day. She briefly turned on the news. Another school shooting, another missing person, and the Democrats and Republicans shouting at each other wasn't what she needed to hear, so off it went. Answering phone calls, messages, and e-mails were things she wasn't ready for either, so she stayed away from those devices.

Lori was curious about the mail, though she realized nowadays with all the digital devices most of the mail consisted of throw-aways. She rose from the table and went to fetch the mail. There were a few envelopes and a small brown box at her feet. Taking her bundle of mail and her lemonade with her, she walked out to her ample patio. She sipped her cold lemonade, leaned back in her white wicker lounge chair with the rose padded cushion, and admired the clear Wedgwood blue backdrop that enhanced the spellbinding brown and purple shades of her majestic mountain. Birds flew to her feeder, long-eared rabbits scampered along, lizards ran over the desert sand, and cacti stood up straight proud to show off their spring flowers. The comical brown and white roadrunner sped by, and in the distance, coyotes howled. Being home gave Lori a feeling of peace even though she knew, like her daughter's death, Josh's murder would haunt her memory until her dying day.

Rain had taken good care of her home, keeping it clean, watering her plants, stocking her refrigerator, and collecting the mail. She was just getting to the end of her mail pile now, and she tossed the new letters and box onto the pile of old mail. The first thing she looked at was the *Ventura Weekly Activity Newsletter*. Monday was Travel Club; Tuesday, Games; Wednesday, Exercise; Thursday, Genealogy; and Friday, Book Club.

A sharp pain shot through her hip, and she wondered if she would ever be able to join an exercise class again. Just walking was difficult.

She hoped the name of the Arizona doctor she needed to make an appointment with was still among her papers. *That takes care of exercise.*

Games would have to be taken off her list too. There was no way could she concentrate on bridge. Now Mah Jongg would be a real treat. Two of her Mah Jongg-playing friends spent most of the game complaining. Could she really listen to them whine? "You called that tile wrong. You're too slow. Call the league!" And she was certain she could not really stand to listen to Deborah's constant wail of, "No one has as much trouble as I do!"

She could change the newsletter to: Monday, Travel, that one is good. *We could cover the police stations and hospitals of London.* Tuesday would be changed to Murder Mysteries. Wednesday would be Kidnapping. Thursday, she could keep Genealogy; surprise, you have new relatives. Friday, Book Club. *Now there is an idea,* she thought. She figured she could write a book about her adventures! She would have to find a better ending than "The murder was solved, and she lived happily ever after in her retirement community."

But to her, that ending seemed peaceful enough. She had had enough of twists and turns.

Oh, God, she thought, *how long will I be able to keep the masquerade up this time? Better tackle the rest of the mail,* she thought, looking down at the large box of mail sitting next to her. She intended to go through it and finish it today since she knew the box contained bills long overdue. Her son was right; she should have been paying everything on the Internet like the rest of the world. She had actually left the iPad he had purchased for her at home, thinking she would only be gone two weeks. What a laugh. She took another sip of her lemonade.

She thumbed through the box and picked up the little brown package that arrived that morning. Turning it round and round, she found no return address, but she noted the British postage.

Might as well start with a mystery package, she said to herself.

Reaching for the scissors on the table next to her, she cut open the box. Inside, she found a small black cosmetic bag. She frowned upon recognizing it as the cosmetic bag she had left in Josh's hotel room.

Renewed tension and anxiety coursed through Lori like a lightning bolt as she gazed at the bag. The scent of her Channel No. 5 perfume permeated the air. She hesitated before reaching inside it. Shaking her head as though the gesture would shake the painful, disturbing memories away, Lori moved to the small, covered garbage pail sitting on the patio and started to toss the cosmetic bag in there. She hesitated, and then she decided to open it first. Besides her lipsticks and makeup, there was her bottle of Channel No. 5.

When Josh had put his arms around her on their way back to their room after their romantic dinner, he had whispered in her ear, "I could always find you by the scent of your perfume."

She put the bottle down and pursed her lips in an effort to keep the tears from spilling onto her face. She took out the lipstick and other makeup and threw them into the pail. She would only keep the perfume. Although it had unpleasant and sad memories associated with it—Josh had given this particular bottle to her, and it was also her mother's signature scent—she realized it was part of her, and those memories, like so many wonderful memories the perfume evoked, were the memories and experiences that made up a life, her life. It identified her too much to dismiss it outright; a woman's signature scent was her own, and no matter how many other women wore it, it always bore a unique take on each person.

Sifting through the unmarked box, Lori found a small note. It was from Geoffrey Holmes.

Dear Lori,

I hope this letter finds you in good health, as I have been wishing you a speedy recovery.

Due to an oversight on the part of Scotland Yard, your cosmetics bag was left behind and is now being returned to you with our apologies. This was the only item not returned along with your personal items taken from the hotel room. I thought you would like to have it.

I am so very glad we were able to spend some time getting to know one another. You are a strong and remarkable woman, and I do regret our missed opportunity to enjoy the theater together here in London. Perhaps, upon my retirement, I can take a trip to the States and you can show me the marvels of Arizona?

It would be lovely to see you again.

With warm regards,

Geoffrey Holmes

Lori smiled as she folded the note and slipped it into her shorts' pocket. Geoffrey Holmes was a bright light in the whole sordid ordeal. Perhaps something good always did come from a bad experience. Her heart grew light as she thought on his sweet, awkward ways, the warmth of his voice and his smooth English accent, and the kindness in his eyes. She looked forward to the possibility of seeing him again.

"All right, Lori, you hopeless romantic," she admonished herself as she flipped through her mail pile. "Lots to get through here, so keep moving."

Next was a padded manila envelope about the size of a wallet. With the edge of a scissors, Lori sliced open the top and looked inside. There, in the corner, she spotted metal keys. She tipped the envelope and caught two tiny silver metal keys in the palm of her hand. Upon inspection, she noted the keys had tiny numbers etched upon them. She knew they weren't hers. She never saw them before. The envelope, she noted, was processed in California.

Who in California would send me keys? Why? Then her mind sharpened. *Could they be the missing Swiss bank keys?* Her stomach tightened. *No. No more mysteries, please.* She was just easing into the groove of calm, uneventful days, recovering back at home. Now the mail service had brought in the bad energy from her experience, opening up wounds barely healed over.

She sat back and closed her eyes for a moment. In her hands were the very objects five people, Josh being one of them, had been killed for, and for which two others were sitting in jail. The fate of Suzi Brill was likely to be one of another fatality in this tragedy, and, all the while, the world still wondered where Josh Wheeler had hidden the money. Who had sent her these keys? She irrationally thought it might have been Josh, afraid of the Chinese and using her as a decoy.

Still, if Josh hid the keys he couldn't have sent it. Josh was dead. Her pulse raced, and her head throbbed. Josh and this terrible mess had followed her home, and this envelope was the awful tangible proof. What was he up to? Lori's mind, still churning with this new, confusing discovery, came to the sad conclusion that Josh may have been using her all along. Although he had feelings for her, they were of the sentimental kind, perhaps feelings from a long-lost innocence of youth he tried to relive and recapture in those few hours in the hotel room. His life was definitely in chaos when Lori encountered him at the airport, and he acted as though he hadn't a care in the world. He didn't have to take her to the luxurious hotel and sleep with her; he could have simply slipped these keys into her purse while she was in the restroom at dinner.

She turned the envelope around. There was no address, just a postage stamp cancelled somewhere in California. Lori rubbed her temples, weary of the questions in her head. She knew she could call Jordan Gould, and he would figure out this mess. After all, Josh Wheeler's money issues were not a concern for Scotland Yard; this was in the hands of the FBI. She could hand over the keys and be done with this, once and for all. She slipped the keys into the pocket that held Geoffrey's letter.

Lori felt bemused as she sifted through the box and found another piece of mail, this time an envelope, with overseas postage from Britain. She quickly ripped open the envelope and unfolded a letter.

> *Dear Mrs. Brill,*
>
> *I hope you are doing well, and I am truly sorry for the terrible inconvenience and horror you have been put through. You seem like such a nice lady, and I have suffered terribly, wondering your fate. I hope that you can find it in your heart to forgive me and move on with your life and put this terrible tragedy behind you. I guess this letter is a confession of sorts.*
>
> *I have heard via the newspapers and the news programs that the murder of Josh Wheeler has been solved, and Scotland Yard has closed the case. I have followed this case quite closely, and its connection to me shall be revealed now without further delay.*
>
> *My beloved husband Peter was the one who murdered Josh Wheeler. It was not planned. We were in London on holiday, staying at the Palace when we recognized Wheeler as he entered the suite next door to us. Peter did not even know you were in the room until he heard the shower going, and by then, it was too late. The deed was already done.*

Twenty years ago, Josh Wheeler had broken our only daughter's heart. Celia had been a beautiful twenty-year-old girl with her whole life ahead of her, working in Harrods's perfume department, when Wheeler swept her off her feet. He wined and dined her for four months while in London on business. When he left her without a word, she was heartsick and pregnant. And he knew it. My darling Celia committed suicide by overdosing on sleeping pills.

When my husband, a retired Palace Hotel guard, recognized Josh Wheeler as the man staying next door to us at the Palace he fell apart, lost his senses. He took out the gun he always traveled with and, knowing his way around the rooms, picked the lock of the door in the closet between our suites, slipped through, and shot Wheeler. Peter knew the layout of the suites before this latest renovation, and no one was the wiser. I feel I should confess to someone, and it may as well be you, as you are as much a victim of Mr. Wheeler's shenanigans as the rest of us.

Last week, driven by sorrow and guilt, Peter shot himself. It killed him instantly. I feel I may follow suit, as the two loves of my life are gone. I cannot say that I am proud of my culpability in this tragic situation, as much as I feel Josh Wheeler needed to be put down before he irretrievably damaged anyone else's life. I am comforted by the thought that my Peter has found our Celia and her child, and that they have found peace.

I wish you peace and ask for your forgiveness.
Cordially,
Margaret Putnam

Epilogue

ALL MANKIND IS CONNECTED

SUZI WU will die after weeks in a coma. No one will know that she had the keys in her possession, and Josh had the codes in his head. Their meeting and planned disappearance never took place due to his murder. Wu Industries summoned her to China immediately after Josh arrived in London. She quickly mailed the keys to Lori before her Wu Industry escorts arrived. Her infant daughter will someday learn of the family connection to Lori.

JOSEPH LUNT will have a prominent place in British politics. He and his father will have a strained relationship. He will someday learn of his family connection to Lori.

CATE AND JORDAN will have successful careers and a chaotic relationship with each other for years to come.

ROLAND will spend the rest of his life in prison for the murder of Bly and Suzi. He will be deprived of the publicity attached to the murder of Wheeler once Margaret Putnam's letter becomes public.

GEOFFREY HOLMES will retire early, traveling to Australia and Arizona. He and Lori will stay friends for years to come.

LORI BRILL will live a long life, finally at peace with her mother and daughter. She will tie all her family history together before dying. She and Cate will continue to have a very special relationship.

WHEELER MONEY: Only a small amount of Wheeler's stolen fifty million will be recovered.

About the Author

Native Chicagoan Charlene Wexler is a graduate of the University of Illinois. She has worked as a teacher and dental office manager and as a wife, mom, and grandmother.

In retirement, her lifelong passion for writing has led to her creation of several essays, short stories, and novels. Among her books are: *Lori*, *Murder on Skid Row*, *Elephants in the Room*, *Murder Across The Ocean*, and *Milk and Oranges*.

Coming Soon!

CHARLENE WEXLER'S

FAREWELL TO SOUTH SHORE
FARWELL TO SOUTH SHORE SERIES
BOOK ONE

Farewell to South Shore taps into and articulates a woman's emotions related to dealing with a changing society, particularly its expectations of women. Farewell to South Shore creates an instant rapport between the main character and the reader who has experienced change in her own life. It explores the sadness of dealing with divorce, single motherhood, a friend's abortion, a beloved cousin suffering from AIDS, changing mores, and the joys resulting from a loving family, rewarding career, finding new love in middle age, and making the world a better place. The book inspires perseverance and determination to help take charge of one's own life in a rapidly changing world—a world vastly different than the idyllic South Shore of the main character's youth.

For more information
visit: www.SpeakingVolumes.us

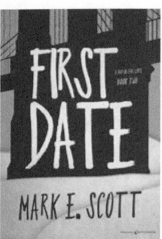

Made in United States
Orlando, FL
02 November 2023